Books by Anette Darbyshire

Single Titles

Love in Another Dimension

I0680955

Love in Another Dimension

ISBN # 978-1-78686-306-5

©Copyright Anette Darbyshire 2017

Cover Art by Posh Gosh ©Copyright 2017

Interior text design by Claire Siemaszkiewicz

Totally Bound Publishing

LOVE IN ANOTHER DIMENSION

ANETTE DARBYSHIRE

Dedication

Thank you to everyone who has believed in me and encouraged me since I started writing this book. I couldn't have done it without your support.

Chapter One

Jemma opened her eyes to find that a little crowd had gathered around.

"It's okay," she mumbled as heat flared up her neck and into her cheeks. "I'm fine."

She gazed up at the anxious faces peering down at her. *Damn, why do I have to be so bloody clumsy?* Her way of dealing with the humiliation that always followed these frequent accidents was to pretend that nothing had happened. Like now. She sat up then straightened her back and tried to look unfazed. If only everyone would stop staring at her. *Isn't it enough that I look a complete fool without these people making me feel worse? Are they laughing at me?* She scanned the crowd again. No, they weren't laughing at all. In fact, they looked horrified.

"She's dead," someone cried.

"Who, me? No, I told you, I'm fine, and will you please stop staring at me?" This was getting annoying now. *Haven't they ever seen anyone fall over before?*

Confused and with growing unease, Jemma started to stand, but instead of watching her, the crowd continued to stare at the spot on the floor where she had fallen. She followed their gazes and that's when she saw what they saw... Her body was lying lifeless on the floor, with a woman checking for her pulse and someone else calling an ambulance.

"But I'm fine," she whispered, although this time she knew she wasn't fine at all.

Stunned, all Jemma could do was stare down at herself in disbelief. This had to be some sort of weird dream.

Then the truth hit her like a slap in the face. She had just died. As her brain scrambled to process what was going on, one question kept poking at her. How could she be dead, but also be standing here looking down at her own body?

"Oh God," she cried as panic gripped her. "I must be a ghost. What the hell am I going to do?"

* * * *

Three days earlier…

"*The bats have left the bell tower.*"

"Huh? Bats?"

Jemma opened her eyes. An intense pain seared through them into the deepest pits of her already sore head.

"I must have died and gone to hell," she groaned, although it wasn't very easy talking when she had grown fur on her tongue.

"Got a bit of a headache?" Alice grinned at her, fresh and chirpy, much to Jemma's annoyance. "Serves you right for finishing off the punch."

"What was in that stuff anyway, rocket fuel?" Jemma raised her head off the sofa. "Ooohhh, my head, turn that racket down, *pleeease.*"

"How can you call this a racket?" Alice looked outraged as she turned down the volume. "It's Bauhaus and they're amazing. Anyway, it's a damned sight better than the rubbish you were dancing to last night. Here, I've made you a coffee."

"Thanks." Jemma reached for the mug and inhaled the rich aroma steaming into her nostrils. She took a sip and sighed as the strong shot of caffeine burned its way to her stomach. *Mmn, that's good.* Feeling more human, she blinked as she became aware of her surroundings. They were in a large, comfy living room strewn with empty glasses, wine bottles and stale crisps – always the sign of a good party. Now that her head was a little clearer, the events of the night before started to come back to her.

"Where's Jack?" she asked before taking another sip of her coffee.

Jack was the guy whose party it had been. He and Alice had hit it off straight away and had spent most of the night putting the world to rights. At four o'clock in the morning, after the last guests had left, Jack had said he didn't want them walking home on their own and had offered to let them stay over.

"Clearing up in the kitchen." Alice grinned and leaned closer to Jemma. "Guess what? He's asked me out."

"Really? That's great, babe." Jemma smiled as Alice's cheeks glowed. Well, at least one of them had struck lucky. They'd been invited to the party last night by a friend and, on the way there, they'd joked how this was the night that Jemma would meet the love of her life. Only it seemed that on this occasion, it was Alice's turn to meet Mister Right.

"Do you remember what we talked about last night?" Alice's voice grew serious.

Jemma took another sip of her coffee. "No, I don't believe I do."

"Come on, Jem, I know you do. We made a pact and I'm not about to let you forget about it."

Jemma shrugged. It was no use acting dumb, as it was clear that Alice wasn't going to let the subject drop. Last night, under the influence of too much alcohol, they'd made some stupid pact about changing their lives. If Jemma remembered correctly, she had agreed to enroll at college and get herself some qualifications so she could get a better job.

At twenty-eight, Jemma's career consisted of a mixture of waitressing, cleaning and shelf stacking. Nothing wrong with that, but it was time to experience the thing called job satisfaction and that meant doing something positive about her lack of career prospects instead of just moaning about being bored and broke. It had been very easy being positive and proactive when she had been enjoying the effects of a tasty punch, but it was quite different the next day when she was nursing a hangover.

"Yeah, all right, but let's wait until we get home. We can discuss it then. Right now all I want are some painkillers and my bed."

"Did someone mention bed?" Jack popped his head round the door, grinning, and Alice promptly went a deep puce.

It was easy to see why Alice fancied Jack so much. Alice liked her men with long hair and Jack's floppy dark curls were just long enough to meet with her approval. He wore the same alternative-style clothing that Alice preferred and had the same taste in music. That was a pretty good start.

"Jack, thanks for the party last night and for letting us crash on your sofa." Alice gazed at him with a demure smile. "So do you still fancy meeting up again some time?"

Jemma nearly choked on her coffee. Alice was never this forward.

"Well, if you're still interested, I'll see you next week. You're coming over on Wednesday, aren't you?"

This time it was Alice's turn to look blank. "Am I?"

Jemma grinned. Alice must have had more punch last night than she'd realized.

"You know, for the psychic workshop. You said you were interested in developing your psychic skills. Remember?" There was no flirtation in Jack's voice, just the friendly, efficient manner of a mentor welcoming a new student.

Jemma glanced at Alice as her friend must have realized that she had mistaken Jack's invitation to join his paranormal group for something more romantic. Poor Alice, she looked mortified.

"She'll be there, won't you, Alice?" interrupted Jemma, knowing that Alice was about to make some pathetic excuse not to go.

"Er, yes, of course. Right, see you next week. We really must go now." Abandoning her coffee, Alice grabbed her jacket and ushered Jemma to the door.

As soon as Jack's door was shut and they were alone, Alice wailed, "Shit, Jemma. I remember now that we talked about meeting up, but I had forgotten the bit about the workshop on Wednesday. I'll never be able to face him again. He must think I'm completely stupid."

"Look, don't worry about it, he's a guy. He probably has no idea that you fancy him and you *will* see him again because we've got a deal. Remember?"

"Maybe we were at bit hasty," Alice backtracked.

"No, I know how much you've wanted to find someone who can help with this psychic thing and now this great guy has invited you to join his group. It's perfect. I'll keep my part of the deal if you do. Tomorrow I'll enroll at college, okay?"

As Alice grunted some sort of agreement Jemma decided to make damn sure that her friend didn't find an excuse to back out.

They walked on in amiable silence, each of them lost in their own thoughts. It was a lovely morning — the roads were quiet because it was Sunday and the warm September sunshine felt welcoming and soothing. They decided to go back via Belsize Park and have breakfast in their favorite café. The coffee there was so strong it could grow legs and walk on its own.

The walk from Swiss Cottage, where Jack lived, to Belsize Park was just long enough to help clear their heads. By the time they reached the café Jemma had managed to convince Alice that Jack had had no idea that she had misunderstood his invitation and that, with a bit of subtle flirting, he was still within reach. With the worry gone, they found an empty table and waited for the server to take their order.

Belsize Park was one of Jemma's favorite areas of London, with its wide tree-lined roads packed with boutique shops. Several cafés and restaurants spilled out onto the pavement, giving the place a Parisian feel where young cosmopolitan couples enjoyed their morning coffee while reading the Sunday papers.

About half an hour later, while Alice was trying to get the waiter's attention so they could order more coffee, Jemma sat back in her chair, closed her eyes and basked in the warm sunshine. It was amazing what some caffeine and a bacon sandwich could do and now, sitting in contentment as the world went by, she started to feel more positive about this college idea.

Ambition wasn't something that had seemed that important to her in the past and she had always been happy to plod along earning her way as and when she could. *Maybe losing Mum at such a young age has left me without the direction I'd needed to work for my GCSEs?* When she had gone to live with her aunt in Tunbridge Wells she had pretty much been left to her own devices and when she had discovered boys, cigarettes and cheap cider she had stopped going to school altogether.

She opened her eyes again and found Alice watching her. "Penny for them?"

"What? Oh, I was just wondering what I'm going to study at college. I'm not exactly the academic type. I'm not really good at anything."

"Don't put yourself down," scolded Alice. "You're a lot more clever than you give yourself credit for and I'll bet there are loads of things you'll be good at. How about doing some sort of foundation course that lets you try out a few subjects before you decide for real? A bit like 'try before you buy'."

"Hmm, I guess I could. In fact, that's not a bad idea. Why didn't I think of it?"

"Because I'm psychic and I know what you want before you do." Alice winked at her and held up her coffee cup. "Here's to us, babe."

Jemma picked up her already empty mug and they toasted their new lives. "What are you going to do after this workshop? If you do have a gift, how are you going to use it?"

Alice's eyes lit up. "Well, I'd love to be a healer and perhaps also help people who have lost loved ones by working as a medium. Maybe the people I meet on Wednesday will be able to help me."

"Oh, so you are going, then?"

"Oh, absolutely. If you enroll at college tomorrow, I'll be there on Wednesday, and I'll be as cool as a cucumber around Jack."

"So what's the story with Jack then? How come he lives in that big house all by himself?"

"Well, I don't know too much about him, but I think he inherited the house from his grandparents. Apparently he lives there alone because nobody else will live there. Every time he finds someone to share with they leave after a few weeks."

"Why, do the ghosts scare them off?" said Jemma, laughing.

"Actually, yes. Seriously, the house is haunted. I felt it last night. That's how Jack and I got talking. I said that I could feel some sort of presence and asked if the house was haunted. He told me that he believes there are two, or maybe even three, ghosts there."

"Oh come on, you're not serious, are you? Alice, there's no such thing as ghosts." Although Jemma begrudgingly accepted Alice's beliefs, she didn't believe in all that stuff herself. "The only spirits I came across last night were in the form of a very potent punch."

"I'm telling you, something isn't right in that house. Anyway, come on." Alice stood up and stretched. "Let's get back to the flat. If you have any more of that coffee you'll be like a hyperactive gecko."

"Gecko?"

"Yeah, climbing the walls."

When they arrived back at the small flat they shared in Camden—well, Chalk Farm really, but Camden sounded so much cooler—Jemma went to her room for a rest. She had a serious hangover to recover from and, besides, it was her turn to do the washing-up. Jemma was allergic to washing-up…and tidying…and cleaning. She had learned a long time ago that if she retreated to her room for 'a rest' the chore would somehow be done by the time she came out again. Poor Alice couldn't bear clutter. She was a complete 'clean freak', the exact opposite of Jemma, who believed that a little bit of clutter never hurt anyone.

After a few minutes of tossing and turning on her bed, Jemma got up again and headed for the kitchen. She was too restless to sleep. Alice had been right about all that coffee.

"Here, let me help you with that." Jemma picked up a tea towel and reached for a glass.

"I thought you were tired," said Alice as she rinsed a plate.

"Couldn't sleep. I can't stop thinking about going to college. Are you sure it's such a good idea? I mean, I'm in my late twenties, totally set in my ways and I'm not exactly the student type."

"That's why you need to do this, hun," said Alice, sighing. "Your age is irrelevant, but you do need to unset your ways and I think you'll find that once you find something you like there'll be no stopping you."

They chatted as they worked and it wasn't long before they had finished the dishes. "It's quite therapeutic, this washing-up lark, isn't it?" mused Jemma.

* * * *

Later that evening, sitting alone in her room, Jemma logged on to her laptop and did a search for colleges. She found a site that listed every college and university in London along with a comprehensive list of their courses.

"Wow," she exclaimed aloud. "I had no idea there are so many subjects." As she scrolled through the website she became more enthused by all the possibilities that seemed available to her.

Eventually she found a small local college that offered a one-year foundation course. They said it would help to improve her general education and offered access to university degrees on completion of the course. Core subjects included English, maths and study skills plus additional choices from a long list of more specialized subjects.

Excitement surged through Jemma as she devoured the information. The more she read about it the more inspired she became. This was the course for her. This was going to change her life. Without giving it another thought, she clicked on the 'enroll now' icon. Ah, just one small problem – the fee. She had forgotten that it would cost money, but hey, it couldn't be that expensive. Another click. "*How much?*" She nearly fell off her chair in shock.

This couldn't be right. The information on the screen said that the one-year foundation course was *one thousand two hundred and fifty pounds*! Deflated, Jemma sighed. She had been so excited about finding this course, but now she might not be able to do it. There was no way she could afford that.

Hang on. One of her credit cards had just had the credit limit extended by a thousand pounds, and last month she had managed to make an extra payment. There was a chance that she might have enough credit available to pay for the course. There was just one problem. Where the heck was the card?

She glanced around her small room. Suddenly the clutter wasn't quite so harmless because somewhere among the piles of clothes, stacks of magazines and heaps of shoes, handbags and makeup was a small plastic card that was the key to her whole future. She had to find it.

Over an hour later her room looked like a hurricane had torn through it. Whereas before the clutter had been relatively organized, now each pile, heap and stack was one giant mound of rubbish, but it didn't matter because she had found the card. It was just a shame that she hadn't searched in her top drawer before turning her room upside down, as that was where she had left it last month.

Once back at her computer Jemma entered the credit card details and held her breath as she clicked 'Pay Now'. Would there be enough money on the card? She hardly dared look. 'Congratulations, your enrolment has been successful.'

"Yes!" She jumped up, sending her chair flying backward. Leaving the chair where it had landed, she rushed into Alice's room and threw herself onto her bed. "Guess what?"

"Go away, I'm asleep." Alice buried her head under the duvet.

"No, you're not. Come on, Alice, wake up."

Alice sighed and appeared resigned to not getting any more sleep for a while. "Go on then, what's so urgent that it can't wait until morning?"

"I've done it. I've enrolled at college. I just did it online now. I found the perfect course and it's only in Hampstead. I've already enrolled and paid for it. And you'll never guess what?"

"What?"

"I start on Wednesday." She prodded Alice to get her attention.

"Yeah right, Wednesday," muttered Alice, yawning. "Great."

"Alice, wake up, dopey. Wednesday is the same day you go to your workshop, remember? Don't you see? This is meant to be. You know, I've got a really strong feeling that this is the start of something big for both of us."

Alice glared at her then seemed to grudgingly accept that Jemma wasn't going to go back to bed any time soon. "Okay, let's make some hot chocolate and you can tell me all about it," she said, sighing as she dragged herself out of bed.

With steaming mugs in hand, they snuggled up together on the sofa and chatted about how their lives were going to change.

It was four o'clock before they got tired. By that time Alice was a world-famous medium with her own TV show. She and Jack had four children and lived in his haunted house while Jemma was Managing Director of her multimillion-pound empire with two male personal assistants to attend her every need.

"It's destiny," mumbled Jemma just before she dropped off to sleep on Alice's shoulder. "This is so right, it's meant to be…"

Chapter Two

On Wednesday morning I roll over in the soft silk sheets and smile up at the gorgeous hunk standing next to the bed. He's holding out a glass of champagne, smiling seductively and wearing nothing except for a small towel wrapped around his waist. There's an irresistible smell of bacon wafting into the room from the kitchen. What more could a girl want? Gorgeous man, champagne and breakfast in bed. It doesn't get much better than this.

"Wake up, Dogsbreath."

"Charming," mumbled Jemma.

"Come on, I've made you a bacon sarnie."

Jemma opened her eyes and found that her beautiful, sexy man had morphed into Alice holding a mug of tea and the silk sheets had turned back into her old Garfield duvet cover.

"I thought I'd treat you on your first day at college." Alice sat down on Jemma's bed and handed her the mug.

"Thanks," she croaked. "Did you mention bacon?"

"In the kitchen. Come on, get up or you'll be late."

Jemma dragged herself out of bed and padded into the kitchen. The bacon sandwich was delicious—it was just what she'd needed. She glanced at Alice, who was already showered and dressed. She wished she was more like her. Jemma was still in her tatty pajamas with yesterday's mascara smudged around her eyes and her hair resembling a bird's nest. It was a typical morning. With one exception.

"So, what time's registration?"

Jemma yawned. "Not sure, 'bout half nine, I think."

"Well, you'd better get a move on, it's a quarter to nine already."

"What?" screamed Jemma. "Why the hell didn't you wake me earlier?"

Jemma dived into the bathroom and emerged ten minutes later with her long auburn hair tucked into a towel and her face now clear of the previous day's makeup. After another fifteen minutes she returned to the living room dressed, makeup on and hair dried. Not bad, all things considered.

Alice sat back with an amused grin as Jemma ran around the flat trying to find the bag she'd packed last night with her notebooks and pens. When she was ready and about to rush out of the door, though, Alice said, "Oh dear, did I say a quarter to nine? Sorry, hun, I meant to say a quarter to *eight*."

"You did that on purpose. Why the hell did you do that?"

"Duh, if you thought you had loads of time there's no way you'd be dressed and ready to go on time." Alice chuckled as she made her way into the kitchen. "Now, you've got time for another cuppa."

After two more mugs of tea and a quick tweak of her hastily applied makeup, Jemma studied herself in the mirror and frowned. *Who am I kidding? I'm nearly thirty years old and am about to go back to school with a bunch of teenagers.* She considered her trendy skinny fit jeans and the tight T-shirt that showed off her generous cleavage and the words 'mutton' and 'lamb' sprang to mind.

She didn't only wish that she could *be* more like Alice, she wished she *looked* more like her as well. They couldn't be more different. Alice looked like an elf—petite and pale—whereas she was tall with a natural tan. They loved to tell people they were twins so they could laugh at their shocked reactions.

Alice sauntered up behind her and gave her arm a squeeze. "You look great, hun."

"Thanks. So do you. Hey, are your eyelashes longer?" Jemma noticed for the first time that Alice seemed to have made more effort with her appearance today. Her shoulder-length blonde hair had been blow-dried into a stylish bob and she had applied a little discreet blusher on her porcelain cheeks. Her blue eyes appeared huge thanks to eyelashes that were suspiciously longer than they were yesterday.

"Yep, I knew that ultra-lengthening mascara I bought in the sale would come in handy one day," said Alice, fluttering her lashes at Jemma.

"You do that at Jack, young lady, and you won't have to try and seduce him. He'll be seducing you."

"I'm going to play it cool with Jack, remember? I don't want to scare him off." She glanced up at the clock. "Hey, you'd better get a move on, it really is time to go now."

It was only two stops on the Tube to Hampstead and Jemma arrived with time to spare. As she walked through the gates of Hampstead College of Further Education countless butterflies fluttered in her tummy. *Am I nervous or excited? Probably a bit of both.*

Inside, crowds of students rushed across a large entrance hall. Some were young and trendy, but there were people of all different ages, nationalities and cultures, some of whom looked just as lost and nervous as she felt.

Halfway down a musty-smelling corridor Jemma stopped and froze. She took a deep breath to steady herself as memories of school taunted her. She'd been happy at school when she was younger. Although she hadn't been as brainy as some of the kids she had been able to hold her own. In fact, the only negative comments on her school reports had been that she needed to concentrate more and chatter less. She had fond memories of her form tutor saying that if talking was on the curriculum Jemma would be a grade-A student.

But her smile faded and her eyes misted over as her thoughts drifted back to the fateful day her world had fallen apart. She had only been fifteen when she had come home from school and been met by a police officer. He had been waiting outside the house for her and her gut instinct had known something was wrong by the serious expression on his face. He had tried to break the news as gently as he could, but that didn't stop her from becoming hysterical when he told her that her mum had been killed in a road accident that afternoon. Her beautiful, kind, loving mother had been taken from her and she had been left alone. She had never known her father — he had left when she was a baby — so her mother had been everything to her. A wave of grief threatened to engulf her now as the pain stabbed at her heart again.

She jumped as her thoughts snapped back to the present and willed herself to think of something else. *Damn, this is not the time to get emotional.* But it was too late, she had allowed herself to think of her mum and now she couldn't stop. "Oh, mum, I wish you were here with me now. I could really do with a hug," she whispered.

Her mum's funeral had been the second most devastating day of her life, the first being the day she had died. Afterward she had gone to stay with her mum's sister, Aunt Tess, but she was ten years older than her mum and the two sisters had never been very close. Aunt Tess had meant well, but she didn't have any kids of her own and just hadn't known what to say to help her cope with her grief. It was Alice who had been there and given her a shoulder to cry on. That was when they had grown close. Alice had tried to help her, but she had been a lost cause and their friendship hadn't been enough to stop Jemma from getting in with the wrong crowd. It hadn't been long before she had started bunking off, drinking, smoking and drifting further away from the secure, happy past she'd known at school.

"Excuse me?" On hearing a voice, the memory burst and she found herself back in the corridor of the college. "Do you know where room 3G is?"

"Er, no. Sorry." She smiled and glanced at the clock. She'd better get a move on or she'd be late for her first lesson.

The rest of the morning flew by. After a couple of wrong turns, she had found her way to her classroom, just in time for registration. The first lesson had been study skills and, to be honest, it was all a bit obvious. But that was probably just to make everyone feel that they weren't in over their heads on their first day.

At lunchtime she joined a few of her classmates in the canteen. She was surprised at how nice it was — she had half expected stale old sandwiches and vending machine coffee. However, there was hot food including fish and chips, curry, jacket potatoes, and it was all quite cheap too. So over egg and chips, Jemma joined in the eager conversations that ranged from a debate about whether their teacher was gay or not, to speculation about what they'd be doing during the afternoon.

The room was full of enthusiastic energy, everyone keen to get to know one another and work out who they had most in common with. Some people ate packed lunches while others tucked in to the canteen food. The atmosphere in the room buzzed with excited chatter and Jemma loved it. She was a part of this — she was one of them. It had been a long time since she'd felt as if she belonged somewhere. It felt good.

She glanced at her watch and wondered whether Alice had arrived at Jack's yet. She had been annoyed when Alice had played that prank on her with the time earlier, but she could see the funny side now. Only Alice knew her well enough to know that she needed to tell a little white lie in order for Jemma to be ready on time. She hoped that the meeting at Jack's worked out for her. Since returning from her travels in America Alice had seemed a bit lost, unsure of what to do next. Then her parents had invested in a flat in Chalk Farm — correction, Camden — and had agreed to rent it out to Alice and herself at a reduced rate. At first they had been so excited about sharing a flat together that jobs and careers hadn't seemed all that important. It was only at Jack's party last weekend that they'd gotten their acts together and made the decisions that led them to where they were today.

"Earth to Jemima Haley."

"What? Oh, I'm sorry. I was miles away." Jemma turned her attention back to the conversation, which had moved on to the male students in their class. "What did you say?"

"Is there anyone in our class that you fancy?" asked Kirsten, a bubbly blonde with an Australian accent. She took a sip of her Coke and let out a little belch. "Oops, sorry."

"Not really, they're not my type." Jemma wasn't paying attention any more. She had noticed a group of students heading for the door with cigarettes and lighters in their hands. She could kill for a fag right now. Alice would go mad if she knew she still smoked the odd little ciggie, but here she would never know.

"Sorry, guys, but I'm just going to nip outside for a minute. See you back in class." After making her excuses she left the others to their gossip.

As she made her way across the canteen she searched in her bag for her secret stash. She had to make sure her cigarettes were well hidden so Alice wouldn't find them. She knew Alice meant well, but sometimes it got bloody annoying when she kept on nagging her about her smoking. She had often accused Alice of being more like an overbearing mother than a friend, but she didn't really mean it. Deep down she was thankful that someone liked her enough to care. Nevertheless, when it came to smoking, it was so much easier just to play along and pretend that she had given up.

Jemma was so preoccupied with her thoughts that she didn't notice the coffee that someone had spilled on the floor earlier, and it wasn't until her foot slipped on the small puddle that she became aware that something was wrong. She felt herself falling backward, legs sprawling in the air as she landed with an ungraceful bump on her backside. Everything seemed to be happening in slow motion until her head hit the edge of a table, and after that everything went black.

And now, standing next to her body, trying to get to grips with what had just happened, Jemma could only stare in horror as the moments that had led to her death kept replaying in her head again and again.

After what felt like an eternity she started to move away from the crowd, stepping backward, unable to take her eyes off her body. Then she noticed that the people she had just had lunch with were coming over to see what all the commotion was about. She watched their curiosity turn to shock when they saw that it was their new friend who had just died.

With one final glance at her body, which was now lying in a pool of blood that was trickling from her head, she turned and walked away in a daze, not knowing what to do or where to go. The panic was growing, threatening to overcome her.

"Alice," she cried out in desperation. "I've got to find Alice. She can help me." She didn't know why she thought Alice could help, but it was the only thing she could think of.

Jemma had no sense of time as she made her way to Swiss Cottage. It didn't seem to exist anymore. Everything seemed muted, sounds were muffled, sights were a little blurry. It was as if she were inside a giant bubble, detached from the real world, which was carrying on without her. When she arrived at Jack's house, she paused outside and thought sadly of the last time she'd been there. She and Alice had been so full of optimism as they'd set off on their walk to Belsize Park that morning with Alice still reeling from her faux pas with Jack.

Now, she stood alone, hesitating before reaching up for the doorbell. Nothing happened — her finger went right through it. "Oh yeah, I'm dead," she muttered and tried to stifle more panic that kept coming in waves. She tried the door handle, but as she'd suspected, the same thing happened. She raised her hand and placed it on the door. She gasped when it disappeared from sight. *Shit!* Then she stuck her foot through and eventually her whole body. She felt nothing – it was as if the door wasn't there.

Once inside she crossed the hallway and stood by the closed living room door, feeling like an impostor. On the one hand she didn't want to interrupt Jack's meeting, but on the other she didn't know where else to go.

She stepped toward the door and paused for a moment before stepping through it into the living room. She found Alice sitting next to Jack, transfixed by everything he was saying. Jemma stood still for a moment and observed what was going on until she could decide what to do next.

About a dozen people were sitting around Jack in a circle, except for a couple of people sitting near the window. There was also a lone man slouched in an armchair in the corner, away from the others and looking as if he didn't want to be part of the group.

The air was heavy with the sweet smell of lavender wafting up from an oil burner, and the half-drawn curtains gave the room a subdued feel. Several candles had been lit, their flames throwing shadows that danced against the wall, creating a calm and tranquil atmosphere.

The only sounds were from an old antique clock ticking on the mantelpiece and Jack's velvety voice talking to the group.

"You need to clear your minds of everything," he was saying. "Remember, you wrote your problems and negative thoughts on that piece of paper earlier and threw it away. There is nothing to stop you from focusing on that imaginary blank screen in front of you."

Jemma stood behind Alice as she contemplated what to do. She somehow had to make Alice aware that she was there, but how?

"Hey, Alice," she whispered in Alice's ear, hoping that she would somehow turn around and say 'Oh, hi, Jem, what are you doing here?'

But, of course, there was no response. Nothing.

"Alice, it's me," she said a little louder.

Still nothing. Alice remained quiet, with her eyes shut, listening to Jack. There wasn't even a shiver of reaction to Jemma's presence. "So much for your bloody psychic skills," she muttered.

She took another glance around the room. Everyone looked as if they were concentrating with their eyes shut, except for the two people near the window. On closer inspection, Jemma noticed that one of them was a young girl, probably about ten or eleven years old. *How odd that someone would bring a child to something like this.* The other person was a man who appeared to be in his late twenties, maybe the girl's dad. Actually, he was quite cute. He had a beautiful sculpted mouth, a bit like Johnny Depp, and the most striking green eyes she had ever seen.

"Hello, Hot Lips," she murmured, forgetting her ordeal for a brief moment and enjoying the fact that she could say whatever she liked without anyone hearing her. "I bet you know how to kiss a girl."

She glanced over at the solitary man sitting in the corner of the room. His cold, beady eyes seemed to stare right at her. An uneasy shiver ran through her as she turned away. "I bet you're a barrel of laughs," she muttered.

Turning back to the group, that looked like they'd gone to sleep, Jemma sighed. How the hell was she going to get Alice's attention?

She tried everything she could think of. She prodded her, pulled her hair, shouted into her ear, but there was no reaction. A rush of despair threatened to overwhelm her. If she couldn't talk to Alice she'd be all on her own. She needed Alice to tell her what to do next. And she needed a hug.

Maybe she'd have more luck with Jack. She ran over and stood behind him.

"*BOO!*" she shouted. Nothing.

"You're doing it all wrong."

She screamed at the voice that had come out of nowhere. *Who the hell said that? Is it talking to me?* She swung around to see who it belonged to and was horrified to find herself face-to-face with Hot Lips.

"Are you talking to me?" she asked. *Maybe he'd been talking to Jack?*

"Of course. Who else would I be talking to?"

"You mean you can see me?"

"Oh yes, I can definitely see you." He grinned, his beautiful eyes crinkling at the corners.

"Why? I mean, how come? Are you psychic?"

"No, I'm dead. Just like you. Oh, and I haven't had any complaints."

"About what?"

"The way I kiss a girl."

Oops. "Sorry about that," she mumbled, heat surging to her cheeks. Did ghosts blush? Well, it certainly felt that way.

"Don't be, I'm flattered." Hot Lips grinned. "So, when did you die?"

This was turning out to be one hell of a weird day. Hearing the man ask her in such a casual way when she'd died brought her plight back to her with a start. Her life had just been snatched away from her and here she was flirting with a ghost and discussing death as if they were having a casual chat in the local supermarket.

Overwhelmed and biting back threatening tears, she smiled. "Actually, I just died today."

She had been about to crack some sort of joke about how this sort of thing happened all the time, but she couldn't think of anything else to say. She was drained—it was all too much.

"I don't want to be dead," she whispered as the first tear rolled down her cheek. "I don't want to be here, I just want to go home. I need Alice. Oh God, what am I going to do?" More panic enveloped her as the reality of what was happening gripped her once again.

"I'm so sorry," said Hot Lips, his voice gentle. "If it's any consolation, I know just how you feel. I died over twenty years ago and I still haven't gotten over it. By the way, my name's Tom."

Jemma stared at Tom with wide eyes. "Twenty years? That's awful. But why are you here? Aren't you supposed to go to heaven or something?"

Tom shook his head. "I can't move on because I can't accept the circumstances of when I died, so I'm stuck here forever, trapped in this damned dimension."

Is that what this is, a dimension? Surely it's just a case of the good go to heaven and the bad go to hell. End of story. So what's this stuff about a dimension? Are there other dimensions? Is heaven in another dimension?

"Will I be stuck here too?" she whispered. There were so many questions spinning around in her head, but she wasn't quite sure how to ask them. This was all way out of her league.

"Well, I don't know, to be honest. As you're here with us now it looks like you've either got unfinished business in the living world or you weren't meant to die in the first place. Once you're here it's practically impossible to leave so I'm afraid it looks like you are stuck here."

The thought of being trapped in some strange void forever, aware of her presence and yet knowing that she no longer existed, was too much to bear. Tom seemed like a decent guy, but it angered her that there didn't seem any fight left in him. Why couldn't she move on to wherever it was she was meant to go?

"No," cried Jemma with renewed strength. "I can't accept that. There must be something I can do. I won't stay here forever."

Tom put a hand on her shoulder, his eyes kind. "I'm afraid you haven't got a choice."

"Oh no? Well, you just wait and see. This can't be all there is. There must be something more than this, somewhere better, and I'm going to find it. And I'll tell you one thing, Tom, I'll never give up. I *will* find my way out of here if it's the last thing I do."

Chapter Three

"I'd offer you a cup of coffee, but you wouldn't be able to drink it." Tom's attempt at humor didn't amuse Jemma at all.

"Great," she grumbled. "Not only am I a bloody ghost, but I'm a starving ghost." The thought that she wouldn't be able to eat or drink again did nothing for her already pessimistic mood.

She was now more determined than ever to get the hell out of there. Her mind raced as she scanned the room. She had to do something, but what? Alice must be able to help her. All she had to do was get her attention. Okay, so her attempts to talk to her and Jack had been unsuccessful so far, but this was meant to be a psychics' meeting, after all, so surely there'd be other people there who would be more receptive.

Her eyes settled on the young girl she had spotted earlier. She had a vague memory of Alice once mentioning something about children being more in tune with their psychic side. If she could somehow communicate with the child, maybe she could act as a medium between her and Alice and, together, they could exorcise her or something. Then she could move on to the next place, wherever that might be. It was worth a try.

Ignoring Tom's protests, she strode up to the girl and stopped as close to her as possible. In fact, they were so close that they were almost touching noses.

"Hello?" shouted Jemma in as loud a voice as possible. "Hello, can you hear me?"

"I'm not bloody deaf," the girl shouted back.

Jemma was so shocked that she stumbled backward. "Oh no, not another one," she groaned. "Don't tell me. You're a ghost, right?"

"Yeah, and I'm sorry if I frightened you, but you looked so funny," said the girl, her giggle exposing an endearing dimple on each freckled cheek. "I'm Susie."

"Hello, Susie. So are there any more of you or are you done with frightening the life out of me?" She wasn't sure she could cope with any more scares today.

Mischief glinted in her eyes as Susie replied. "Well, actually, you haven't got any life left in you, remember? Anyway, there's just Max over there. He's a grumpy old sod."

She turned to see who Susie was pointing to and saw that Max was the miserable one with the beady eyes. *Great*!

"Susie, don't be rude," scolded Tom. "Max is just a bit quiet, that's all." When he saw Jemma's expression, he added, "Don't worry, Max is just a harmless old spook. Aren't you, Max?"

"Get lost," growled the scowling old man.

"I've *so* got to get out of here," muttered Jemma. "Okay." She turned back to Tom. "You said earlier that I was doing it wrong when I was trying to talk to Alice. Would you show me the right way?"

Tom looked thoughtful. "It's not as simple as that. First I have to explain a bit about where and what we are. Susie, you always accuse me of getting too technical, do you want to explain?"

"Okay, get ready because this is going to blow your mind." Susie jumped up, shaking back her long, light brown hair, eager to show off her knowledge. She rolled her eyes up as if preparing to recite a script that she had learned by heart. "You may think that there are only three dimensions, four if you include time, but there are in fact eleven, most of them just folds in space and time. Simple really, but it sounds a bit weird." She glanced at Tom as though seeking confirmation that she was on the right track. He smiled and

Susie continued.

"Once you die — really die I mean, not like us — people become free beings of energy that can move through most of those dimensions. The reason *we're* here is that we're trapped in one of them." She leaned over to Tom and whispered, "Is that right?" When Tom nodded Susie beamed.

"So how come we're trapped here? Why couldn't we just become some of those free beings of energy?" Jemma frowned as she tried to get her head around what Susie was telling her. *She must be some clever kid to know this stuff.*

"That's the problem, you can only become a free spirit if you were at peace when you died. Some of us weren't meant to die and some of us can't accept we're dead, while others can't move on because they have some sort of unfinished business back with the living. It's sort of like being in an in-between state, neither in one place or the other." She glanced at Tom who, once again, nodded his encouragement.

"So can we ever leave?" asked Jemma.

"I think so, but it depends on the circumstances of your death. Until you sort out the reason you're here in the first place I'm afraid you ain't going nowhere," stated Susie in dramatic fashion.

"Okay, so how is all this linked to the way I make contact with Alice?"

"I'll let Tom talk you through that. It gets harder now and he's better at that bit than I am."

Jemma glanced across at Tom, keen to learn everything she could.

He cleared his throat. "Before I tell you about touching the living there's something you need to know about the dead. Right now there's no physical barrier around you to prevent us touching you. Apart from the fact that it's both natural and comforting for us to feel the touch of someone else, even if it is a ghost, it also leaves you highly vulnerable. Anyone could look inside you right now, read

29

your thoughts and even take over your mind and soul."

"Oh." Crap, that didn't sound good.

"Don't look so worried." Tom smiled. "There's an easy remedy to that. You need to erect a barrier of energy around you. Once you've done that, keep it there always. Here's what you do. Close your eyes and imagine a white light, deep inside you."

Jemma did as Tom said and closed her eyes. She conjured up an image of a light and concentrated on keeping it there.

After a moment or two Tom continued. "Can you see the light?"

It was now a brilliant white light that shone inside a vast dark void. She nodded.

"Now, imagine holding that white light in your hands then wrapping it around your body. Imagine you can *feel* its glow."

Jemma took the light and enveloped herself as if she was swathing herself in a big fluffy blanket. It was comforting in an odd sort of way, a bit like being cocooned in a light bulb, but without feeling trapped. Not that she'd ever imagined being trapped inside a light bulb.

Tom waited until she opened her eyes and when she did, he moved over to her and touched her near her elbow. Rather than passing through her, his hand rested on her arm. She jumped at the feel of him. The relief at having real contact was so unexpected that a lump formed in her throat. That had felt so good. And a little overwhelming. Tears pooled behind her eyes but she blinked them away.

"Good, it seems to have worked. That'll stop any unwanted intrusions and will allow you to test your theory." Tom's sharp eyes seemed to penetrate her soul as if there was no barrier of energy to stop him.

"What theory?"

"Whether I know how to kiss a girl."

Damn, she was blushing again.

"Oddly, this will also enable you to retain some physical actions, like breathing. Try to blow on your hand." He waited for her to lift her hand. "Go on, try it."

She took a breath, surprised that her lungs did seem to fill with air, then blew into her palm. Cool air tickled her skin, sending goose bumps flurrying up her arm. "Wow."

"Don't ask me why we can breathe when we don't need air. Nobody knows." He grinned as he took a step closer to her. "They say that kissing is just as real as well."

Jemma's stomach almost hit the floor as she imagined him planting those lips on hers. *Get a grip.* Forcing down another rush of heat to her cheeks, she tried her best to look unimpressed. "Right. Maybe we can get back on track now?" she asked, keeping her tone as even as possible.

Tom nodded. "Sure. Oh, and you should still be able to feel temperature as well. Anyway, back to how you touch Alice. Imagine that everything in the universe is made up of an invisible field of energy. Well, *our* energy is part of that field too, as is everything else in the universe, and you can control that energy just by thinking about it. Consciousness controls reality."

"Oh yeah, right." Jemma laughed. *If only it were that simple.*

"Just listen. When the living see a ghost they're witnessing one of three types of entities. The first, and most common, is a residual haunting which is basically just an event imprinted on the edge of a dimension that replays over and over. Boring.

"Then there's the free spirits, the ones who can move *beyond* the dimensions. These entities can manifest and communicate easily because they have access to unlimited energy. However they cannot communicate with us because they can't penetrate the boundaries of some dimensions, including this one.

"And then there's us. We can also communicate with the living, but it's much harder for us. So what you have to do is concentrate very hard. You have to use your mind to make it happen, but that takes lots of energy, which we don't have. The trouble is the more you concentrate the more you need. That's when you have to draw it from the field and that takes practice. However, you can cheat by using things like lights, batteries and even body heat from the living."

Whoa, surely that's the stuff of science fiction? "How do you know all this?" Jemma frowned, uncertain whether to believe him or not.

"By talking to others who have been here for decades, even centuries. Then when you experience it for yourself it all falls into place. It suddenly seems so obvious. It does take time to be able to communicate effectively with the living, though. You have to start with something simple like a gentle touch and once you know how to do that you'll find it gets easier with practice."

"Okay. Will you show me now on one of these people here?"

"Yes, of course, but first I want to ask *you* a question."

"What?"

"Why are you so desperate to talk to Alice? I mean, what makes you so sure that she can help you?"

Jemma wasn't sure what to say. How could she explain that Alice always knew what to do, had always advised and helped her whenever she got into a muddle—which was quite often—and that Alice had a profound intuition that hinted at her innate spirituality? It could well be that Alice wouldn't be able to help, but just hearing her tell her that she would be okay would be a huge comfort and might give her the confidence to fight her way out of this place. But she couldn't possibly expect Tom to understand that. So she just shrugged and said, "I just do. Please, Tom, show me."

Tom strode over to one of the people in the group still in deep meditation. Jemma couldn't help appreciating his tall, athletic build as he moved across the room. His clothes were a bit dated, but seeing as he died over twenty years ago she could forgive him that. His dark brown hair was quite short, framing his handsome face, and that smile of his did funny things to her insides. How ironic that now she'd met a hunky guy he was a bloody ghost.

"I'm going to make this woman feel my hand brush against hers. Watch."

And she watched. And she saw the deep concentration on his face as he thought about what he needed to do then, at just the right moment, he ran his fingers along the woman's hand. Jemma smiled as the woman jumped and glanced down at her hand in surprise. She must have thought she'd imagined it because she shut her eyes again and resumed her meditation. But Jemma had seen Tom make contact with a living person and it gave her hope.

Susie clapped at Tom's success and rushed over to tickle a man on the nose, although nothing happened.

"Damn," she exclaimed. "I can hardly ever do it, it's so annoying."

"You're too young to concentrate that hard," explained Tom. "Keep trying, don't give up. You will get better at it."

"How old are you, Susie?" asked Jemma.

"Eleven, although I'd have been thirty-one now if I'd still been alive."

It didn't take a genius to work out that Susie must have died twenty years ago then. Around the same time that Tom died. Were they related? What was their connection? How did they die? She had so many questions. Like why were they trapped in this dimension and why were they haunting Jack's house? What were these unusual circumstances relating to Tom's death that he couldn't accept? And what about Max? Who was he and why was he there?

She'd have plenty of time for questions later – if she was still around. Right now she just wanted to make contact with Alice while she was still there. She raced over to where her friend sat and stood behind her. Just before she started to clear her mind, ready to concentrate, she glanced up. Tom gave her an encouraging smile, sending a shiver through her body. She smiled back and lowered her gaze to hide her reaction to him.

It was a long time before she felt she was ready. Then

when her body relaxed she willed her mind to become more focused. She felt heavier and heavier as she concentrated as hard as she could. Somehow, she knew when she was ready then leaned over Alice, pursed her lips and blew on the back of her neck.

"Oh shit," cried Alice as she jumped up in shock. Everyone opened their eyes and stared at her.

"I'm so sorry," she mumbled, embarrassed.

Jack came to her rescue. "Tell you what, guys, let's have a break. I'm sure you could all do with a drink. We'll lighten things up for the last hour."

As everyone dashed for the kettle and the loo, Jack came over to her.

"Are you all right?" he asked, his gorgeous brown eyes showing genuine concern.

"Oh, Jack, I'm sorry about that, but I felt something on my neck. I've been feeling quite uncomfortable for a while now, and that was just the last straw."

"What do you mean by uncomfortable?"

"I'm not sure to be honest, but something's not right. I can feel a really strong presence and it's making me feel odd. I can't describe it."

"It's interesting you say that, because I've felt something too. Normally the presence here is quite calm, but this afternoon it's distinctly unsettled. Something's changed. Look, seeing that we're both experiencing similar feelings, why don't you stay after everyone's gone and we'll try to work out what's going on?"

A warm glow wrapped itself around her like a giant hug. Jack wanted her to stay after everyone else had left.

"Sure. Okay, if that's all right," she replied, trying to sound more casual than she felt.

While Jack checked that everyone had what they needed, Alice wondered how Jemma was getting on at college. She was tempted to send her a quick text, but Jack had asked everyone to turn their mobiles off before they started and she couldn't be bothered to dig it out of her bag now. And anyway, by the time she'd switched it on it would be time to switch it off again. No, she'd wait until they'd finished then send her a text. She might suggest that they snuggle up on the sofa with a takeaway and a bottle of wine tonight. Then they could tell each other every single detail of their day.

An hour and a half later the meeting was over and the last of the group had left. Alice and Jack were chatting while clearing away in the kitchen when Jack stopped, turned around and glanced behind him.

"What's wrong?"

"I don't know, I just felt like I was being watched. I suppose I should be used to it by now. How about you? Do you still have the same feeling you had before?"

Alice nodded. "It's really strong. I *know* that something or someone touched me before."

As she finished drying a mug she glanced out of the window. *How strange.* There was a young boy standing outside in the garden, looking in and staring at her.

"Who's that?" she asked, glancing over her shoulder at Jack.

"Where?"

"Outside. The young boy. Does he live here?"

She turned back to the window, but the boy had gone. *Oh well, he's probably some neighbor's kid.*

"Never mind, he's gone now. Is it all right if I make some more coffee?"

Jack grinned. "Yes, that'd be great."

Armed with their coffees, Alice and Jack went back into the living room and exchanged stories about their spiritual experiences. It felt good sitting next to him on the sofa and listening to him talk about his house, the group and the resident ghosts. But something still wasn't right.

"Jack, you do believe that something touched me, don't you? It was very deliberate and I'm in no doubt that it was specifically intended for me. Don't ask me why, but I just have this really strong feeling that something's not right."

"There's no doubting your psychic skills. But what about me? I'm the one who's got to sleep here on my own tonight."

Was that a hint? Was he making a pass at her? She glanced up at him but, once again, his face was deadpan. *Damn!*

Then, out of the blue, Alice felt something brush against her leg. "Argh," she screamed and jumped up in fright.

Jack laughed as he picked up a very fluffy white cat. "Sorry about that. This is Casper. Where have you been all day, puss?"

Casper glared at Alice before jumping down from Jack's arms with a grunt.

"I guess that's my cue to leave." Alice smiled, getting up from the sofa.

"Oh, don't take any notice of Casper, he just wanted to check you out."

"It's not Casper — he's lovely. I really do have to go. If the spooks get to be too much before our next meeting, let me know and I'll come over and chase them away for you." She giggled as she switched her phone on and checked the display.

"I might just take you up on that. What's wrong?"

"I'm not sure. I've got about ten missed calls and four messages." Alice dialed her voicemail and played back the messages. When she'd finished she stared at her phone with a worried frown.

"What?"

"The messages are all from Jemma's college asking me to call them urgently. Apparently she had put me down as her next of kin. Oh, Jack, something's wrong."

A dark sense of foreboding crept into Alice's bones as she called the number the college had left for her. The tiny knot of concern that had formed in her stomach a minute ago was growing into a harder, tighter ball of fear. Something was very wrong. It seemed to take forever before she was put through to the principal of the college, but she only heard his first words before everything went black.

Chapter Four

"Alice. Alice. Wake up..." As Alice became aware of the distant voice calling her name she opened her eyes and looked up into Jack's concerned face, his image becoming blurred as tears welled in her eyes. She tried to sit up, but her head was spinning so much that she nearly passed out again.

Snippets of her conversation with the principal of Jemma's college flashed back to her. Terrible accident. Died instantly. Didn't suffer. It had to be a mistake.

"I only saw her this morning," she gasped, as great wracking sobs took over her body.

"Who? Alice, what's happened?"

"It's Jemma. Jemma's dead. Oh my God!" Alice lost all sense of time and place as grief overwhelmed her. She clung to Jack, desperate for him to tell her that the college had just called back and said they had made a mistake, that Jemma wasn't dead. But of course, he didn't. He just held her while she cried like she'd never cried before.

It was a couple of hours before she regained her composure, stood up and thanked Jack for taking care of her. As if in a trance, she picked up her coat, ready to leave.

"Where do you think you're going?" he demanded.

"Home. I've burdened you enough already. Thanks again." She was on autopilot and her voice was monotone and flat.

"Are you going to stay with your parents?"

"No, they're away right now. I'm going home to our flat. My flat."

Jack looked incredulous. "No way! You're not going

anywhere. You can stay here with me. You shouldn't be on your own right now."

"Oh, Jack, that's really sweet of you, but I'm not exactly good company at the moment and…" Alice's voice trailed off as she ran out of things to say. She was drained and didn't have any strength left to argue. The grief was blunted by the shock, she knew that, but she was only too well aware that when all this hit her, she shouldn't be alone.

So Jack showed her to the spare room, jumped into his car and drove to her flat to pick up some clothes and toiletries. When he returned he made her some beans on toast and plied her with endless cups of sweet tea.

One day blended into another. She had no idea if it was Monday or Friday. She didn't care. Jack left her alone when she needed to cry and listened with endless patience when she wanted to talk. He became her rock.

Then, a few days later, on a bright and sunny morning, he knocked on the door to her room and brought her a mug of tea. "How are you feeling?"

"Okay." Her voice sounded distant, as if it didn't belong to her. She was sitting by a dressing table putting the final touches to her makeup. It was a peaceful room, small and uncluttered, with cream walls and pale blue curtains. The only furniture was a single bed, a wardrobe and a dressing table with a stool. It was all she needed.

Jack's kindness had touched her. She had known him for such a short time and yet he had let her stay with him, in his house, in this safe, calm room. She somehow felt closer to Jemma here. She wasn't sure why, but it was a comfort to her.

But today was the day she had been dreading. How was she going to face everyone, to smile through her grief while burying her best friend?

"We need to make a move." Jack strode over and put a hand on her shoulder. "It'll take a couple of hours to get down to Kent and we need to allow for traffic."

"Okay." She nodded and got up from the stool. "Thank

you, Jack," she whispered. "I don't think I could have coped with this if it wasn't for you."

Jack smiled and squeezed her hand. "Come on, let's go."

They didn't talk much during the journey to Stenhurst, a pretty little village in the heart of Kent. Jemma's Aunt Tess had wanted to bury her there, close to the town where she had grown up and near to her mother's grave. Tess had offered to organize everything, which had been such a relief. Alice dreaded to think what kind of funeral Jemma would have had if she'd been left to sort it.

"Will your parents be there?" asked Jack, glancing across at Alice as they drove through the Blackwall Tunnel.

"Yes, they really like Jemma." She swallowed a sob. "I mean, liked."

As they left London behind and reached the pretty Kent countryside, Alice's mind started drifting back to when they had been children. Her mum and Jemma's mum had known each other through a sports club. They used to meet every Thursday morning to play tennis while the girls were at school. One day, during the school holidays, the mums had brought their ten-year-old daughters along while they played.

The first time Alice had met Jemma she had been a little intimidated by the tall, confident girl. She'd had the longest, wildest hair she had ever seen, the dark red waves making her look exotic and exciting. But her eyes had resembled a teddy bear's — big, soft and brown.

'Hello,' she had said with a crooked grin. 'Do you like princesses, fairies and pink stuff?'

'Er, no, not really,' Alice had replied.

'Oh, thank God for that. I hate all that soppy girly stuff. Do you like sport and music?'

Alice had been thrilled to meet a kindred spirit. 'I love sport, especially swimming. And music. Do you like…boys?'

'Yuck, no way!'

And that had been the start of their friendship. They hadn't been best friends at first, that had come later, but they'd had fun when they'd seen each other and had been delighted when they'd both ended up at the same secondary school.

"Shall we go to Tess' house first or straight to the church?" Jack's voice dragged her back to the present.

"Erm, I told Tess that we'd see her at the church. I couldn't bear to have to go in one of those black cars behind the hearse. They're so depressing."

"Okay. Well, this is Stenhurst and we're early. Let's find somewhere to park then pop into that pub over there for a drink. You look like you could do with one."

The village was quiet for a Thursday afternoon and they had no trouble finding a parking space. As they walked in silence toward the welcoming pub, Alice glanced around. She remembered coming here with Jemma to visit her aunt back in the summer. It was such a pretty village with its cute cottages and immaculate gardens. There was a lovely little duck pond at the end of the High Street, and if she stood at a certain spot she had the most incredible views across miles of rolling countryside. A couple of oast houses stood tall in the distance, leaving no doubt that she was in the heart of Kent.

Jemma's mum, Rosie, and her sister, Tess, had grown up in this village so when Rosie had died, Tess had arranged for her to be buried there, alongside their parents. Shortly after Jemma had moved to London, Tess had left Tunbridge Wells and moved back to the village — and was still there.

Once seated in the pub, Alice surveyed Jack as he ordered their drinks at the bar. He had been amazing since Jemma had died and now he was by her side as she was about to face the biggest challenge of her life. If only things had been different and she had gotten to know him under happier circumstances. Who knew what might have happened? But romance was off the cards now. She needed time to mourn her best friend then, when she was ready, she might just pack her bags and go traveling or something.

As he returned with the drinks, he gave her a warm smile

and her stomach did a little somersault. God, he was cute. She took a deep breath. *Here goes.* "Jack? You've been so kind, but I've imposed on you long enough. I'm going to stay with my parents for a few days before deciding what to do about the flat. Is it okay if I stay tonight and then leave tomorrow?"

"Of course it is. You can stay for as long as you like. You know that, don't you?"

Alice took his hand in both of hers and smiled. "Yes, I know, and I really appreciate it. These last few days have been the worst of my life, but you've helped me through them and I'll always be grateful to you. But I need to move on. You do understand, don't you?"

"Of course. I admire your strength, but remember I'm not far away and you can always come round whenever you want. And anyway, I need you to keep those ghosts in check."

As soon as they'd finished their drinks Alice stood, brushed her coat down and stuck her chin out. "Right, let's do this."

Walking toward the church, they saw that the hearse had already arrived and was parked outside the gates. Alice hesitated before continuing. This was not going to be easy.

Alice had never been inside the church before and as she stepped through the thick, wooden doorway she stopped for a moment and looked around. There was a huge stained-glass window behind the altar throwing colored light toward the congregation. Several smaller windows along the sides snuck extra light in. From the very high vaulted ceiling hung two enormous brass chandeliers, and candles were lit at the end of each ornately carved pew. It smelled like a church ought to smell, a mixture of musty old wood, candles and fresh flowers. It was both beautiful and comforting.

As she scanned the small congregation she spotted her parents sitting in the second row, talking to Tess. The church was by no means full. In fact, there were fewer people than she had expected. She recognized some of the faces, distant family and old school friends, but there were some unfamiliar ones there as well. Alice wondered who they were before her eyes settled on a strangely familiar face. The boy was watching her, but made no attempt to talk to her. He was young and very pale, almost ethereal. Where had she seen him before? She couldn't remember. The next time she searched for him, though, he had gone.

Jack took her hand and led her to the front pew. She glanced back at her mum, who gave her a loving smile. "Are you okay?" she mouthed at her daughter.

Alice nodded and turned back to face the coffin. Tears filled her eyes as she imagined her friend lying in the wooden box, alone and lifeless.

"Oh, Jem," she whispered. "I miss you so much. What am I going to do without you?" As she closed her eyes, a reassuring hand rested on her shoulder. She turned around to see who it was, but there was nobody there.

"*Yes!*" Jemma punched the air when Alice reacted to her touching her shoulder. She had tried several times to repeat her success since last week, but it was a lot harder than she'd first thought. This was the first time she had done it since and she was so glad that she had been successful at such a poignant moment.

"That's my Aunt Tess," Jemma said to Tom, pointing to a smart-looking lady in her sixties, "and those people over there are from my college. I can't believe they came, they only knew me for half a day."

It was very surreal, being at her own funeral. Although she was touched by the genuine grief of some of her friends and family, she couldn't help thinking how funny it would be if she could jump out of the coffin shouting, "Ha ha, only joking."

The trouble was, nobody would find it funny. Except maybe Alice. She stared at Alice's pale and drawn face. *On second thought, maybe not.*

She stole a glance at Tom, who was listening to the vicar introduce himself. She was thankful that he had come with her today. Apart from offering her moral support, he had also helped her to travel — ghost style, as Susie liked to call it.

When she had walked to Jack's house the day she had died, she hadn't known that there were other ways she could move around. Tom had shown her how to travel in an instant from one place to another. She just needed to concentrate very hard on where she wanted to go and, hey presto, she was there. The first time she had tried it she had felt like a Starfleet officer transporting herself back onto her starship. It had been an exhilarating experience.

Tom had been good to her since she'd arrived and had helped her get used to the reality of being a ghost. He had seemed keen to know more about her and she had been glad of the chance to tell him all about her former life. He had made her feel welcome and she was grateful for his friendship. The thought of going through all this alone was unbearable.

There was something about Tom that intrigued her. Maybe it was the air of mystery always hanging over him, or perhaps it was just because he was so damn cute. She often found herself staring at him when he wasn't looking. Even though there was nothing romantic going on, she was sure there was a connection between them that pulled her toward him, a bit like a magnet. If he felt it too he didn't let on. She had no idea if he liked her or not. In fact, she still didn't know very much about him at all. When she asked him about himself, he became elusive and always managed to change the subject.

Susie, on the other hand, had been only too happy to talk about herself. Jemma had learned that she and Tom were not related, but that he had taken the young girl under his wing when he died. Tom had found her wandering aimlessly along Finchley Road at Swiss Cottage, lost and frightened. Susie had explained that she had died just a couple of months earlier than Tom in an accident, and that the reason she was trapped in this dimension was because it had not been her time to die. She was a great girl. Cheerful, funny and bright. Jemma had asked her to come along today, but she had declined, saying that funerals depressed her.

While the vicar continued talking, Tom gave Jemma a nudge. "Hey, are you all right?"

"I'm fine. I think. I'm just wondering what they're going to say about me." Suddenly she didn't want to know. What if they said horrible things?

'Jemma was reckless, lazy and pretty stupid for getting herself killed in such an ordinary and unexciting accident. She had no job, no money and no boyfriend. In fact, Jemima Haley was a total loser.' *Is that really what people will say? Surely Alice will say something nice about me?*

"Jemma was such a lovely girl." She glanced up to see her Aunt Tess talking. She was saying how brave Jemma had been when her mother had died and how she felt that she had let her down by not being more of a parent to her when she was younger.

Jemma gasped. She hadn't realized that her aunt cared that much, but there was no mistaking the genuine sadness in her voice as she spoke.

Then it was Alice's turn to speak. Jemma braced herself as Alice walked up to the pulpit and spoke in a small, trembling voice.

"Jemma was a very special person…" She paused, looking as if she was trying to hold herself together. "She was funny and kind and loyal and she—" Alice's voice was barely audible and the catch as she broke off showed just how much she was suffering.

Jemma's heart broke to see her friend so consumed by grief. She made her way over and put her arms around her, willing her friend to remain strong. And Alice did seem to pull herself together, as if she had somehow sensed Jemma's support. Alice took a deep breath and continued.

She didn't speak for long, but what she said was touching

and evocative. She ended her speech by saying that Jemma had been like a sister to her and that it was wrong that she had died so suddenly and so young. "She was so full of life," cried Alice with passion, "and there's no way she was ready to die. This should never have happened."

As the congregation then sang *Amazing Grace*, Jemma turned to Tom and frowned. His shoulders were slumped and his head bowed as if he was scrutinizing the stone floor.

"Tom, what's wrong?"

"Nothing."

"Is it this song? Did they sing this at your funeral?" She was so curious to know more about him. Maybe the intense atmosphere in the church meant that he would loosen up a bit and tell her a bit more about himself.

"Jemma, this is your funeral. I don't want to talk about me." Although he was smiling, his tone made it clear that she needed to change the subject.

"At least tell me how you died," she persisted. The more evasive he was the more she wanted to know.

"For God's sake, will you leave it? I don't want to talk about it." This time he wasn't smiling.

"Sorry," she mumbled. Why the hell was he so secretive? His constant refusal to discuss his past was bloody infuriating. She refocused on what was going on in the church, but she'd be damned if she was going to give up.

It was a nice ceremony, emotional but dignified. Afterward, Jemma watched from a distance as the congregation gathered around the empty grave outside. Jack had his arm around Alice, supporting her as she grew ever more distressed. Even Aunt Tess was crying, something Jemma had never seen before — Aunt Tess had never cried, not even when her own sister had died. At least, not that she had been aware of.

Then all the voices faded from her mind as Alice's words rang in her ears. '*She was so full of life, there's no way she was ready to die. This should never have happened.*'

"That's it," cried Jemma, and jumped up from the tree

stump she'd been sitting on.

"That's what?" asked Tom.

"That's why I'm here. I was never meant to die. This is not my time."

"Okay, but why are you so happy about that?"

"Don't you see? Now that I know *why* I'm trapped here, I can do something about it."

"Like what?"

"I don't know. Yet. But do you remember when Susie said that until I know why I'm here I won't be going anywhere? Well, now I know. Surely that's a start?"

"Yeah, I suppose," said Tom. "But right now you need to decide if you want to go to your wake. Look, everyone's leaving."

"Oh." In her excitement, Jemma hadn't noticed the most important part of the funeral—her burial. And now they were about to leave to go to the wake. Did she want to go? As she watched her friends getting into their cars, Jemma didn't want to leave them. Somehow, the finality of today was making her uneasy, like she wasn't ready to let go just yet.

"Do you mind if we tag along?" she asked.

"Of course not. I'm hardly in a rush to go anywhere. I heard someone say it's at your aunt's house. Let's do our Star Trek thing and beam ourselves over there."

Chapter Five

"I'm bored," sighed Jemma as Jack emptied the washing machine. Watching his mundane chores around the house, day in and day out, had become her only source of entertainment, and it was becoming depressing. She knew what he ate for breakfast, how he stacked the dishwasher and which brand of toothpaste he used. Even though she had been tempted, she had drawn the line at watching him in the shower. Some things were meant to be kept private.

It had been less than a month since her funeral, but it already felt like she had been dead for an eternity. She couldn't eat or drink, she couldn't have a bath, and even reading a book proved futile as she couldn't turn the pages. Tom wasn't around much, Max was creepy and Susie, although she was a lovely girl, was only eleven. She needed a distraction, something to keep her occupied until she figured out how to leave this place. She had been so determined to leave at first, but without even realizing it she had settled into something of a routine and her plans had somehow become something she would think about the next day, then the next... She had been glad to accept Tom's invitation to stay with them after the funeral. She couldn't face being on her own at the flat watching Alice cry herself to sleep every night.

Susie jumped down from the kitchen table. "Today is Saturday so there should be plenty to watch on TV tonight. Jack has downloaded the next series of *The Big Bang Theory*, so that should kill a few hours over the weekend."

"So our only entertainment is eavesdropping on someone else's TV programs? I can hardly wait," grumbled Jemma, her spirits sinking even lower. If she didn't do something interesting soon she would go mad.

"Oh, it's not that bad." Susie grinned, her face full of mischief. "I often amuse myself by winding Jack up. It's quite funny changing the channel in the middle of a film he's watching. Trouble is, he's gotten used to it now and just tells me to go away. I'm better at touching things than people, I don't know why. I'm great at knocking things off shelves and stuff."

"How do you manage to do that? Whenever I try to touch anything my hand just passes through to the other side." As if to prove her point, Jemma clenched her fist and tried to knock on the kitchen table but, as usual, her hand went straight through.

Susie laughed and flicked a teaspoon into the sink, making Jack look up.

"How do you do that?" Jemma frowned.

"It's easy, but it takes practice. As I said, I'm better at touching things than people. I've been here for twenty years and I still can't touch living things properly. Tom says it's because I'm a child. It's so annoying. Anyway, I'll show you what to do, then you can have a practice when we go out haunting later. You basically use the same technique that you use for touching the living, you just do it in a slightly different way. You still need to focus all your energy on whatever it is you want to touch, but instead of concentrating on a person, you direct all your energy to a specific point on whatever it is you want to touch. Like this." Susie stared at the table for a moment before clenching her fist then knocking on the table's surface. Jack stopped folding his washing and frowned. Then he opened the kitchen door and disappeared into the hallway, probably to check if there was anyone at the front door.

Susie laughed. "You try it. Knocking on something is a bit hard at first, so try moving that cup over there."

Jemma focused her energy on the cup, willing it to move. At first nothing happened but then the cup went flying across the room and crashed next to a sleeping Casper, who woke with a startled meow. "Yes! I did it," she cried and high-fived Susie.

"You need to learn to adjust the amount of energy you focus depending on what you want to touch, but you've basically got it. Now you can join me in having a bit of fun."

"That's what I like about you." Jemma said with an affectionate smile. "You're always so positive and funny. But Tom's very serious, isn't he? I thought he was fun at first, but he's been really quiet and withdrawn since my funeral."

"Tom's okay. He just has a lot of stuff to deal with and I reckon that being at your funeral might have brought back a few bad memories."

"Memories from his own funeral, you mean?"

"He didn't go. He says he wouldn't have coped with the grief."

"It's never easy watching your family suffer. Funerals are sad at the best of times, but to watch your loved ones grieve for you…" Jemma shook her head as memories of Alice's distress crept back into her heart with an icy chill.

"No, his family didn't go to the funeral either. That's what he couldn't deal with — his mum's rejection."

"Oh, that's awful," cried Jemma, stunned. "How did he die?"

"Brain tumor."

"Why on earth would a mother turn her back on her own son when he'd just died of a brain tumor? That doesn't make sense. Had he done something wrong?"

Susie shrugged. "I shouldn't be talking about this. Tom would go mad if he heard. Just remember, he's a good guy. He's looked after me from the moment he got here and although he can be a bit quiet at times, he's kind, honest and even has a sense of humor every now and then."

Jemma tried to hide the frown she knew would be giving away her frustration. She was more curious than ever, but it was clear that she wasn't going to get anything else out of Susie for now. It did seem odd that Tom hadn't told her about his death himself. After all, what was wrong with dying from a brain tumor?

"Where is Tom, anyway?" asked Jemma. She hadn't seen him all morning.

"Dunno, he's probably gone to the cemetery again. He often goes there to be with his dad. Come on, you and me are going to have some fun."

"Where are we going?"

"You'll see. There are advantages to being able to walk through walls and being invisible, you know. Let's go do some haunting."

"In the middle of the day? Aren't we supposed to wait until midnight?"

"Oh no, that's a myth. Ghosts are around all the time — it's just more fun haunting at night because people get scared more easily." Susie had that mischievous glint in her eye again. "A bit of harmless spooking is just what we need right now. And later, when Jack's fallen asleep on the sofa, we'll go and wind up a group of ghost hunters at the Marling Hotel."

"What's that?"

"A hotel, dummy. It's really old and is famous for being haunted so a couple of ghost hunting groups meet there regularly. Jack goes sometimes. Some of the people from his group are members of a ghost-hunting society. There are a couple of boring old resident ghosts there, but they never do anything scary so I help out every now and then by providing a few bumps and screams during their vigils. It's a right laugh."

"Susie, you are bad — but I can't wait. So, who are we going to haunt now, then?"

"You'll see." Susie giggled. "Let's go shopping."

"Huh?"

Jemma was still wondering what Susie was up to as they wandered into a supermarket. It was busy with Saturday shoppers weaving in and out of the crowded aisles, some with shopping lists, others with confused and stressed expressions on their faces, but all with one common goal—to get out of there as soon as possible.

They watched as a very young boy, sitting in the seat of a trolley, begged his mum for a packet of sweets. The young mother was adamant that he wasn't having them and thrust them back onto the shelf, leaving the poor child looking crestfallen.

"Oh, poor thing, it's only a few sweets. Let's give him a hand." Susie ran over to the shelf, fixed her eyes on the packet of sweets and managed to knock them off the shelf and into the trolley just as the woman was about to move on.

"But won't the mum notice at the tills and refuse to pay for them?" asked Jemma.

"Oh no, she'll be so busy loading everything onto the conveyor belt and then packing them into bags on the other side that she won't notice a small packet of sweets. And when she gets home and unpacks the shopping, she'll think that she must have put them in the trolley after all and let the boy have them."

"How do you know?"

"You don't think this is the first time I've done this, do you?" Susie snickered. "I once swapped a posh lady's fillet steak for a tin of Spam. You should have seen her face at the checkout when she saw it."

"Susie, you are incorrigible," scolded Jemma, suppressing a hidden smile.

When they returned to the house a couple of hours later, Jemma felt much better.

"Did you see that man's face when I knocked those books off the shelf in the library?" cried Jemma, tears of laughter rolling down her face.

"And the librarian thought it was him and nearly threw him out," howled Susie.

"Actually, that wasn't on purpose. I was trying to help him. I heard him ask her where the books on Monet's paintings were and I felt sorry for him when he couldn't find them. That's why I knocked that book down — it was a book about Monet. Only, I haven't quite perfected the technique yet so the whole bloody lot came down. Poor man, he did look shocked."

"At least he found his book."

"Thanks, Susie. I needed that."

"That's okay. I'm so glad to have a new friend. Tom's sweet and I love him to bits and all that, but he's very grown-up and sensible, isn't he? You're much more fun."

"Are you trying to say that I'm not grown-up and sensible?" teased Jemma.

"Oh no, not at all. Put it this way, when you first came, I didn't really like you very much. You seemed so angry and uptight, but now that you've come to terms with being here, you're a lot more chilled."

"Susie, I'm still leaving. The reason I was so uptight was because I'd just died and I was scared. I may have 'come to terms with being here' as you put it, but I'm still planning on finding a way out eventually."

Susie's face dropped. "Please don't go," she whispered. "Don't get a big head or anything, but I sort of like you being here."

Jemma ran over to Susie, put her arms around her and gave her a hug. She wanted to protect this young girl who had died so young. But then Susie burst into tears and tightened her arms around Jemma.

"Hey, I didn't mean to make you cry," soothed Jemma. This was a side of Susie that Jemma hadn't seen before. Poor girl, there must be more behind her cheeky smile than Jemma had realized.

"Sorry. It's just that I haven't had a hug since I died. Tom's been like a father to me, but sometimes a girl just needs a motherly hug. I miss my mum, Jemma. I just want to go home. I was never meant to die."

Jemma hugged Susie tighter and tried to think of something positive to say. It had never occurred to her that this funny young girl was so lonely. As she stroked her hair, though, a thought struck her.

"I wasn't meant to die either, so I'm going to do something about it. Come with me, Susie. I'll help you get home."

"But what about Tom? I'm not leaving him here."

"Can't he come too?"

Susie shook her head. "You and I weren't meant to die, but he died of a brain tumor. It *was* his time to die. But he can't accept certain things that happened around the time of his death so I don't think he can ever leave, because of what happened."

"Well, if he won't even talk about it then he'll never know," snapped Jemma. She cursed Tom for being so damn secretive. His stubborn refusal to face his demons was keeping Susie here. "I think it's time I had a little chat with him."

"Jemma, don't give him a hard time. There's a lot more to it than you know…"

"What do you mean?"

"Nothing. Forget it." Susie stood, indicating that she had said enough, then left the room.

Later that afternoon, Susie said something about going to the house next door as the kids who lived there usually watched Tracy Beaker, whoever she was, on a Saturday afternoon, and Jemma found herself alone. She wandered around the house, which was now very quiet. Jack had gone out and Tom still wasn't back. Warmth swept through her as she thought of Tom—handsome and warm on the one hand, aloof and elusive on the other. She wished she could get him to open up to her, to trust her enough to tell her about himself. She pictured his intense green eyes softening as he poured his heart out. She would put her arms around him to let him know she understood, then his beautiful perfect lips would seek hers and they would kiss—

"What're you smirking about?" growled a voice from the corner of the living room.

Jemma snapped back to reality with a start. She had never

spoken to Max. He always looked so angry and hostile. He'd never made any attempt to talk to her either and she had been careful to avoid him.

"Oh, nothing. I was just thinking about something Susie said," she replied, trying to sound casual. She didn't want to start up a conversation with him. He gave her the creeps so she reinforced the protective barrier of energy around herself, as if he might somehow attack her.

"Bloody kid, always up to no good," he grumbled, his cold, beady eyes devoid of any expression. "Where's Tom?"

"Erm, I don't know. You know Tom, always popping out without warning."

"Hmm, he always was a wanderer. When he was a youngster he walked right out of the front door without telling no one and he was gone for hours. His ma was mad as hell."

"How long have you known him?" Jemma asked, puzzled.

"All his life. Watched him grow up."

"How did you know him? Are you related?"

"No, you daft girl, I've been dead over a hundred years. I just saw him grow up here, that's all."

"Tom grew up here? In Jack's house? So that's why he haunts this house, it's his home."

"'Course it bloody is. Why else would he be here?"

Good point. Max glared at her and she shifted under his cold gaze. There was something about him that unnerved her. Even though he was being civil with her right now, his eyes hinted at something dark, even menacing, and she found herself wondering if he was as harmless as Tom had said he was.

"Are you still leaving?"

"Oh yes, definitely. I've just got to find a way."

"You want to find a wormhole, then."

"A what?"

"Wormhole," snapped Max. "It's the only way out of here."

"How? What exactly is a wormhole? How do I find one?"

But before Max could answer, Tom walked through the wall. "Find what?"

"Max was just telling me about something called a wormhole. He said it's the only way out of here."

Tom smiled. "I'm afraid it's not that easy. Wormholes are notoriously difficult to locate and even harder to manipulate. I wouldn't get your hopes up."

They all jumped when the front door banged shut. Jack had returned, laden with shopping bags. Leaving Max behind, Jemma and Tom followed Jack into the kitchen and watched as he started unpacking the shopping.

"He'll be watching television later," said Tom.

"I know."

Jack made himself a cup of tea and rifled through the biscuit tin while trying to stop Casper from jumping up onto the worktop.

"Why is Max haunting this house?" asked Jemma, interrupting the bored silence.

"Max? He's been here for a long time. Did you know that I grew up here, in this house?"

"Well, Max did mention something just before. I wasn't snooping, honestly, it just came up."

"That's okay. My parents moved in when I was a baby and I lived here until I was eighteen. My grandparents owned the house originally, but they wanted to move to the country when Grandpa retired so my mother and father bought it off them. I always felt that this house was haunted, but whenever I mentioned it to my parents they just said it was my imagination. There were times when I heard unexplained noises, lights would switch on and off and I had the distinct feeling that someone was watching me. The only person who ever believed me was Grandpa. He said he'd felt it too. Anyway, I got used to it and when I left home I forgot all about it. And then I died—and met Max. He never says much, but he did make it abundantly clear that he blames my family for his death."

"Why?"

"I don't know. Only that it's to do with my grandfather. Apparently it's his fault that Max died. My father died the year before I did and when I died my mother sold the house to Jack's grandparents. That's all I know. Max won't talk to me."

"Hello? Alice? It's Jack. I just wanted to see how you're doing." Jack's voice interrupted their conversation.

"Oh, Tom, he's phoning Alice," said Jemma.

"Good. Well, you know where I am." Jack paused as he listened to whatever Alice was saying. "What are you doing tonight? Why don't you come round for a bite to eat? No, of course you wouldn't be intruding. Great. About sixish? Right, see you later."

* * * *

Alice stared at the phone as she ended the call. Wow, Jack had just rung and asked her to dinner. Okay, maybe not dinner. But a bite to eat was a start.

She had a sudden urge to talk to Jemma, to tell her about Jack's invitation and get her advice on what to wear. The lump that seemed to have taken up permanent residence in her throat swelled and fresh tears once again stung her tired and swollen eyes. She blinked them away and decided to put some music on to cheer herself up. She found her favorite album on her iPod and smiled as the dark, heavy guitars introduced the first song on *Gothic Doom Anthems*, a compilation of the darkest, heaviest gothic tracks past and present.

She had no idea why, but somehow the darker the song, the more it cheered her up. She caught a glance of herself in the mirror and thought that she would make quite a good Goth, with her pale, drawn face and dark circles under her eyes. All she needed was to dye her hair black and she would fit in well with the trendy crowds in Camden.

As the first chords of the next track started, though, the tears once again returned. This had been the song that she and Jemma had been dancing to at Jack's party last month. *Has it really only been a month?* She had returned to the flat soon after Jemma's funeral, telling Jack that she was going to stay with her parents for a while. She'd felt bad about lying to him, but she'd needed some time alone and Jack would never have let her come back to the cold, empty flat all by herself. She had sent him the odd text to let him know that she was all right, but she hadn't seen him since. The last psychic meeting at Jack's house had been canceled. The next one was the following week so she had supposed that that would be when she would see him again. He had always replied to her texts soon after she'd sent them, telling her to let him know if there was anything he could do.

The thought of Jack brought a smile to her face as she hunted through her wardrobe for the skinny black jeans she'd bought on sale a couple of months ago. They made her legs seem longer than they were and went perfectly with her new white top. The black suede kitten heel boots finished off her classy and sexy, but 'I didn't go to any trouble' look. As she put on a simple silver necklace and matching earrings, she surveyed herself in the mirror, decided that a little lip gloss was needed along with a squirt of lemon-scented perfume, and she was ready.

"Wish me luck, Jem," she whispered just before she left for the Tube station. She was going to be lazy and go one stop on the Tube then walk to Swiss Cottage from Belsize Park. She loved that walk, along the same road that she and Jemma had walked down the morning after the party.

Once in the station she waited on the near empty platform. A slight breeze ruffled her hair. Suddenly, a rush of goosebumps ran up her arm. She glanced around her, certain that someone was watching her, but the only people were at the other end of the platform. She could have sworn there had been someone standing behind her. In fact, she had been sure of it. It was with huge relief that she heard the distant rumble of an approaching train. She boarded it as soon as it stopped and opened its doors. The carriage was quiet, with only a handful of passengers sitting distantly from each other. Alice put on her air of detachment—an essential requirement for Londoners traveling on the Underground—using it as a protective cloak, warning others not to talk to or look at her.

She flopped into a seat, lost in her thoughts, and as the train pulled into the tunnel, she stared at her reflection in the window opposite. Suddenly she froze and a cold shiver ran through her as she gazed at the dark tunnel speeding past. Sitting next to her and staring at her through the reflection was the strange boy she had seen before—pale and a little blurry in the dirty window. She whipped her head round to look at him, but the seat next to her was empty. There was nobody in that section of the carriage at all. She blinked. He *had* been there, she was sure of it.

At last the train pulled into the station and stopped. Alice got off as fast as she could and made her way to the lifts as the train disappeared back into the tunnel. Nobody else got off and she was alone. The only sound was her heels clicking on the stone floor. It seemed like ages, but at last the lift arrived and she hurried inside, letting out a sigh of relief as the doors started to close. But then Alice glanced up and spotted the boy again, standing in silence outside the lift and disappearing as the two sides of the doors met.

Chapter Six

The walk to Jack's house seemed much longer than it had before. Dark shadows spooked her and distant noises made her jump. She couldn't stop glancing over her shoulder every few steps, convinced that she was being followed. But the pavement behind her was empty except for a lone cat pacing through the crisp fallen leaves. She drew a breath and dug her hands deeper into her pockets, shivering in the autumn chill. The air was cool and carried a subtle smell of burning leaves. It brought to mind a time when she and Jemma would make a bit of extra pocket money by sweeping up leaves in neighbors' gardens. They'd almost always ended up throwing themselves into the huge pile they'd worked so hard to gather and have to start again. A smile spread across her face as the memories came flooding back.

By the time she got to Jack's house she had calmed down and her initial unease had been replaced with anticipation at seeing Jack again. As she rang the doorbell a flutter of excitement ran through her. Would he be pleased to see her?

"Hey, you." He beamed as he opened the door, allowing a delicious aroma of tomato, garlic and herbs to waft out. "Perfect timing. Come and try the sauce for me. I hope you like spaghetti Bolognese?"

"Ooh yes, I love it, thank you." Alice followed him into the kitchen, enjoying the warmth as she took her coat off. "It smells fantastic."

As Jack opened a bottle of red wine she admired the uncluttered and immaculate worktops, not unlike her own.

Jack was very much like her—he also hated clutter and was always tidying up after himself.

"What do you think?" he asked, holding a spoon of steaming sauce to her lips.

It was very hot so she blew at it, raising her eyes to Jack's as she tasted it. She couldn't help wondering what would happen if a bit of sauce dripped and fell onto her white top. Would he offer to clean it for her? Of course, that would mean taking it off…

"Mmm, delicious," she murmured. She ran her tongue over her lips, hoping the gesture would stir something in him.

"Great." Jack turned away, looking pleased with his culinary efforts and oblivious to Alice's not-so-subtle signals.

She rolled her eyes. What would she have to do to get his attention? She wasn't about to make the first move, though. She wasn't that brave. And anyway, what if he didn't fancy her? What if he was wishing that she'd get the message that he was only being nice to her because he felt sorry for her?

Dinner was lovely. Jack was an excellent cook and an attentive host, making sure her wineglass was topped up and that she was comfortable. After they'd eaten he introduced her to his favorite television series about a lovable bunch of geeks. It felt so right, the three of them sitting on the sofa together—her and Jack, and Casper curled up on Jack's lap after licking his plate clean.

When they had watched three episodes in a row, Jack stood, stretched, then took the plates out to the kitchen. Alice followed him and hovered in the doorway, watching him as he fed Casper. Jack was everything she could ever wish for in a man. Apart from the obvious—his good looks and excellent taste in music—he was also kind, warm-hearted and sensitive. In fact, he was perfect. Except for one thing—he didn't seem to fancy her.

"By the way, have you moved back to your flat?" Jack's voice interrupted her hopeful thoughts.

Oh shit, I'd lied about that. "Er, yes. I *was* going to stay with my parents, but I needed to be on my own for a bit. Sorry, I should have told you."

"Hey, it's up to you what you do. I only asked because I care."

"Do you?" *Did he just say he cared?* She moved a little closer to him and looked up into his face, hoping for some sort of sign that he cared a little bit more than he was letting on.

Jack hesitated then gazed into her eyes. "Yes, I do, as it happens."

They were standing very close now, so close that she caught a whiff of his faint musky scent. She raised her face to his and closed her eyes, waiting for her much-anticipated kiss.

But Jack turned around and the moment slipped away — again.

"Oh no, you don't," she growled and pulled him back toward her. She planted her lips on his before he had a chance to object and kissed him, tentatively at first, but then with more urgency as he responded. Warmth spread through her blood, making it sizzle as Jack took over the kiss. Nobody had ever reached so deep that her heart fluttered as though someone was tickling it from the inside. It was everything she had dreamed it would be and more.

"Wow," he gasped, when he pulled away.

Alice grinned as she tried to steady her thundering heartbeat. *Had I really just made the first move?* "Sorry about that. I was beginning to think you were never going to kiss me."

"Oh, I've wanted to. I came pretty close a couple of times tonight, but I didn't want to push you. You've been so fragile since Jemma died, the last thing you needed was me as an added complication."

"Complication? You silly thing, that's the last thing you are. I thought you didn't like me."

He wrapped his arms around her and held her. "I've fancied you from the moment we met at the party, but I thought you were just interested in the psychic group. Then Jemma died and it didn't feel right. I didn't want you to think I was taking advantage of you."

"I'd never think that. I don't know how I would have got through all this without you. I do feel a bit guilty, though, feeling the way I do when my best friend has just been buried." She sighed and wished she could remain in their first embrace forever, with Jack's heart pounding against her chest.

Jack pulled away and traced his finger along the outline of her lips. "That's why we have to take this slowly. You've still got to come to terms with everything that's happened. You're special, Alice. I don't want to risk losing you because we rushed into this before you're ready."

Leaving the dishes in the sink, which was uncharacteristic of both of them, they returned to the living room and cuddled up on the sofa. She snuggled in to him, leaning her head against his chest, and became hypnotized by the rhythmic beating of his heart. Happiness that her feelings for Jack were reciprocated rippled through her, but she couldn't hold back waves of guilt from drowning out the moment. Surely it wasn't right, feeling like this so soon after her best friend had died in such tragic circumstances?

Much later, as Alice dozed in his arms, Jack groaned. "Oh no."

"What?" Alice raised her head off his chest and gazed up at him, loving the way his long, dark hair was disheveled, with a stray wisp flopping over his eyes. She brushed the offending hair away, delighting in the pleasure such a simple act gave her.

"I completely forgot, I promised to meet a few people at a ghost-hunting vigil at the Marling Hotel. I'll ring them and tell them I'm not coming."

Alice was intrigued. *Ghost hunting?* Suddenly, she didn't feel tired anymore.

"No, don't do that. Why don't I go with you? It could be fun, I've never been ghost hunting before."

"Are you sure? I mean, it's already late and we won't be back until the early hours."

"I'm not tired and anyway, tomorrow's Sunday. We can have a lie-in."

Jack raised an eyebrow. "We?"

* * * *

The Marling Hotel was smaller than she had imagined. It probably used to be a private house, a rather large private house, but not the grand, imposing building she had been expecting. In fact, it was quite beautiful with its Victorian bays and sash windows.

"How many rooms are there?" she asked, staring up at the dark façade.

"Fourteen. There's a small bar, restaurant and reception area on the ground floor and that's about it. It's the two bedrooms at the top that make this place so interesting for ghost hunting."

"What about the guests, won't we disturb them?"

"Most of the rooms are vacant on Saturday nights. This isn't really a tourist area so it's mostly businesspeople who stay during the week then go home for the weekend," he explained, taking her hand in his. "The owners only use the two haunted bedrooms if they're really busy because they got so fed up with frightened guests coming down in the middle of the night demanding to be moved to a different room."

"Why, what happens?" asked Alice, trying to ignore the first twinges of apprehension.

"That's what you're about to find out," replied Jack. He led her up some marble steps.

As they entered a small reception area, a bohemian-looking lady wearing a long, flowing purple dress came rushing up to them.

"Jack, darling. We were beginning to think you weren't coming." She flung her arms around him and squeezed.

"Hello," said the lady, turning to Alice. She had wild, flame-red hair and reminded Alice of a fortune teller that she might see at an old-fashioned fair. Every finger on both hands was adorned with rings set with bright, colorful stones and her wrists rattled with numerous bangles and bracelets. Round her neck was a large, silver pentagram resting against her tan chest and on her right shoulder was an old, faded tattoo of some Egyptian-looking symbol that she guessed might be an ankh.

"Alice, this is Maggie, ghost hunter extraordinaire, and Maggie, this is Alice, a good friend of mine. She attends my psychic group," he added.

"You'll know Chris and Mary then?" She smiled and took Alice's hand. "Now, love, have you ever been on a vigil before?"

"No, I'm afraid I'm a complete novice," replied Alice, warming to this wonderfully eccentric woman.

"Don't worry, just watch what we do and enjoy yourself. I'm a medium, by the way. Not all ghost hunters use mediums, but my gifts have come in useful a few times."

Alice glanced at Jack and he squeezed her hand.

"Are you up for this?" he asked.

"Definitely. I can't wait."

They followed Maggie into a small room with a modest bar in the corner and a scattering of old round wooden tables and stools. The walls were flowery, as were the carpet and curtains. With the subdued lighting, it looked a bit like an old pub. Sitting at one of the larger tables were six people, all busy chatting while they were finishing their drinks. Alice recognized Chris and Mary from the group and smiled as Jack introduced the others. The atmosphere was warm and welcoming, which helped her to relax as they discussed the plans for the night ahead.

"John and Mary, can you start with EVPs tonight? Chris and Janet, you take the EMF meters. Jack, would you set up the IR cameras, please." As Maggie delegated with military efficiency, Alice wondered what on earth EVPs,

EMF meters and IR cameras were. "Emma and Julie, are you okay helping the others set up while I fill Alice in on all our paraphernalia?"

As the group headed for the stairs carrying their heavy bags and equipment, Maggie sat back down next to Alice.

"You'll hear us talking about EVPs. That's electronic voice phenomenon. We leave digital voice recorders running in both the rooms and sometimes, if we're lucky, we find voices recorded on them that you can't hear at the time. The voices are usually those of the spirits. Sometimes we ask questions, other times we just leave the recorder running to see what happens."

"Wow, do you really get voices from ghosts on those recorders?" asked Alice, fascinated.

"Oh yes, love. Not every time, but we often get something. Now, EMF meters are simple devices that measure the electromagnetic field in the room. The energy from a spirit can affect the electromagnetic field and these meters have become an important tool for a lot of ghost hunters. IR cameras are just infrared cameras that can see in the dark. We leave them running then go over the footage afterward. We also carry handheld video cameras."

"I had no idea there was so much technology involved," mused Alice. "I just assumed it was a group of people walking around an old building waiting for something spooky to happen."

Maggie grinned. "I'm afraid this isn't the most exciting venue tonight, but that's not a bad thing, it'll give you a gentle introduction. We don't want you getting so freaked-out that you never come back. We believe the two bedrooms at the top are haunted by two different spirits. We've managed to make contact a few times, but they're not always in the mood to comply so it can be very quiet. However, occasionally we connect with a child and she's anything but quiet. Right, are you ready?"

"Yes." Alice stood up and waited for Maggie to lead the way. *This is going to be fun.*

"Wait. Just one more thing." Maggie rummaged in her large bag and pulled out a small purple card. "As you know, I'm a medium. If you ever need a reading or any guidance spiritually, just call me."

Alice took the card and studied it. It was a homemade business card with Maggie's name and mobile number on it. She wasn't sure why Maggie would think she'd need her guidance, but she thanked her and popped the card into her coat pocket.

When they joined the rest of the group in the first bedroom on the top floor, the equipment had been set up and they were just about ready to begin. The atmosphere was charged with excited expectation and the group exchanged jovial banter as they finished checking the cameras.

"Okay, guys, lights out," called Maggie. A moment later the room was thrown into darkness.

Jemma smiled as she watched Alice hold Jack's hand in the dark. She was so glad they'd gotten together—they were made for each other. It was good to see Alice smiling again. That alone made coming tonight worthwhile. She wasn't in the mood for spooking a group of ghost hunters, especially now that Alice was one of them, but Susie had persuaded her at the last minute. Although the room was pitch black, she was still able to see who was doing what, which was handy. The advantages of being a ghost were wasted on the dead.

"Is there anyone here?" called Maggie, her clear voice breaking through the silence. "Who are you? Did you die here?"

"Here we go," said Susie. "Better not disappoint them." She knocked on the table next to her.

"Are you a child? Knock once for no and twice for yes."

Susie knocked twice and laughed when she saw the excited reaction of the group.

"Are you alone?"

Susie knocked once and the group gasped.

"Are there others here with you?"

Two more knocks led to more excited gasps. It was fun at first, but about ten minutes into the investigation Jemma started to lose interest. She'd rather explore the rest of the building, so she wandered away from Susie and left her to her spooky games. As she passed through the nearest wall she found she was in the second room that was being used by the ghost hunters. The cameras were running, filming in silence any possible movement. They wouldn't see her, though, as she wasn't using enough energy to make herself visible to the living world. She stopped and cast her eyes around the room, then noticed that a voice recorder had been left on. She approached it with caution aware that it was there to catch the disembodied voices of ghosts. Ghosts like her.

"Alice?" she said into the recorder. "It's me."

She stayed still for a moment, staring at the recorder. She had tried so many times to make contact with Alice and failed — why should this time be any different? It was time she accepted her fate — she was dead, trapped in a dimension she wasn't meant to be in and unable to talk to her best friend. She could only watch as Alice continued her life. But one day Alice would grow old and die, of natural causes she hoped, and move on to her next world, then what? She'd still be here, still trapped, still alone. Only she wasn't alone. She had Tom and Susie, but Tom was wrapped up in his own troubles and Susie, although fun and sweet, was always going to be a child. Was this really her fate? She recalled the moment at her funeral when she had realized that she had never meant to die so young. She had assumed that that had meant an easy way out of this place. But she was still here, still no wiser as to how she was going to leave.

Except she did have a clue. Hadn't Max told her to find a thingy-hole, whatever that was? Surely that was a start? All she had to do was find out what it was then find one and work out how the hell it was going to get her out. Easy. But if this thingy-hole could get her out of here, where would she go? Would she end up in yet another dimension or her final resting place, wherever that might be? Or maybe she'd find herself in a different universe altogether. She'd heard about parallel universes, but she'd never paid much attention. Maybe it was time she had another chat with Max. He seemed to be the only person who knew anything about this, or at least the only person willing to talk about it. Tom had known what Max had meant, but had dismissed it. Why wouldn't he help her?

The thought of talking to Max again reminded her of the unease she had felt the last time she had spoken with him. She would rather not have to talk to him unless she had to. He still gave her the creeps.

"Hey." Susie popped her head through the wall. "Why are you in here on your own? You're missing all the fun."

Jemma smiled at her young friend and put her thoughts to the back of her mind. "I just felt like looking around the hotel."

"There's not much to see," said Susie. "Do you want me to show you around?"

"Okay, but what about your ghost-hunting friends? Won't they be wondering where you are?"

"They've got more than enough evidence to sift through next week. Anyway, I'm getting bored. Come on, let's go."

A few minutes later they were back in the bar, having finished the short tour of the small hotel.

"Shame about Tom not coming tonight," said Susie, sitting on top of the bar with her legs crossed.

At the mention of Tom's name, Jemma's cheeks flared. Not that anything was going to happen with him. He'd been so flirty with her when they'd first met but since that first day, he had been friendly but distant. "Mmm. Tell me about Tom. Was he married when he was alive?" asked Jemma, trying to sound casual.

"No. Why? Do you fancy him?"

"No, of course not," she lied.

"Yes, you do." Susie jumped up and flapped her arms. "*Jemma fancies Tom*," she sang.

"Susie, shut up," snapped Jemma. "Anyway, what do you know about Max?"

"Oh my God, don't tell me you fancy Max as well?" Susie looked horrified.

"Don't be silly, of course I don't. I'm just thinking of having a chat with him, that's all. He seems to be the only one who can tell me how to get out of here."

"You need to watch Max." Susie's expression was serious now. "I wouldn't trust him as far as I could throw him."

"You said that he was just a harmless old spook."

"That was Tom, not me. Look, Max is bad news, Jemma. Be careful."

"I have to talk to him in order to get information out of him. Nobody else is going to tell me. Surely he can't be that bad?"

Susie's voice had a new, urgent pitch as she replied, "Jemma, Max is dangerous. In fact, I'd go as far as saying that he's evil. Stay away from him or you might just regret it."

Chapter Seven

The following morning Jemma sat alone by Jack's kitchen window staring out into the garden, which was now a spectacular scene of stunning colors—brown, yellow, orange, red... Every autumnal shade imaginable. It was ironic that something so beautiful did, in fact, come from death. The dry, crisp, fallen leaves had once been vibrant and alive—a bit like her. She had been so full of life and vitality and now she was just like the leaves. *Dead.*

Being dead was nothing like she'd expected, not that she had ever dwelled on it. Although she had never considered herself to be religious, she had assumed that when she died she would go to heaven and be reunited with her mum. But this? This was worse than she could ever have imagined. She couldn't be with her loved ones who were living nor be reunited with her dead family. Was this purgatory? Was this punishment for not being a better person? If she was here because she hadn't been meant to die then why had she died in the first place? The questions spun around in her head, tormenting her, leaving her with a sense of desolation and hopelessness.

"Hi." Tom's voice interrupted her pensive mood. "Are you all right?"

"Mmm, just thinking." She didn't turn around.

"How was the ghost hunting last night?"

"Okay." She sighed and turned to face Tom. "Actually, I was a bit bored. Spooking people is all right at first, but you quickly tire of it."

"I know. That's why I didn't come."

"Alice was there, with Jack. They were together. You

know, properly together."

"Really? That's good, they're well-suited." He frowned as he seemed to study her. "What are you up to today?"

"Oh, I don't know. I don't really feel like doing anything."

"You look like you could do with a distraction. Why don't you come with me to a special place I go to when I'm in need of cheering up?"

"Where?"

"You'll see. Come on, it'll do you good."

"Okay." Nothing would cheer her up right now, but it was easier going with Tom than thinking of an excuse not to.

"Hold on to my hand and close your eyes."

When she opened them again she was standing on the most beautiful beach she had ever seen. The wide expanse of soft white sand stretched for miles and the deep blue, calm sea sparkled in the sun as if someone had sprinkled silver and gold glitter onto it.

"Wow," she cried, forgetting that she was still holding on to Tom's hand. "This is fantastic. Where are we? Seychelles? Bahamas?"

"Norfolk," replied Tom, looking pleased with her reaction.

"You're joking." Jemma glanced around, noting the absence of a funfair, donkeys and amusement arcades, things she'd always associated with an English seaside. In the distance, a lone figure walked along the water's edge with a dog running ahead, looking like a tiny blot on the unspoiled, serene landscape. Away from the water were huge sand dunes with clumps of long grass waving in the gentle breeze. They were so tall that she couldn't see what was on the other side, adding to the feeling of isolation. The bright October sunshine reflected off the sand and bounced back onto the water, making the whole scene a shimmering image of perfection.

"How do you know this place?" she asked, still drinking it all in.

"I used to come here as a boy for family holidays. There's

a row of Victorian cottages just on the other side of those sand dunes, less than a five-minute walk away. One of them was owned by some friends of my parents and every summer we'd come and stay for two weeks while the owners went abroad."

"You're very lucky to have come somewhere like this as a child." Jemma's only memories of seaside holidays were weekends at Brighton and Hastings. Although she had always had fun, they had been filled with noisy, overcrowded beaches and kiss-me-quick souvenirs.

"I've got many happy memories of here. I spent hours playing on this beach, building more sand castles than you could imagine. My brother and I used to hide behind the dunes there, pretending they were fortresses. We were hunting dragons and demons. My father would sometimes pretend to be a monster and would chase us into the water where we'd play-fight. Then my mother would find some shade by the dunes and lay out a picnic for us." Tom's face dropped as he recalled his nostalgic memories.

"It sounds like you were all very close," said Jemma, confused. That wasn't the image of his family she had imagined after what Susie had told her about his mother's absence at his funeral.

"Yes, we were once. It's different now. My father died the year before me and my brother moved to Manchester after he graduated so my mother is on her own. She never comes here now. That perfect happy family doesn't exist anymore."

An overpowering wave of affection for Tom as she turned to look at him took Jemma by complete surprise. She wasn't sure where the feeling came from, whether it was pity, empathy or something deeper. Afraid that she was going to say something stupid, she gave his hand a comforting squeeze. "Susie said something about you visiting your dad at the cemetery. Are you buried there too?"

Tom's eyes clouded over again as he gazed into the distance. "No," he muttered, a note of bitterness creeping into his voice. "It was my only wish and she wouldn't even grant me that."

"Who? Your mum?"

"Yeah. She knew I wanted to be buried next to my father, but she had me cremated and got rid of the ashes. I think that's one of the reasons I'm here."

"What do you mean?"

"I *was* meant to die, Jemma, unlike you. I died of a brain tumor. It was diagnosed a week before I died and my last request was that I be buried next to my father." He stared out at the vast sea.

"Tom, I'm so sorry. I don't know what to say." Jemma peered up into Tom's handsome face, which was now marred with a mixture of anger and pain. She wanted to ask why his mother had been so cruel, but didn't want to upset him any further. She'd keep her questions for another time, but that didn't mean she was going to give up. Right now, he needed her support, so she remained quiet as she stood next to him and stared out at the distant horizon.

After a few moments she stole a discreet sideways glance at him and studied his profile. His nose was straight, his jaw strong and those eyelashes… She couldn't see his eyes, but she didn't need to. She knew them by heart now, the deep emeralds that flashed with fierce passion when he was angry, but that also showed a man who was intelligent and kind. It was the way they sparkled as he smiled, though, that Jemma loved the most. The corners would crinkle as they hinted at his sense of humor and good-natured temperament. Did ghosts fall in love? Maybe, but the chance of something romantic happening with Tom was pretty remote. *Shame.*

"Let's walk," she said and linked her arm through his.

As they strolled along the water's edge, Jemma told Tom stories of her antics with Alice and how her friend had been her rock when she'd needed her most. "Apart from my Aunt Tess, she was the closest thing I had to family," she said. "My death hit her hard, which is why I'm so glad she's found Jack. He seems like a really nice guy."

"How about you?" said Tom, smiling down at her. "Did you have a boyfriend?"

"No. I never met anyone who liked me enough to stick around for long."

Tom's eyebrows shot up in surprise. "Really? I find that hard to believe. You're gorgeous."

Jemma flushed and tried her hardest not to look overjoyed at Tom's compliment. "Thanks."

Tom stopped then turned to face her. His face was alive with emotion, his eyes burning with something Jemma couldn't quite decipher as he stared at her for what seemed like forever. She gazed back, transfixed by the energy that crackled between them. She opened her mouth to say something then closed it again. No words could express how she felt at that moment. Like the way her heart was fluttering and her head spinning. *Is he going to kiss me?*

Instead of kissing her, though, Tom pulled her into his arms and held her in a tight embrace. "I wish we could have met under different circumstances," he murmured. His lips touched her earlobe, tickling it with his airless breath. Or had she just imagined that?

"So do I," she whispered. "Although, there's no reason why you can't show me that you really do know how to kiss a girl."

He laughed but, instead of planting his lips on hers, he pulled away then took her hand and started walking again. "I'm sorry if I've been a bit distant lately," he said as if he hadn't heard what she'd just said. "When you arrived you were like a breath of fresh air. I think both Susie and myself needed someone like you to come and ruffle our feathers. It's easy to become complacent and drift through each day on autopilot. Your refusal to accept your fate gave us a bit of a shake-up. But it also brought back memories of when I first arrived. You've forced me to ask myself some questions that I'd been avoiding for a long time."

Jemma stopped and stared at his strained face. "Is the fact

that you're not buried next to your father the only reason you're here? I get the feeling there's more to it."

He sighed. "Yes there is, but I don't want to talk about that now."

"Why?" Jemma frowned. "Don't you trust me?"

"Oh, Jemma, of course I trust you. But it's not about trust. It's something that I can't talk about, to anyone. It's personal."

"That's all well and good, but it's not just you this affects. What about Susie?" she demanded.

"What about Susie?" Tom stared at her with a look of genuine confusion.

"She's lonely, Tom. She misses her mum and desperately wants to go home. I think it's possible that she could come with me when I go, but she won't even consider it because of you. She doesn't want to leave you behind on your own. Don't you see? Because you won't face whatever it is that's troubling you, you haven't got a chance of ever moving on, and that means you're stopping Susie from moving on as well."

Tom glared at Jemma, his eyes narrowing as they became cold and angry.

"I see, so it's my fault that Susie's unhappy, is it?"

"No, I didn't mean it like that. All I'm saying is that Susie misses her mum and she may have a chance of getting out of here with me. But she's loyal and won't leave without you."

"What makes you so sure that you can help her leave anyway?" snapped Tom. "You have no idea how to get out of here yourself, if I remember correctly."

"Not yet, but at least I'm prepared to try to find out. Tom, stop being so bloody stubborn and defensive. I'm not your enemy. I was only trying to let you know that Susie is feeling a bit down. I'm trying to help."

"By accusing me of keeping her here against her will?"

"Oh, for God's sake. I didn't say that." Jemma's voice had gone up an octave, which was a strong indication that she was on the verge of losing her temper. It took a lot for her to get so pissed off, but when she did she flew off the handle and often said things she later regretted. In an attempt to diffuse her anger, she kicked the sand with the full force of her frustration. To her amazement, the action resulted in the sand flying through the air the way it would have done if she were alive. She stopped dead in her tracks, her irritation forgotten in an instant.

"Wow, did you see that?" She turned to Tom in excitement. "I just made the sand move."

Tom's anger also seemed to dissolve as he smiled. "That takes a lot of energy. You must have been really pissed off."

Jemma grinned back at him with relief. She would leave the subject of Susie for now, but she wasn't going to let it drop for good. So instead she would find out what he knew about this thing that Max had spoken of.

"Sorry, I didn't mean to upset you."

"That's okay. I will think about what you said. I didn't realize that Susie was unhappy."

They started walking again, watching in amusement as a flock of seagulls fought over a dead fish that had washed up on the beach.

"Tom, do you remember Max talking about these…" She paused, trying to remember the name she was looking for. "Slugholes or something?"

"You mean *worm*holes. Yes, I remember. Don't tell me, you want me to tell you what a wormhole is, right?"

"Well, yes. Max said it's the only way out of here, but he gives me the creeps and I'd rather not ask him unless I have to." She shuddered at the mere thought of him. Susie's warning last night hadn't helped.

"I can tell you a little bit, but to be honest you're better off talking to Max. He's been here for a very long time and has actually helped people leave."

They strolled over to some tall sand dunes and sat down. Jemma turned her face up toward the sky and closed her eyes, enjoying the warmth of the bright autumn sun on her face.

"Oh my God," she said with sudden realization. "I can feel heat. Tom, I can actually feel the heat from the sun."

"That's because the sun is pure energy. It's nice, isn't it? If you concentrate hard enough, you can almost imagine you're alive."

"Mmm, it's lovely. Right, tell me what you know," she demanded, closing her eyes again.

"Okay. A wormhole is a tube that connects one region of space-time to another. Basically, a wormhole allows you to travel backward in time, but it's not as simple as it sounds. You either have to locate an existing one and manipulate it to take you to a specific point in space-time or you can create a wormhole by warping space-time, but either way it's dangerous."

"Wow, you're saying that time travel is possible?" Jemma couldn't believe that the science fiction she had watched on TV when she was a kid might have had some truth to it.

"Yes, time travel is possible, and the only way you can leave here. You'd have to go back to the point in time just before you died and stop the incident that killed you from happening. This can only be done if you weren't meant to die in the first place, of course. Another thing to bear in mind is that if you went back to your specific time, that's not going to help Susie get back. You'd have to find a separate wormhole for her, so it's not as straightforward as you think."

"Tom? There's just one more question I want to ask you. Please don't be cross with me, but I think it's important. If *you* went back in time, is there any way that you can change what happened to you, whatever that might be, so that you would be able to move on and be at peace after you die? What if you could be buried next to your dad?" Jemma braced herself for Tom to start shouting at her again, but instead he gave her a sad smile.

"Jemma, I hear what you're saying and I thank you for caring enough to ask, but I really don't want to talk about it." He shrugged, stood and held out his hand to help her get up off the sand, leaving her in no doubt that the subject was closed.

They spent the rest of the day exploring a small town nearby that Tom used to visit on his holidays and getting to know each other better. All too soon, though, it was evening. As they took one last stroll along the beach Jemma found herself reflecting on the day. She felt so comfortable with Tom. It was as if they had known each other for years and yet... She sighed as Tom's refusal to open up reminded her that they clearly weren't as close as she would like to think. But there had been no mistaking the chemistry between them earlier. He had hinted that he liked her, yet when he'd looked as if he had been about to kiss her, he had withdrawn again. Well, she wasn't going anywhere for a while so she resolved to just enjoy his company for now and see if anything might develop later. She was pretty sure that the attraction wasn't just from her side.

She squinted at the setting sun as it threw bright rays of orange and red light onto the sea, which was a lot livelier now. Small white peaks danced to the fading light and the seagulls screamed hungry cries for their supper.

As Jemma took Tom's hand to return to Swiss Cottage, she sighed with the first hint of happiness she had felt in a very long time.

"Thank you," she said. "I can honestly say that this has been one of the nicest days of my life." They both laughed at her choice of words. "Let me rephrase that. One of the nicest days of my life – and death."

Chapter Eight

Sunday evenings were meant to be quiet, designed to recover after a busy weekend and prepare for the new week ahead, and this one was no different. Alice was snuggled up against Jack on his sofa as they watched *Antiques Roadshow*. They had just eaten a cheese and spinach omelet that Jack had prepared for them and had polished off some cake that Alice had bought earlier.

They hadn't arrived back until gone four in the morning after their ghost-hunting adventure and they had been exhausted. Alice hadn't thought about the fact that all the equipment had had to be packed away at the end of the night and when she had been delegated the tedious job of winding up the electric cables, she had cursed herself for being so keen to come along in the first place. The last hour had been very quiet with no paranormal activity, so when Maggie had suggested they wrap up and go home, she had been relieved. Once all the equipment had been packed away, the group had then continued to talk in the bar for another hour, by which time Alice could barely see, let alone hold an intelligible conversation.

When they'd gotten back to Jack's flat she had collapsed on his bed with all her clothes still on and had slept until eleven o'clock that morning. Waking up next to Jack had been a pleasure. Well, it had been until she had seen herself in a mirror across the room and realized that she still had yesterday's makeup smeared over her face while her blonde hair looked like candy floss. He had laughed when she'd screamed and run into the bathroom, slamming the door behind her. When she had re-emerged, clean-faced with her hair washed and brushed, he had handed her a cup of tea and some toast with a flirtatious grin and a bit of gentle teasing.

Later in the day they had walked to Belsize Park to get the Sunday papers and had ended up having coffee in the same café that she and Jemma had gone to the morning after the party. That had felt strange. The memory of her last visit was still fresh, but she had coped well and hadn't cried as she had feared she might. Perhaps having Jack there with her had helped soften the edges of the grief that still threatened to overcome her every now and then.

When they'd returned to the house, they had spent the rest of the day reading the papers, listening to music, drinking several cups of tea and finishing off a packet of digestive biscuits. Alice had enjoyed the day and it was now with regret that she needed to think about heading back to her flat.

She looked up into Jack's relaxed face. "I'd better make a move."

"What? You're not staying?" The disappointment in Jack's voice was clear, and knowing that he didn't want her to leave warmed her insides.

"I need to get back. I've got things to do tomorrow and, besides, you've got two articles to finish, remember?"

Jack was a freelance music journalist, which involved writing album and concert reviews and investigating new up-and-coming bands, as well as interviewing the more established, successful artists. She knew he loved his work, not just because it gave him relative freedom and flexibility, but because music was a passion of his and what he didn't know about it wasn't worth knowing. He was successful too, earning continuous commissions from all the big music press organizations. The benefits of his job were numerous, but the best had to be the free concert tickets that were always landing on his mat. Not just any old concert tickets either. They were usually accompanied by backstage passes and invitations to the after-show party. Alice had been impressed when he had shown her the stack of unused tickets in his bottom drawer.

"That can wait," he argued, giving her an irresistible puppy-eyes look.

"No, it can't. Anyway, I need an early night and I know I'm not going to get much sleep if I stay here." She planted a firm kiss on his lips then stood, letting him know that her mind was made up. He must have gotten the message because he let out a sigh of defeat before dragging himself from the sofa.

"Okay, but I'm driving you home."

"You don't have to do that."

He glared at her then pulled her into his arms. "I'm not about to let you walk home on your own. I'm giving you a lift and that's that."

"Okay, thanks."

A few minutes later they stopped outside her flat. "Are you sure you don't want to stay over at mine?" His eyes twinkled as they reflected the streetlights and she was more tempted than ever to tell him to take her back, but she kept her resolve and instead kissed him one final time.

"Yes, I'm sure, but why don't you come here tomorrow evening? I could cook us something for dinner then perhaps we could go to one of the wine bars in Hampstead and have a drink."

"Sounds great. It's a date."

She let herself into the flat and was once again hit by the emptiness left by Jemma's absence. The heavy atmosphere seemed to reach out and touch her as she headed into the living room and she shivered despite the warmth blazing from the radiators. Damn, maybe she should have stayed at Jack's after all. But she had a reason for needing to be home tonight and it wasn't just to let Jack work in peace tomorrow.

She wandered into her bedroom, opened her wardrobe door and stared at the dresses hanging in a neat row on the rail. Should she wear jeans and a nice top or would that be too casual? Maybe she should wear a dress? She settled on a pair of smart black trousers and a green jumper. Not too casual, just smart enough to make her look as if she'd made an effort.

She surveyed herself in the mirror and tried to ignore the butterflies fluttering in her belly. She needed something to bring her luck. She had always been a great believer in lucky charms. Although she wasn't sure how much of it was psychological reassurance more than actual luck, she found that wearing one did have the desired effect. She didn't need to think too hard about what her charm would be. She already knew. Jemma had given her a beautiful silver bangle for her birthday last year and she always wore it on special occasions. It had been a while since she had last worn it, though. *Where have I left it?* At that moment nothing was more important than finding the bangle.

She rifled through the drawer that she kept her jewelry in, but the bangle wasn't there. *Shit, where is it?* A sense of unease crept into her as she rummaged with more urgency It had to be there. This was the last present Jemma had given her while she was alive. It might not have cost the Earth but, to her, it was priceless. She stared at the drawer, then at the dressing table, trying to remember when she had last worn it and where she could have put it. By the time she had searched every inch of the floor and every drawer, shelf and bag she was in tears.

"Oh, Jemma, what am I going to do? I can't find the bangle you gave me. I *have* to find it," she cried out loud.

And then she felt it—cool air drawing her across the room, back to her dressing table. A fine mist clouded the mirror for a brief moment before disappearing. She was sure she hadn't imagined it. Goosebumps tingled on her arms as she stared in disbelief at the dressing table. There, in the middle of it and in full view, was the missing bangle. But she was sure it hadn't been there before. How did it get there? Instinctively she knew.

"Thank you, Jemma," she whispered, more tears welling

in her eyes. "Thank you."

Rather than unnerving her, Alice found that her brief encounter with Jemma had given her an odd sense of calm. There was no doubt that it had been Jemma who had helped her find the bangle. It confirmed her suspicions that her friend's spirit was still nearby. *Is she at peace?* She would give anything to talk to her one more time.

She fiddled with the bangle and smiled to herself. Now that she had her lucky charm she would be fine tomorrow. She had never been good at job interviews, which was why she hadn't told Jack about it. If he didn't know about it he wouldn't need to know if it didn't go well. On the other hand, if she got the job it would be a great excuse to celebrate. It was only a waitressing job in a bistro in Camden, but it was the first job she was going for since returning from America and her CV wasn't exactly impressive. Her advantage was that she had worked in several restaurants in New York and was used to a busy, bustling environment. This job would be ideal for her. The hours were split between three day shifts and two evening shifts a week. Her weekends would be free as they had regular weekend staff. And it was local — she could walk to work, saving on travel costs. It was perfect. She *had* to get this job.

As she climbed into bed later that night, her phone bleeped, telling her she had a text. She smiled as she read Jack's message.

Night night gorgeous.

Warmth glowed inside her as she reread the words before snuggling under the duvet. Her last waking thoughts were of Jack gazing down at her, his eyes full of love.

Jemma sat and watched Alice as she slept. She was glad she had been able to help earlier with the bangle. What Alice couldn't have seen was that it had been pushed behind the mirror on the dressing table. All she had had to do was use just enough energy to push it back to the middle where

Alice would see it. It had been a very special moment for her when Alice had thanked her, letting her know that she knew it was her who had helped her find it.

She wished more than ever that she could talk to her friend, to wish her luck with her interview tomorrow and to tell her not to wear that hideous green jumper. She gazed across at the clothes, laid out with Alice's usual precision ready for the morning, and frowned. There was no way she was going to let Alice wear that horrible thing. The green made her face look pasty and washed out — it was one of the most unflattering colors she could possibly wear — and it did nothing for her figure either. No, it would never do, she had to do something. She made her way over to the pile of discarded clothes that Alice had left on the chair while deciding what to wear. On the top of the pile was a lovely dark red blouse that was fitted at the waist. It would show off Alice's slim figure and complement her porcelain complexion. Why the hell hadn't she chosen this to begin with? She sighed at her friend's hopeless sense of fashion and, with enormous effort, managed to push the offending green jumper under the bed and replace it with the red blouse. She grinned to herself as she pictured Alice's puzzled face when she found the swapped top in the morning. She hoped Alice would get the hint.

She stayed with Alice for another half hour or so before heading home. It crossed her mind that the flat should feel more like home. After all, it was where she had lived before she died. However she liked it at Jack's house. Alice would be there more often now that she was going out with Jack. Then there was Susie. She had started to think of her as a little sister and had grown very fond of her. Most of all, though, it was because of Tom that she had stayed. Tom, who made her laugh one minute and drove her mad the next. He was gorgeous, sexy and charming, yet haunted by a tragic past that prevented him from moving on to a better place. She wanted to help him, but she was beginning to realize that a person could only help someone if they wanted to be helped, and it was becoming more and more obvious that Tom had given up the fight a long time ago. Still, she couldn't help wanting to persist, to keep chipping away at the shell he had encased himself in, confident that one day she'd break through and he'd open up to her. She wasn't going to give up on him. She had developed feelings for him that went deeper than anything she had ever felt for anyone and she was going to stand by him, whether he liked it or not.

"Hello, stranger," he said, giving her a warm smile as she returned to Jack's house. "Where have you been?"

"With Alice. She's got an interview tomorrow and she needed a bit of help with her outfit." She chuckled as she thought of Alice turning up at the interview looking like a little green elf. She hoped she had hidden the offending top well enough for Alice not to find it when she discovered it was missing. "Where's Susie?"

"I'm not sure. She said something about visiting a friend." He sighed as Jemma sat down next to him. "I had a chat with her. You know, about her mum."

"Oh."

"You're right. She is unhappy and I feel awful, because it never occurred to me that she would still be feeling sad after all this time. She always seems so bright and cheerful."

"She knows you have a lot on your mind. She doesn't want to burden you with her problems."

"Oh God, that makes me feel even worse."

Jemma touched his arm. "I'm sorry about the way I told you. I should have been more tactful. Tact isn't exactly my strongest quality, in case you hadn't noticed."

"You're honest, that's all, and that's something to be proud of. How am I going to help the poor kid?"

"Would you be okay if she were to leave without you?"

A shadow crossed his face before he answered. "Yes, if it were possible. I'd miss her dreadfully, but I hate to see her so unhappy. If there's a way for her to go back without me, then I'd be happy for her."

That was good enough for Jemma. If Tom was happy for Susie to go back, then that was all that mattered. She smiled, thankful that Tom had seen sense. When he smiled back a strange sensation fluttered somewhere deep inside her, reminding her of the day at the beach. How she longed to kiss those beautiful lips. There was a very good reason she'd called him Hot Lips when she'd first got here. That seemed like such a long time ago now, even though time in this dimension didn't exist anymore.

"I might as well go and talk to Max straightaway. I keep putting it off, but I suppose now's as good a time as any."

"Do you want me to come with you?" he asked, raising his eyebrows. *Is he worried about me?*

"No, if he doesn't like you, he may not want to talk. I'll be fine. Thanks."

As she walked through the open door to the living room, though, she wished she had taken Tom up on his offer. Max scared her and, on top of that, she couldn't get Susie's warning out of her head. As she looked at him now, the same unease that she always got around him crept back. He had an air of danger about him — or was it evil? Either way, it unsettled her and it was with enormous effort that she swallowed her fear and smiled through her nerves.

"Er, Max?" She hesitated, trying to think of what to say. *Remember, he's just a harmless old spook.*

He stared at her in silence, his icy eyes boring into her. Jemma shifted from one foot to the other, raised her head and met his chilly gaze. She blinked when she caught something like pain flash across his face, but before she could be sure he had fixed an angry glare on her.

"What do you want?" he growled, his voice deep sounding as if he had swallowed a bucket full of gravel.

"Erm, I was wondering if I could talk to you about something?"

"What?"

She coughed. "Er, well, as you know, I want to leave this place and you told me before that there's only one way out and that's through a wormhole. I was, well, I was wondering if you would tell me how I'd locate…" She trailed off when she saw the hostility on Max's face.

"Think you're so fucking clever, don't you?" he snarled.

"Oh, no, I just…"

"Come here," he growled.

Jemma had never been up close to Max before and the thought terrified her. But something about this sinister man intrigued her so, taking her time, she moved closer to him, growing more uncomfortable with every step, until she stood in front of him. Up close, she was surprised to see that he wasn't as old as she had first thought. And he looked wet. His old-fashioned clothes, possibly early twentieth century, clung to his body as if he had just climbed out of a swimming pool.

"Are you wet?" she couldn't help asking, her quest forgotten for a moment.

"Of course I bloody am. I drowned, didn't I?"

"Oh, I didn't know. What happened?" she asked, her curiosity replacing her fear.

"I was on a boat, a big boat built for the rich. I got a job on it, shoveling coal in the engine room. Bloody hard work it was, but it was a job and there was the chance of staying in America and starting a new life. But the bloody boat sank." He paused then threw Jemma a glare that chilled her bones. "They said it was unsinkable."

"Oh my God," whispered Jemma. "You were on the Titanic?"

He gave a slight nod. "The night it happened, I had gone up onto the passenger deck. We weren't allowed up there, but it was late and I needed some air. There was a married couple, walking on the deck, but I didn't take much notice of them. When we hit the iceberg, the missus slipped and fell onto the deck. I went over and helped him pick her up. She was a bit shaken, but all right. *I helped them,*" he spat with vehemence.

Jemma shook her head, stunned that she was talking

to someone who had been on the Titanic. She had seen countless films and television programs about it, but here she was, getting the story first-hand from someone who had been there.

"When we were in the water," continued Max, "I saw a lifeboat and tried to swim toward it, but it was so cold. Someone was sitting in the boat looking into the water for survivors. I managed to get quite close and saw it was the man whose wife I had helped. I called to him for help, but he ignored me. He turned away and got someone else out of the water, leaving me to drown. I had helped him and his wife and then he left me to fucking drown." The fury in Max's voice had flared so fast that Jemma shrank away from him. But then he stopped talking and the room filled with a deathly silence as Jemma stared at him, his eyes now filled with a rage that must have been festering for a hundred years. Jemma searched for something appropriate to say, but how the hell should she respond to something like that?

"It was his fault that I died. He could have saved me, but he left me in that water and he's going to pay." The dark menace he radiated was terrifying and Jemma knew, without a doubt, that he meant it.

"Who was he?" she asked, somehow dreading the answer.

"It was him, wasn't it? George *fucking* Cresswell. Tom's grandfather." He spat the words out as if they were poison.

So that was why Max was haunting Jack's house. He must have followed George back here so he could get his revenge. Jemma wanted to know more, but now probably wasn't be a good time to persist. Max's face was red with simmering rage. She needed to get away from him before his anger erupted. There was no way she wanted to be around if that happened. So she said she was sorry to hear his story and bade a hasty goodnight before getting out of the room as quickly as she could.

When she was on her own again, their conversation replayed over and over in her head. Max's revelation had left her in no doubt that he wanted revenge. She knew that Tom's grandfather wasn't in this dimension, probably because he had done nothing wrong. It was very likely that he hadn't even seen or heard Max in the water. After all, it must have been very dark and Max would have been so cold that his voice wouldn't have had enough strength to be heard. And yet Max had been adamant that Tom's grandfather was going to pay one way or another. But if George Cresswell wasn't here, how would Max exact his revenge? Jemma already knew the answer. A dark sense of foreboding gripped her as she realized that there was only one person Max *could* get his revenge on. Tom.

Chapter Nine

Alice stopped outside the restaurant and smiled as she read the sign over the window — *Glitz*. The silver and gold letters sparkled as if they were made of thousands of tiny crystals. It was glamorous and, well, glitzy. She peered through one of the windows, which was surrounded by tiny white fairy lights on the inside, and saw a colorful, stylish eatery with tables of various sizes placed around the room for customer comfort and privacy. The place looked fun and she longed to be a part of it — and she hadn't even walked through the door yet.

She glanced at her reflection in the window and was glad she hadn't been able to find that green jumper this morning. It was very odd how it had disappeared like that. She remembered she had put it on the chair before she had gone to bed and was sure she hadn't picked the red top out. But whatever the explanation, it had done her a favor because the red top looked so much better and that, along with her lucky bangle, had given her a much-needed confidence boost.

She checked her watch. *Two minutes to ten. Perfect.* She pushed open the door, stepped inside and was greeted by the distinctive sound of Abba. She loved Abba, so that was another good omen.

"I'll be right with you," called a voice from behind a door.

Alice took in her surroundings with a rush of excitement. This place was fantastic, with its twinkling lights, delicious smell of fresh coffee and friendly mood — and that was without the buzz of customers. The walls were covered with mirrors and pictures of seventies and eighties pop stars. The bleached oak tables were laid with stylish plain silver cutlery and shiny wineglasses. White candles and clean linen napkins finished off the uncluttered but stylish table decor. The red velvet-covered seats were just right and gave the place a feeling of comfort mixed with a hint of decadence.

"Sorry about that," called the voice as its owner emerged from behind the door. "You must be Alice. I'm Oscar, named after the great Oscar Wilde. Actually, my mum tells me I was named after my granny's dog, but Oscar Wilde sounds so much better, don't you think?" he said, with a wink.

"Absolutely," Alice grinned, "unless the dog was very clever and very beautiful."

"He was a wire-haired sausage dog."

"Oh. Oscar Wilde it is then." Alice laughed, liking this bubbly, flamboyant man. He was tall, with his blond hair styled in an immaculate quiff and his hands manicured and smooth. The black T-shirt he wore had ABBA written across it in silver glitter. In fact, his blue eyes sparkled almost as much as the glitter on his T-shirt.

"Would you like a coffee? I'm desperate for another cup. I can't function until I've got at least three shots of espresso inside me."

As Oscar produced two cups of steaming coffee from the large espresso machine, he glanced over at Alice.

"So, tell me about yourself. Do you like Abba?"

"Yes, I love Abba," she enthused. Jemma had often teased her, saying that people who liked alternative music weren't supposed to like Abba. That was bullshit. She loved Abba as much as The Sisters of Mercy.

"Good, who's your favorite member?"

"Oh, I'm not sure. The blonde one, I think."

"Agnetha? She's great, but I love Frida. I met her once, you know, she was so nice. She's an amazing lady. Did you know she's a princess now?"

This was the most unusual interview that Alice had ever

been to. When Oscar had asked her to tell him about herself, she'd assumed that he had meant her work experience. She certainly hadn't expected a discussion on which member of Abba she liked best.

When she left, over an hour later, she still didn't feel like she'd just been to a job interview. They had chatted about music, food, New York and his boyfriend, Dean, who was the cook at Glitz. She didn't recall Oscar actually telling her that she had got the job, but guessed she probably had when he asked if she could start the following week.

Now, as she walked up Camden High Street, Alice felt like skipping. She had just gotten a job. And not just any job. Glitz was the most amazing restaurant she had ever been to and Oscar was going to be so much fun to work with. She couldn't wait to tell Jack. She would cook him a nice meal and, later, they would go up to Hampstead for a celebratory drink.

She grinned at a couple of punks strolling past her. She loved Camden, with its quirky shops and eccentric shoppers. As she strolled past a shop selling alternative-style clothing, her eyes were drawn to a gorgeous black corset style top hanging in the window. It was gorgeous, just the type of thing she loved, but she couldn't afford to buy clothes right now. Maybe after her first payday... She was about to turn and walk away when a voice inside her head screamed 'buy it, buy it'. It wouldn't do any harm to go in and have a closer look, although she didn't need another top. Anyway, twenty-five quid was too much. But it was a really nice top. Oh, what the hell. Making her mind up, she smiled at the girl behind the counter as she entered the shop and asked to try the top on.

By the time she got back to her flat, laden with ingredients for tonight's dinner, a couple of bottles of wine and the top, she was exhausted. If only she could have told Jemma about the interview. She would have loved Oscar. She would also have approved of her spontaneous purchase. She wasn't sure what had made her buy it when she knew she couldn't afford it, but she was glad she had. It had almost been as if Jemma had been with her, willing her to buy it. But of course that was ridiculous. It was a comforting thought, though.

She pushed the kitchen door open with her foot and was about to put the shopping bags down when a movement by the sink made her glance up. She dropped the bags in shock as the young boy she had seen before took a step toward her. A scream stuck in her throat as she froze. *How the hell did he get in? And, more to the point, what does he want?*

"Who are you and how did you get into my flat?" she demanded, when she got her voice back.

The boy just stared at her, silent and mysterious. Alice gaped back, as if she was under some sort of spell. It was like she was in a trance, unable to move or speak, no longer in control of her actions. Her body tingled as if some sort of energy was probing her, searching for something inside her, demanding her compliance. As she gazed at the boy, she noticed that his skin appeared almost transparent and that his blue eyes were so bright that they radiated a light that seemed to bore deep into her soul. The room was cold, unnaturally cold, and Alice shivered as she became more aware of the intense silence surrounding her.

"*Alice.*" Although the boy had not moved his lips, she knew it had been him who had whispered. *How does he know my name?*

But before she was able to ask, a loud shrill noise thundered through the silence, making her jump and breaking the spell. Alice glanced over at the ringing phone but returned her eyes to the boy straight away. He had gone. He'd just vanished. One minute he was there and a split second later, he wasn't.

Fear chilled her bones as she gripped the back of a chair for support. It had been one thing seeing the boy in a garden or Tube train, but it took on a whole new level when he appeared in her flat and even knew her name. It was obvious that this was no ordinary boy. The way he had disappeared like that meant that he must have been some sort of apparition. Was he a ghost? Probably, but why on earth was he following her? She had the distinct impression that he had been about to communicate with her, but why?

The phone had fallen silent again, but Alice remained rooted to the spot, alone and diffident, shaken by what had just happened. If it had happened at all. *Had I just imagined the whole thing? It had seemed so real and yet…*

She sank into a chair, the shopping bags forgotten, and stared at the empty space where the boy had been standing. With shaking hands, she picked up her phone and dialed Jack's number.

"Hello." His voice smiled through the earpiece. "I just tried to call."

"Oh, it was you." Alice's voice broke into a sob.

"Hey, are you okay?"

"Yes… No. Jack? Can I come over?" She didn't want to be alone. She needed to get out of the flat and, more than anything, she needed to be with Jack.

"Of course you can. I stayed up half the night finishing those articles so I could get them out of the way. I called to ask if you fancied coming over for lunch."

"That would be lovely. I'm on my way." Alice ended the call, grabbed her bag then ran out of the flat as fast as she could.

Twenty minutes later, Alice was in Jack's kitchen, clutching a mug of tea and telling him about the ghostly boy. She reminded him about the time she had seen him outside his kitchen window and told him about seeing him on the Underground and in the church at Jemma's funeral.

"I didn't imagine it, Jack, he was right there in front of me." She ran her hand through her hair. *What if Jack thinks I'm making it up?*

But he took her hand in his, stared her straight in the eyes and said, "It does sound as though the boy is trying to communicate with you. Look, there's another psychic meeting on Wednesday. Why don't you mention it to the group then? Someone else may have had a similar experience and be able to offer some advice."

Anyone else might have laughed at her and run a mile, but not Jack. She leaned forward and kissed him.

"Thank you, I'll do that. Oh," she cried, remembering her exciting news. "I completely forgot to tell you. I've got a job. I went for an interview this morning and it was amazing…"

Jemma watched Alice and Jack eating their lunch while Alice told Jack all about her new job. She had listened with curiosity when Alice had spoken off this strange boy who had visited her at the flat. She could have kicked herself for not following Alice home after her interview, but once she had persuaded her to buy that top she had gone back to Jack's house. *If Alice is seeing – and even hearing – ghosts, then why can't she see me? And who is this boy anyway?*

She left the two of them to finish their lunch and wandered into the living room. In the corner, as usual, sat the scowling and hostile shadow of Max. He still gave her the creeps.

"What do you want?"

She flinched – he sounded so angry. "Nothing," she replied and left the room again. Back in the kitchen with Alice and Jack, she strolled over to the window then stared out into the garden. She couldn't forget Max's hateful words the last time they had spoken and wondered just how real a threat he was to Tom. She needed to be alone, to find her own private space she could go to when she wanted a bit of peace and solitude. Even though Tom was out and Susie was watching next door's TV, the house still felt crowded. She longed for somewhere she could go to that was away from this house and the people in it. Tom was at his beach in Norfolk, so she couldn't go there – heaven forbid he might think she was stalking him.

A memory of a place her mother had taken her to when she was a child flashed through her mind. Ashdown Forest was a beautiful forest high on a hill in Sussex where her mother used to take her for picnics in the summer. The views from one particular clearing were out of this world and on a clear day it was possible to see the planes coming in to land at Gatwick. But best of all, Ashdown Forest was the home of one of her favorite childhood characters, Winnie The Pooh. Her mother would read her favorite Pooh stories to her, lying on a picnic blanket with full bellies, and afterward they would go and find the places they had just read about in the book. As a child she had never quite understood why she never got to see the bear or his friends, but her memories of Ashdown Forest were nonetheless magical.

She decided that she would go to the clearing with the beautiful views. There used to be a bench there that would be the perfect place for her to sit and ponder for a few hours. She hoped it was still there. She turned away from the window and jumped as she came face-to-face with Max. "Oh."

He stood very close to her, close enough for her catch the smell of stale seawater on his clothes. A spark of fear flickered in her as his eyes bored into her. "Was there something you wanted?" she asked, trying to keep her voice from trembling.

"No."

"Oh. Well, I've got to go somewhere. Bye." She closed her eyes, ready to transport herself away.

"I will get my revenge, you know."

She snapped them open again and stared at him. "Pardon?"

"Revenge. One way or the other, Tom will pay for what happened to me."

"Why Tom? He hasn't done anything wrong."

Max laughed, a dark, malevolent snarl. "He's a fucking Cresswell and that makes him guilty. Make no mistake, he will pay, one way or another. When he's least expecting it, I'll be there. I've been biding my time. I'm just waiting for my moment and it will come, just you see."

Jemma had heard enough. She had to get the hell out of there, *now*. Closing her eyes again, she imagined herself in the heart of Ashdown Forest and, in a fraction of a second she was there, leaving Max behind at the house. *Oh, it's good to be back.* She started to walk along the path, glad that it was such bad weather. The icy wind and relentless rain meant she had the place to herself. It wasn't long before she became lost in her thoughts, her solitary figure throwing the occasional ghostly shadow against the trees as she ambled along the muddy track.

Max's outburst had unsettled her. Her thoughts flitted from one person to another — Tom, Susie, Alice, Max. What was she going to do about Max and his threat to Tom? When she had told Tom what he had said, he had just laughed and said that if Max was going to do something, he would have done it a long time ago. Then, of course, there were her feelings for Tom. Feelings that were growing stronger every day but might never be reciprocated. Did she want to return to a life without Tom? If she did manage to persuade Susie to leave with her, he would be left alone with Max.

And what about Alice and the mysterious boy? Why was a ghost following her? Could she be in any danger?

Deep in thought, she didn't notice the woman sitting on the bench when she got to the clearing. It was only when she turned to approach it that she saw she wasn't alone. Even in the pouring rain, the woman was dry, like herself, and her hair remained still as the strong wind rushed past her. It was obvious that she was a ghost, which meant that the lady would be able to see her. Sighing, she turned around to walk away, resigned to finding another quiet spot, when the lady spoke.

"Don't mind me," she said in a soft voice. "There's plenty of room for both of us."

"I don't want to intrude," replied Jemma, keen to get back to her thoughts.

"You're not. To be honest, I'd be glad of a bit of company. It gets a bit lonely up here, day in and day out."

"Are you here all the time then?" asked Jemma. She sat down next to the lady and turned to look at her. She had the saddest eyes she had ever seen—troubled and lonely.

"I've got nowhere else to go. So, how long have you been here, dear?"

"Oh, not long. About five minutes."

The lady smiled. "I didn't mean *here*, I meant, how long have you been dead?"

"Oh, sorry. It must be over two months now. What about you?"

"I died in 1937," said the lady, with a note of sadness. "Robert, that's my husband, and I had agreed to meet here, at this very spot, when we eventually died. We promised that we'd find each other again in the next world and that we'd spend the rest of eternity watching the sun setting from this bench."

"That's so romantic," said Jemma with a sigh. She loved a good love story. "So what happened? Where's Robert now?"

"He died about five years after me. But he didn't come, he went somewhere else. I don't know where. I think he's lost." She stared out across the trees before turning back to face Jemma. "It had never occurred to us that we'd end up in different places. He's gone and I'm here, alone, and I don't know why."

"Haven't you tried to find out?" asked Jemma, recalling her own refusal to accept her fate when she had first arrived.

"I just sit here and wait for Robert, hoping that one day he'll let me know what to do."

Jemma's heart went out to this desolate and lonely woman. She was probably in her late fifties, petite and delicate-looking, and was smartly dressed in a 1930s-style blue dress. Thick silver streaks contrasted with her nearly black hair, giving her a distinguished appearance.

"I don't know why I'm here either, but I'm trying to find out. I'm pretty sure I wasn't meant to die and I plan to leave here one day when I've worked out how to use a wormhole. When I've figured it out, I'll help you if you like."

"That's very sweet of you, but I can't leave. What if Robert comes and I'm not here? No, I'm staying, but I hope you find your way out. I'm Claire, by the way."

"I'm Jemma. I used to come here with my mother when I was a child. It's nice to be back."

It was so refreshing to talk to someone new and Claire listened with patience as Jemma told her about her unfortunate death, her futile attempts to talk to Alice and her crush on the handsome and troubled ghost who lived in Jack's house. She didn't tell her about Max, though. There was no need to spoil things.

Much later, Jemma stood to leave. She needed to get back to Susie. "Can I come and see you again?"

"Of course you can, that would be lovely. You know where I am."

Jemma was in a much better mood when she got back to the house. Meeting Claire had been a lovely surprise — she hadn't expected to make a new friend. She found it intriguing that Claire was content with just sitting in the same place, day in and day out, waiting for her husband who was probably never going to turn up. Why was Claire in this dimension? Maybe she wasn't meant to have died, or did she have some sort of mysterious reason for not being able to move on? Claire hadn't been very keen to talk about herself and somehow most of the conversation had been about Jemma.

"Hello. Where have you been?" Susie was lounging in an armchair as Jemma appeared in the living room.

"I went for a walk. Have you ever been to Ashdown Forest?" she asked as she sat down next to Susie.

"No. Why?"

"Just wondering. I'll take you there one day. It's lovely." Jemma reached out and brushed a stray strand of Susie's fringe to the side. It was an affectionate gesture, but one that resulted in Susie bursting into tears. "Hey, Susie, what's wrong?" Jemma put her arms around the crying child and held her tightly.

"My mum used to do that," she sobbed, reminding Jemma

that, for all her bravado, she was still only eleven.

"Oh, you poor love." Tears pricked Jemma's eyes as she felt Susie's heartbreak. "We've got to get you home. Did Tom talk to you about you leaving?"

"Yes, and I told him not to be so stupid." Susie's voice was sharp, which was unlike her.

"What? Oh, Susie, why did you say that? He's trying to help," scolded Jemma.

"Because there's no way I'm leaving without him."

"Will you stop being such a bloody saint? Tom wants you to leave, he wants you to be happy. What's the problem? I'll stay here with him if that's what's bothering you."

"Yeah, right," snapped Susie.

"I mean it, Susie, if that what it takes to make you agree, then I'll stay." Jemma was only too aware of the enormity of what she was saying.

"Now you're the one being a saint," retorted Susie. "And I wasn't being a saint *actually*. I was just stating a fact."

"What do you mean?"

"Nothing. It's complicated. Just leave it."

"No. Susie, listen to me. You have a chance to go home, to leave this place and be with your family again. Tom wants you to go and I'm going to find out how to do it because I know it's possible. What's so complicated about that?"

Susie glared at her, her eyes brimming with more tears as she whispered, "I can't leave without Tom, not ever."

"Why not?" demanded Jemma.

"Because..." Susie paused then took a deep breath. "It's because of Tom that I died."

Chapter Ten

"Did you kill Susie?"

Tom stared at Jemma, his face frozen in shock. "Why on earth do you ask that?"

"Sorry, I didn't mean for it to come out like that. I know that you wouldn't have deliberately killed her, but—"

"But you still think I killed her," interrupted Tom, with a chill creeping into his voice.

"Well, that's what I heard. Look, will you just answer my question? Did you kill her?" Jemma was determined to get an answer from him, whatever it took. She'd had enough of being fobbed off with his excuses and elusiveness. She could sort of understand that he found certain parts of his past painful to talk about, but if he did have anything to do with Susie's death, even if it was an accident, it was about time he was straight with her.

"Of course I didn't kill her. How can you even think that?" His eyes had clouded over, masking the warmth she had grown so fond of.

"So why did Susie say you did then?" demanded Jemma, trying her hardest to keep her voice calm.

"What exactly did she say?"

"That it's because of you that she died."

"So she didn't actually say that I killed her?" he challenged.

"Well, not in those exact words, no."

"Perhaps you'd better check your facts before accusing people of murder, then," he snapped. His brows had drawn together, his features now dark and angry.

"I never said I thought you'd murdered her, I know you wouldn't do that. But Susie wouldn't elaborate and you never talk about it so I'm left to draw my own conclusions. If you had told me what happened we wouldn't be having this conversation now." Her voice was trembling now with the effort of not losing her temper. *Why is he so bloody defensive?*

"And if you were my friend, you wouldn't be accusing me of killing Susie," he shouted before storming out of the room.

"If I really were your friend you would have told me yourself," she yelled after him.

Susie had also been evasive, saying that she shouldn't have said anything and that it was up to Tom to tell her. Jemma expelled a frustrated sigh as she replayed the argument in her head, pacing back and forth across the room. But as she started to calm a little, she was beginning to see why Tom had been so upset. Her question had been too direct, almost accusing, which was the last thing she'd meant. *Damn, why do I always storm in and cause carnage before thinking?* She should have explained what Susie had said then asked him, in a calm and rational way what had happened. Perhaps he would have told her everything and she could have given him her support. Instead they had fallen out and this time it was for real. Her temper had always gotten her into trouble when she had been alive and now it had just lost her a good friend. Would he ever forgive her? She wouldn't blame him if he never spoke to her again.

She had a strong urge to get away from the house so she could work out how she was going to make amends. She liked Tom a lot. In fact, when she had told Susie that she was willing to stay behind she had been glad of an excuse to stay with him. And now she had blown it. *Shit.*

In a split second, she found herself back in Ashdown Forest, thankful for the fact that it was quiet again. She roamed from one end of the forest to the other, her mind racing with snippets of her argument with Tom. Why had she been so tactless? She knew without a doubt that he would never hurt anyone, but her question had come out all wrong and now he thought she was accusing him of murder. She cursed herself over and over until she felt like screaming.

After a while she found herself back at her favorite spot. As she stared out across the expanse of trees and gorse, a soft voice spoke behind her.

"Hello again."

"Huh?" Jemma had been so absorbed in her thoughts that she had forgotten about Claire. She turned around to greet her new friend and was comforted by her warm smile and welcoming gesture to sit down.

"You look like you've got the weight of the world on your shoulders," said Claire. "Are you all right?"

"Oh, Claire, I've just done something really stupid and now I've blown it with Tom," she cried, flopping down next to Claire.

"Surely it can't be that bad. Just say you're sorry and I'm sure he'll forgive you."

"I accused him of killing a child. I didn't mean it, but I more or less called him a murderer." Oh God, it sounded even worse saying it out loud.

"And did he?"

"Oh no, of course not. Tom would never hurt anyone."

"So why did you accuse him?"

"Because I'm stupid." Jemma sighed. "I always do this. I open my big mouth before I think about what I'm saying. In this case, I was frustrated with Tom for being so secretive and I suppose I thought I could force it out of him. Instead I've really hurt him and now he hates me."

"You may have hurt him, Jemma, but he won't hate you. Tom will calm down and when he does, make sure you grovel like hell then tell him what you just told me. He'll understand."

"Really?" Jemma wasn't so sure. Tom had been very angry. In fact, she wouldn't blame him if he did hate her now. The thought filled her with panic. Tom's friendship was more important to her than she had thought and it was only now that she was beginning to understand the depth of her feelings for him. She didn't just fancy him. She didn't just want him as a friend. It was as if they were always meant to have found each other. He was her soulmate. Tears pooled in her eyes as the realization brought more despair.

"I've got to go." She jumped up, now desperate to find Tom.

"Oh." Claire's face fell. "Do you have to go so soon? It's just that I'd forgotten how nice it is to have a bit of company."

"I'm sorry, Claire, but I need to get back to Tom. I have to talk to him. You do understand, don't you?"

"Of course. Don't worry about me. Go and find Tom, but will you let me know how you get on?"

Jemma looked at Claire's sad eyes with a pang of sympathy. Although she needed to find Tom as soon as possible, she didn't want to leave Claire alone when it was obvious that she was in need of a bit of companionship.

"Come with me, Claire. Come back to the house and meet Tom and Susie. You'll really like them and I know they'll welcome you."

"That's very sweet of you, Jemma, but I can't leave here. What if Robert comes?" Claire's soft brown eyes were filled with concern that she might miss her beloved husband. Jemma didn't have the heart to tell her that it was unlikely he was ever going to turn up. It was probably the only thing keeping her sane in her lonely existence.

"Tell you what. Just come for a short while. It'll only take a split second to get there and once you know where we are, you can come back whenever you like. If Robert should turn up and you're not here, he'll wait. You've waited all these years, why shouldn't he wait for a little while? Come on, Claire. Come with me. Please."

"I suppose a few minutes wouldn't hurt." Claire seemed to be torn. In the end her loneliness must have won because she agreed to come back to the house.

"Tom's not here, obviously, but Susie and Max are so I'll introduce you to them before I go and find Tom," said Jemma a second later as she showed Claire into the kitchen.

"Max?"

Jemma pulled a face and pointed to the wall separating the kitchen and living room.

"Yeah, he's this creepy old spook who just sits in there and hates everything and everyone. We'll get him over with first then we'll go and find Susie."

"Max," called Jemma as she and Claire walked through the wall into the living room. As usual, Max was sitting in his chair in the corner looking damp and miserable. Jemma forced a smile onto her face. "This is my friend Claire."

"Hello, Max," said Claire, with a smile.

"Hmph," growled Max.

"Nice to meet you too," said Claire, as Jemma led her back to the kitchen.

"Don't take any notice of him," said Jemma when they were safely out of his hearing. "He's like that with everyone. Ah, here's Susie. Susie, come and meet my friend Claire."

After Jemma had introduced Claire to Susie, she left them to get to know each other while she went off to find Tom. The most obvious place to start searching was Norfolk. She was there in an instant and was soon scouring the long, sandy beach hoping to find him. The sea was rough today, the wind throwing huge waves with high white crests crashing against the shore, creating a noisy and dramatic backdrop. Straining her eyes, she scanned the area, but nobody was there, living or dead. She was beginning to despair that she wouldn't find him when she turned toward the dunes and spotted a solitary figure sitting in the shelter of the long, waving grass. The same place that she had sat with him last time they had been there. Her heart flipped when she saw him, shoulders slumped, head bowed and deep in thought.

"Hi," she said with a hint of caution as she approached him.

"What do you want?" he asked without looking up.

"I came to find you. To apologize." She swallowed, not sure what to say. "Can I sit down?"

"If you must."

"Tom, I'm really, really sorry about what I said to you earlier. I never meant to imply that you would ever deliberately hurt anyone. I know you wouldn't. I just wanted to ask you about what Susie had said, but it came out all wrong."

She waited for him to say something, but when he remained silent, she continued. "I should have kept quiet and respected your wishes not to discuss it. I'm sorry." She hesitated as she racked her brain for something else to say that wouldn't do any more harm. She was only too aware of her ability to say the wrong thing and that was the last thing she wanted to do right now.

Desperate to make him believe her, she said, "You are the most decent, kind and honest person I've ever met. You're also the most important person in my life and it's killing me that you're so cross with me."

"That's not possible," he said, breaking his silence.

"What?"

Tom finally looked up at her, the faintest hint of a smile twitching on his lips. "It can't be killing you because you're already dead." He grinned, the last shadows on his face dissolving as his anger seemed to melt away. "Did you mean it when you said that I'm the most important person in your life?"

Jemma's eyes filled with tears as she nodded. Tears of relief that he was talking to her again and tears of joy at the overwhelming love she felt for him.

"Yes, I meant it. Tom… I love you." There, she'd said it. She hardly dared glance at him as she waited for his response. Tom reached out for her hand and entwined his fingers with hers. After what felt like forever, she plucked up the courage to gaze into his eyes. He didn't need to say anything for her to know, but nonetheless, she was ecstatic when he replied, "I love you too."

* * * *

Alice opened her eyes and smiled up at the dark gray sky above her. She had thought Jack had gone mad when he had suggested a picnic on Hampstead Heath in December, just weeks before Christmas.

"Jack, it's freezing outside." She had shivered just thinking about it. "No one has picnics in December."

"Oh, come on. Where's your sense of adventure?" Jack had said, laughing at her reaction.

"Adventure? I left it next to the bloody central heating boiler," she'd grumbled.

But Jack, of course, had been right. He had packed a thick, waterproof blanket, along with a flask of soup, hot baked potatoes wrapped in foil to keep them warm, and salt and vinegar Pringles. They had put on layers of jumpers under their winter coats and Jack had even brought a blanket to cover their legs. It had been the best picnic she'd ever had. They had snuggled up on the blanket, which protected them from the chilly breeze, and talked while sipping their cups of steaming-hot tomato soup.

As the light started fading and the flask emptied, Alice had lain down next to Jack, savoring the warmth of his body under the fleece. Now, staring up at the sky, she sighed in contentment as he chatted about his job.

She was amazed at the intensity of her feelings for him. He just had to look at her with those big brown eyes and her stomach flipped. He made her feel as if she were the most beautiful woman in the world and she was in no doubt that he would do anything for her, as she would for him.

It felt so right when he leaned over and kissed her, gently at first, then with more urgency as she responded with a passion she hadn't known she had. She was a little embarrassed when he slipped his hand under both of her chunky jumpers. After all, they were out in a public place, but when he traced the contours of her breasts with his fingers before sliding down to the button of her jeans, she forgot all about any modesty. Alice moaned as he continued down, caressing the delicate skin between her legs. She clung to him, desperate for him to make love to her, not caring anymore where she was. When he slipped his finger inside her knickers her insides tightened as her need intensified. "Jack…"

"Shh, be quiet and just enjoy yourself. You can thank me later," he growled in her ear.

A rush of butterflies scattered through her belly as she surrendered to his touch. It was only afterward that she felt the cool air brushing against her skin, which felt deliciously sensuous next to the heat of their bodies under the blanket.

"I can't believe you just made me come," she giggled. "On Hampstead Heath of all places."

Jack propped himself up on his elbows and smiled down at her, his eyes radiant. "I can give you another one if you like," he murmured, stroking her cheek.

Tempting though it was, Alice was becoming aware of her surroundings again and the thought that some dog walker might stumble across them was enough to stop her from accepting his sexy offer. No, they would wait until they got home. Then she would thank him once they were in the warmth and privacy of the bedroom.

"Why don't we head back?" she whispered into his ear. "I believe we have some unfinished business to take care of."

As they walked hand in hand back through the Heath, which was now in complete darkness, happiness swirled through Alice. She was in love with the most perfect man in the world. He was gorgeous, sexy and sensitive. He even shared her interest in the paranormal. Her only regret was not being able to share her good fortune with Jemma. It seemed ironic that losing Jemma had led to her and Jack becoming closer. And yet, sometimes it felt like Jemma was still around. Sometimes, she would catch the scent of her perfume or think that she could hear her voice. She often felt her presence in both Jack's house and their flat. Maybe, if she could continue to develop her psychic gift, she might one day be able to say a proper goodbye to her friend. The psychic meeting was scheduled for the following day so she might learn more then.

"By the way." Jack interrupted her thoughts. "Do you remember Maggie from the ghost-hunting group?"

"Yes, of course."

"She's coming to the meeting tomorrow. Apparently she has something she wants to show you."

"Ooh, that sounds interesting. I'm glad she's coming, I liked her."

"She liked you too. She said that you have a natural gift and that she can help you develop it. Are you going to tell her about the boy?"

"Yes, I think if anyone will know why he's following me, she will." Just thinking about the ghostly child made her uneasy again. She gripped Jack's hand harder as they approached a small pond near the edge of the heath. They stopped for a moment to admire the lights from the houses opposite reflecting on the smooth surface of the water. All of a sudden, the peaceful atmosphere seemed to change, the shadows from the trees becoming darker, the air heavy and silent. A gray mist crept across the pond, dark and menacing. It seemed to be reaching out to her, its cold, bony fingers beckoning her to come closer.

"Come on, let's get out of here." Alice snapped out of the spell and pulled Jack toward the distant, lit road.

"What's up?"

"Didn't you see it? The mist?"

"Alice, it was just mist. I think talking about the boy has spooked you a bit. I don't sense anything out of the ordinary here."

A few minutes later, as they strolled up Pond Street, Alice stopped and turned around, convinced she was going to see the boy following them. But there was no one there. *I must be imagining it.* Jack put his arm around her and pulled her closer.

"Come on. Let's get you home."

Back in the warm, cozy kitchen at Jack's house, Alice reflected on what had happened by the pond. Jack was right, it really had just been mist. Her imagination was beginning to play tricks on her. Had she also imagined the boy in her kitchen? And on the Tube? She was beginning to doubt what was real and what wasn't.

She filled the kettle then flicked the switch on. A nice hot chocolate was just what they needed. Then they would go upstairs to finish off what they'd started on the heath. As she planned what naughty things she was going to do to Jack later, she turned toward the sink to wash out a mug, when something outside the window caught her attention. She screamed and dropped the mug into the sink as the pale, eerie face of the ghost-boy stared back at her through the glass.

Chapter Eleven

"What's wrong?" By the time Jack rushed into the kitchen Alice was cowering on the floor by the sink.

"He's there, Jack. Look, he's there. Outside. He's watching me." Fear had tightened its grip around her throat and she was finding it hard to breathe.

"Alice, there's no one there. See for yourself." Jack put his arms around her and helped her back to her feet.

"But he was there. He was definitely there, Jack. Why's he doing this?" Shaking, she pointed to the window. "Look," she cried, unable to stop the rising panic. But as she returned her gaze to where she'd seen the boy, she saw for herself that there was nobody outside. All she could see was hers and Jack's reflections against the dark background.

"Alice, there really is nobody there. Do you want me to go out and check?"

"Oh yes, would you?" She held her breath as Jack unlocked the back door, but a new fear took hold as he pulled it open. "Jack, be careful." Even though she knew that a closed door wasn't going to stop the boy if he was determined to come in, she felt a lot more vulnerable with it wide open.

After a minute or two Jack came back in, shaking his head. "I've checked everywhere, There's no one there."

"You do believe me, don't you?" Oh God, he was going to think she was crazy.

"Of course." Jack led her into the living room then sat her down on the sofa. "I'm going to make that hot chocolate, then you'd better get some sleep." Before he left the room he gave her a reassuring smile, but there was something in his eyes that hadn't been there before — doubt. He was beginning to doubt her. He must have known that she wasn't making it up on purpose, but could he be starting to think that it was all in her mind? After all, nobody else except her had ever seen the boy. Maybe that was it. Maybe the strain of the last few months had affected her more than she had realized and she really was imagining it?

"Here. Drink this." Jack came back in soon after, handed her a cup of steaming-hot chocolate then sat next to her. "Are you all right?"

"Yes. I'm sorry. I was so sure I saw him, but now I don't know what to think. I'm beginning to doubt what's real and what isn't."

He squeezed her arm and kissed the top her head. "You've had a lot to deal with lately. Try not to dwell on it."

Alice stayed in the kitchen with Jack while he finished clearing away the last few dishes. As he worked, she noticed him gaze out of the window. His reflection stared back, his expression grim and eyes still showing the hint of doubt she had seen earlier. When he suggested that she go up to bed she didn't argue. She didn't remember her head hitting the pillow before sleep claimed her.

* * * *

The following morning she woke in Jack's arms. He was still asleep. His steady breathing soothed her as she lay with her head on his chest. The previous night's scare played over in her mind, but now that the sun was streaming through the crack in the curtains she couldn't help questioning why she had overreacted the way she had. Yes, it was strange that this boy was following her, but he was just a child, for God's sake. What could he do to her? She closed her eyes and snuggled into Jack's warmth. Well, she wasn't going to let the kid spoil things between her and Jack. From now on she would ignore him if she saw him again and if he wanted to talk to her he would have to make more of an effort.

She must have drifted off to sleep again because the next thing she knew something cold and wet was nudging her cheek and rattling so loud that it sounded like someone had brought an old diesel engine into the bed. She opened her eyes to find Casper staring at her, purring loudly, and Jack sitting next to him. Water dripped from his wet hair onto his muscular chest, which was exposed where his bathrobe fell open. Something stirred deep inside her, causing her heart to pump harder. He looked gorgeous.

"Hello, sleepyhead," he said, holding a cup of tea out for her. "Feeling better?"

"Mmm. What time is it?" she croaked, taking the cup.

"Eleven-thirty."

"Really? The last time I looked it was seven o'clock and you were snoring your head off."

"I don't snore," he protested, playfully ruffling her hair.

"You so do." She took a sip of her tea before putting the cup down on the bedside table. "Come here."

"Hey, not in front of the cat." He chuckled and nudged Casper off the bed. Casper stuck his nose in the air and stalked out of the bedroom.

Jack slid off his bathrobe and let it fall to the floor. Alice let her eyes roam from his broad shoulders, down his firm torso to his hard...erm, thighs. He climbed onto the bed, straddled her then pinned her arms down with a firm grip. "Now where were we? Oh yes, I was about to ravish you."

* * * *

An hour later she joined him in the kitchen, where he handed her a mug of fresh coffee.

"Mmm, I could have spent all day in bed." She smiled, her body still tingling with the pleasure Jack had just given her.

"That would have been interesting. Especially as we've got eight people turning up for the meeting in just over an hour."

"Oh yes. Do you think they'll guess? About us, I mean?"

Jack shrugged. "Nah, why would they? You were here last time. As far as they're concerned, nothing's changed. Do you want to tell them?"

"Do you?"

"If you do. Look, I really don't mind what people think, but if you want to tell them, it's fine by me."

"Let's play it by ear then," she said, clearing the breakfast dishes away.

An hour later, as Jack opened the front door to the first of the guests, Alice strolled into the living room, now set up to accommodate the meeting. She glanced at the chairs arranged in a circle, then glanced across at the spare armchair in the corner, wondering if she should pull it into the circle too. She shivered. Jack never used the chair, Casper wouldn't go anywhere near that part of the room and the one time she had sat on it, she had felt so uneasy that she had never gone near it again. No, the chair would stay where it was. She'd bet there was a spirit residing in that corner and she couldn't help wondering who it might be and why it was haunting this house. Apart from the episodes with the boy, things had been quieter during the last couple of weeks, with only a few bumps now and then. But the presence of the spirits, whoever they might be, was always there.

Once the group were seated in the living room with their cups of tea and biscuits, Jack started the meeting. Maggie wasn't there, though. That was a shame, because Alice had been looking forward to chatting with her again. Then the doorbell rang and Alice nodded to Jack that she would get it.

"Hello, love. Am I late?" Maggie beamed as Alice pulled open the door.

"Hi, Maggie, don't worry, they've only just started. Would you like a tea before you go in?"

"Ooh, yes please." She studied Alice for a minute. "My God, girl, who put that sparkle in your eyes?"

Heat rushed to Alice's face as she turned around to get the milk from the fridge. "Sparkle?" she asked.

"Honey, you've got the look of someone in *love*. I'd know that look anywhere, and if I'm not mistaken that glow in your cheeks wasn't there the last time I saw you either. So, who's the lucky man?"

Alice turned back to Maggie and handed her the tea. She couldn't help the grin that stretched from ear to ear. "Well, now that you mention it…"

"I knew it." Maggie chuckled. "So do I know him?"

"Maybe."

"It's Jack, isn't it?"

"Well, yes."

"Good on you, girl. I'm very pleased for you. He's a sexy lad. If I were ten years younger you'd have competition, I can tell you." She laughed before taking a slurp of her tea. "Now, before we go in and join the meeting, I need to show you something. Do you remember when we were doing EVPs at the Marling Hotel?"

"Yes, that's when you tried to catch voices on a recorder, right?"

"Right. Well, while we were communicating with the child, I left a recorder running in the adjacent room, and when I was going over the footage afterward, I came across something I think you should hear."

"Really?" Alice was intrigued as she watched Maggie rummage through her enormous bag, her bangles rattling.

"Ah, here we are. Now, listen to this," she said and pressed play on the small device she held.

Alice wasn't sure what she'd been expecting, but she hadn't expected to hear Jemma's voice, distant and tinny, but definitely Jemma's voice saying, "*Alice? It's me…*"

"Oh my God," cried Alice. "Oh my God, it's Jemma. Maggie, that's Jemma's voice."

"Yes, I thought so. It seems she wants to talk to you."

"What's all the noise about?" Jack frowned as he opened the door to the living room and stuck his head out. As soon as he saw Alice's face, he rushed into the kitchen and threw his arms around her. "Are you okay? Have you seen the boy again?"

"What boy?" asked Maggie.

"I'll tell you later," said Alice. "Will you play the recording to Jack please?" Apart from the fact that she wanted Jack to hear the recording for himself, she was desperate to hear Jemma's voice again. Maggie handed Alice the recorder.

"*Alice? It's me… Alice? It's me… Alice? It's me…*" Alice kept her finger pressed on the repeat button, needing to hear the recording over and over again.

"I have to talk to her, Jack. I don't know how, but I have to talk to her."

"Oh my God!" screamed Jemma. "She heard me. She bloody heard me. Oh my God, I don't believe it, Alice actually heard me."

She flung herself at Tom, jumping up and down in excitement. "Do you know what this means?" she cried. "This means I can talk to her. It means that she knows for absolute sure that I'm here. Maybe now she'll find out how she can make contact with me. Maybe this Maggie woman can help her. Maybe—"

"Calm down." Tom laughed as they walked back through the wall into the living room. "I'm really pleased for you, but have you thought about what you would say if you did speak to her? A lot has changed since you first arrived and tried to contact her. I think you know now that she won't be able to tell you what to do, which is what you originally wanted. All I'm saying is, if she does find a way to contact you, don't waste the moment by being unprepared. Decide what's important to say to her beforehand."

"Do you know what? I'd tell her that I'm really pleased for her that she's with Jack, and I'd tell her that I'm happy. In fact, I'm happier now than I've ever been and that's because of you." She planted a playful kiss on the tip of his nose before continuing. "I don't want to leave anymore because I'm with you and I never want to leave you. Not ever."

"Wow, you've certainly had a change of heart," he said and kissed her back.

"Too right I have." She glanced over at Susie, who was busy trying to tickle a woman's ear, and Max, who was listening to the meeting with his usual sour face. She had an overpowering need to get away for a while. Not from Alice and her friends, but from the constant hostility from Max. Even Susie's innocent teasing about her relationship with Tom was beginning to get a bit tiresome. She wrapped her arms around him and pulled him close. She wished she could breathe him in, but her sense of smell seemed to have abandoned her when she'd died. She inhaled anyway and imagined a fresh lemony scent would suit him. She could feel him, though. Feel the hard muscles in his arms and chest. Feel the warmth that radiated from every pore in his body despite the fact that he was dead. She let out a happy sigh as he tightened his hold on her. She had heard romantic tales of undying love, but she had never really believed it existed. Until now. At last she was beginning to see what all the fuss was about and she had to admit it exceeded everything she had ever dreamed of. Now that she had found her man, she wanted to spend every spare moment with him. It was just as well they had all of eternity. "Tom? Why don't we go to the beach? I've heard everything I need to hear from this meeting today and right now, I just want to spend some time with you. Alone."

"Sounds good to me. Come on, they won't even notice we've gone." As Tom grabbed her hand Jemma just managed to catch the wink from Susie before they disappeared.

When they materialized on the beach they found it deserted, apart from a couple walking a dog along the water's edge. A surge of happiness ran through Jemma as Tom took her hand in his and led the way along the wet sand. Since she'd confessed her feelings for him her world had become a lighter, more beautiful place. Maybe it had been her time to die, after all? She was where she needed to be. She tugged on Tom's arm and started skipping along the beach, dragging him with her.

"Hey, what's the rush?"

"I'm just so happy. I've got all this incredible energy and I just want to skip and run and jump in the water." She laughed as she caught up with the couple and their dog. "Hello, beautiful dog."

To her amazement, the golden Labrador turned around and ran up to her, barking a greeting.

"Look at Sandy," exclaimed the woman to her friend. "What's got into him?"

The couple stared with bemused frowns as Sandy ran around in circles, tail wagging, barking in excitement at what must have appeared to be nothing at all.

"Isn't he lovely?" said Jemma as she knelt down and patted the dog. "I can't believe he can actually see us."

"They say animals are more sensitive than humans — Casper definitely knows we're around. I don't think Sandy can feel you petting him though, unless you've got very good at channeling your energy."

"He does seem to respond, doesn't he?"

"Yes, he does. Maybe he really can feel you. It takes some of us years to learn to do that and it seems it's taken you less than three months."

"He's gone completely mad," said his owners. "Look, he's rolling over as if someone's tickling his belly, and he's actually licking the air."

"Bye-bye, Sandy," called Jemma as his owners managed to drag the dog away. "Hope to see you again soon."

They continued walking along the damp sand, holding hands and enjoying the winter sun sparkling on the water.

"Isn't it weird," she mused, "that we can walk in the water and not get wet."

"We can do more than that," he said, grinning. "We can walk under the water as well. Don't forget, we don't need air to breathe. We pass through water pretty much the same way that we pass through walls. Come on, I'll show you."

He grabbed hold of her hand then led her farther and farther into the sea, the water level getting higher with every step. When the water reached their heads, they continued until they were below the waves.

"Wow, this is amazing. It doesn't feel any different to being up there on the beach." Jemma stuck her tongue out at a jellyfish as it swam past. "Ha ha, you can't sting me," she said, giggling as they passed through a clump of seaweed.

"Obviously this isn't quite as spectacular as it would be somewhere like the Seychelles," said Tom. "There's no coral or exotic fish here."

"Well, let's go to the Seychelles, then."

"It's not that simple. It's a lot harder traveling over long distances. We could end up anywhere, although it could be fun trying. But not today." He smiled. "Let's just enjoy being in Norfolk today."

"I wish we could eat," said Jemma when they got back onto the beach. "I'd love some fish and chips and a nice hot cup of tea."

"It took me years to get used to not eating," said Tom. "I still miss a good hot curry and pint of lager."

"It's ice cream and chocolate that I miss the most." Jemma sighed. Alice had popped a tub of Bailey's ice cream into the freezer the other day. She'd give anything to tuck into that.

"Let's not think about food. Come on, I'll race you to that dune over there." He bolted away, leaving her laughing. She waited until he was about a meter away from the dune, closed her eyes then transported herself just as Tom approached it.

"Hey, that's cheating." He grabbed her then threw her down on the grassy mound of sand. He kissed her hard on the lips before collapsing next to her. "I never thought I would fall in love here," he murmured. "You're the most incredible woman I've ever met. I can't imagine how I managed all these years before you turned up." He propped himself up on his elbows and gazed down at her. "Do you remember when you called me Hot Lips the day you arrived?"

"Oh no," groaned Jemma. "That was so embarrassing."

"I think that was when I fell in love with you. I nearly kissed you there and then."

"Why didn't you?"

"Are you joking? In the state you were in? Don't forget, you had just died and were traumatized."

"Oh yeah. That seems like such a long time ago now. The only thing I wanted was to get out of here and now the only thing I want is to stay here with you." Jemma sighed as she gazed up at the clouds. *Yeah, I'm home now.*

"Were you happy before you died?" asked Tom as he stroked her arm.

Jemma thought back to her excitement at starting her college course, but that hadn't been happiness. That had been hope. Hope that she could find a way out of the rut she had gotten herself into.

"I don't think I had truly been happy since my mum died," she replied. "I just sort of drifted through school, jobs, boyfriends. I had no ambition and didn't really think too much about what lay ahead in the future. Alice was the only real, solid thing in my life and when she left to go to New York I was completely alone. It was only when she came back and we moved in together that I felt like I had some sort of home. When I decided to go to college the day after attending Jack's party, I finally thought that I was on the right path. And then I died."

"I watched you at that party," said Tom. "I thought you were beautiful, even after you got pissed on that punch."

"Alice said she had felt some sort of presence in that house. Who would have thought that that presence would turn out to be the love of my life?"

"Watch it," said Tom with a grin. "It might have been Max's presence she sensed."

"Yeah, right." Jemma laughed and gazed at Tom in wonderment. She had never believed it was possible to be this happy. Just looking into his eyes sent little ripples of joy through her entire body. She reached out and ran her fingers over his face, loving the rough stubble that had been covering his jaw since the day he'd died. He took hold of her hand then guided it to his lips, kissing her palm while keeping his eyes fixed on hers.

"I love you," he said, his eyes heavy with emotion.

"I love you too." Jemma's stomach clenched as a need to be even closer to him struck her. They had never done anything more than kiss and cuddle. Was it possible to make love as ghosts? She couldn't see why not, but Tom hadn't made any moves to take their relationship to the next level. She wanted more, though. She needed to feel his body become one with hers, to revel in the intimacy of something more physical. If his kiss had such a powerful effect on her she could only imagine what the rest of him could do. She shivered at the thought and opened her mouth to give him a suggestive hint, but before she could say anything Tom kissed her again. This time it was longer and deeper than before, leaving Jemma's blood tingling with longing.

When he pulled away he ran his finger along the outline of her swollen lips. "We'd better get back," he said, with a hint of regret. "I dread to think what carnage Susie might be causing at Jack's meeting."

Jemma sighed. "Okay." Disappointed though she was, she had to agree with Tom. Goodness knew what Susie was getting up to.

When they got back, however, Susie was nowhere to be seen and the meeting had finished. The living room was empty, except for Max sitting in his usual place, looking as grim and miserable as ever.

"Where's Susie?" asked Jemma. She was beginning to feel a little less intimidated by Max's offhand manner, although he still gave her creeps.

"Dunno. She said something about going to see Claire,"

he mumbled.

"Oh." She didn't realize that Susie and Claire were that friendly, or that Susie even knew where Ashdown Forest was.

Damn. She had been dying to tell Susie all about her day with Tom and their new canine friend, Sandy. Tom had gone to visit his dad's grave and she didn't feel like talking to Max so she decided to go to Ashdown Forest herself and find them.

When she got there, she found Susie sitting next to Claire on the bench. They didn't react so they probably hadn't heard her arrive. As they were in the middle of a conversation, she decided to wait until they had finished before announcing her arrival, so she leaned against a tree and waited.

"Don't get me wrong," she heard Susie say. "I'm really glad for Tom and Jemma, but it sort of complicates things."

"Really? How?" asked Claire.

Yeah, I'd like to know that as well. Jemma crossed her arms and waited for Susie to clarify.

"I've never really thought this through before, but now that I might be able to leave I've thought about nothing else. Then it suddenly occurred to me last night, and I'm pretty sure Tom hasn't considered it either…" Susie swung her short legs as she spoke.

"Considered what, dear?"

"I died in an accident," Susie said. "It was a hit and run. The driver was drunk. It wasn't meant to have happened, you know. It wasn't my time to die, but it did happen and Tom got the blame for it."

"Oh dear," exclaimed Claire. "What happened?"

"It was Tom's car, but it wasn't him driving. It wasn't Tom's fault, honestly, Claire, but it was because of him that the drunk had his car. The events that led to his car being stolen ultimately led to my death. So the only way I can leave here would be for Tom to go back in time and change those events so that I don't get killed. But that would mean

Tom would change the circumstances around his own death. I know he died of a brain tumor so he would die anyway, but without the trauma of what happened, he probably wouldn't come back here. He'd be a free spirit, which would be great, but what about Jemma? She'd be left on her own."

The more Jemma heard the weaker her legs became as Susie's words hit home. It seemed that the only way to help Susie get back was for Tom to leave as well. Could fate be so cruel as to lead her to her soulmate after her whole lifetime, then take him away again? She turned her back to Claire and Susie, tears blinding her as she stumbled to get away. Pain stabbed at her unbeating heart and she had to grab hold of a tree to steady herself. When she'd regained her balance, she started running blindly into the forest. She needed to escape the realization that her whole world was about to fall apart.

She ran until she had nowhere left to run. As she became aware of her surroundings the fog in her head started to clear. She was walking down the middle of a road, cars speeding through her as though she wasn't there. What was she going to do? She stopped walking as the answer crashed into her with agonizing clarity. Brushing away a tear, she knew there was only one thing she could do. She had to do the right thing and help Susie go back to her life. She had given the girl her word. But in doing that, she would lose Tom forever. She sank onto her knees as her heart splintered into a million pieces.

Chapter Twelve

Alice woke with a start as a loud ringing noise pierced the silence. With a groan, she rolled over and forced an eyelid open as it dawned on her that the offending noise was the alarm clock. Jack was fast asleep next to her, oblivious to the racket, so it was up to her to switch the damn thing off. She groped in the direction of the sound, waving her arm in the air in a feeble attempt at finding the snooze button, only to send the clock flying across the room. It landed next to Casper, who was curled up on a chair. He jumped up with an astonished howl as the clock landed on the side of the chair with a loud thud then he dived under the bed, his tail swishing in anger.

Alice buried her head in the pillow, thankful that the clock had stopped ringing. And Jack had slept through the whole thing. She was about to doze off again when a nagging voice inside her head kept telling her that there was a good reason for the alarm going off. Then she remembered. Today was the day that she was starting her new job. Thank God she hadn't gone back to sleep.

As she dragged herself out of bed and staggered into the bathroom, she cursed Oscar's cheery call yesterday to say that, although she would normally start at eleven o'clock for the lunchtime shift, would she come in at nine on her first day so that he could show her around and teach her how to use the coffee machine? Yesterday she had been happy to agree that it was a great idea and of course she'd be there at nine, but now she wished she hadn't been so quick to agree.

Once showered and dressed, Alice tiptoed downstairs,

careful not to wake Jack. He had been up working until three in the morning so she didn't begrudge him a lie-in. Still sleepy, she made her way into the kitchen, put the kettle on and looked down at Casper, who had followed her.

"Do you want some breakfast, Casper?" she whispered as the purring cat wound himself around her legs, leaving a thick blanket of white fur on her black jeans. His earlier shock must have been forgiven because he jumped up onto the kitchen counter to help empty the contents of the foil tray Alice was opening.

Once Casper was tucking in to his breakfast, Alice turned back to the kettle to make herself some tea. That was when she caught sight of something out of the corner of her eye. It was a perfect white tulip lying in the middle of the kitchen table. But it was December. *Where on earth would a tulip come from in the middle of winter?* As she picked it up and touched its smooth, velvety petals, a memory came flooding back. Tears welled in her eyes as she recalled the day she and Jemma had moved in to their flat. Jemma had come home from shopping with a bunch of white tulips, laughing that she couldn't afford roses, but she wanted to buy something anyway to wish them luck in their new home. Alice had brought tulips for Jemma's grave at her funeral, and now Jemma was returning the gesture. *This tulip is from Jemma.*

"Oh, Jemma, thank you," she whispered. Jemma had left her a good-luck gift. She put the flower in a glass of water and finished making her tea. Twenty minutes later, she slipped out, careful not the bang the door so as not to disturb Jack.

She walked to Camden—it wasn't too far—and she enjoyed the chance for a quiet think while getting a bit of exercise. She thought about Jack and how much she loved him, about her new job and how much she was looking forward to it. Then there was Jemma's message on the voice recorder and the ghost boy. Would she see him again? By the time she got to Glitz, she was wide awake and ready for anything.

"Good morning, Petal," called Oscar from the back of the restaurant as Alice pushed open the door. "You're early."

"We agreed nine o'clock, remember?" said Alice, taking her coat off.

"Did we? Oh well, now that you're here, I might as well show you the ropes."

Oscar showed her how to make a perfect cup of coffee on the giant espresso machine while chatting away about the morning chores, the customers and a bit about the other staff.

"By the way, here's your uniform," said Oscar, handing Alice a black T-shirt with the word Glitz boldly spelled out across the front in small silver sequins. She loved it. "That's about it, Petal, you'll pick it up fast, I know you will. I've got a really good feeling about you. Tell you what, why don't I pop *Arrival* on before Dean gets back? He hates Abba and if I don't get in first he'll stick *Underscore*, or something equally dull, on then he'll disappear into the kitchen where he can't even hear it."

Alice was just beginning to wonder if she would ever get to meet Dean when the door opened and Oscar waved his arm at a tall, dark and serious-looking man. "Hi, sweetie." He rose then gave Dean a quick peck on the cheek. "This is Alice, our new waitress. She started today."

Alice smiled at Dean and held out her hand. "Hello, I'm pleased to meet you."

Dean shook her hand then nodded at her before disappearing into the kitchen. There was no smile, no warmth or friendliness in his greeting. Alice frowned, a little taken aback by his curt and offhand manner.

"Don't take any notice of him," said Oscar, scowling at the swinging kitchen door. "He's always a miserable sod in the mornings. Come on, let me show you how the till works."

It didn't take Alice long to find her way around the restaurant, and by the time the first customer walked in she had mastered the espresso machine and memorized the menu. Lunchtime was busy, but that didn't faze her in the slightest. The customers were friendly and chatted to her as if she'd been there for years, and the time flew by as she took more orders and delivered the food to the hungry guests with expert ease.

It was only later, as she and Oscar were clearing away after most of the customers had left, that she realized how hungry she was. As if reading her mind, Oscar called out to her, "Alice, sweetie, why don't you make us a drink while I finish clearing the last tables. Oh, and help yourself to something to eat."

A couple of hours later, she was enjoying a cappuccino in Hampstead High Street while filling Jack in on her first day at work. "Oscar's great," she told him as she stirred a spoonful of sugar into her coffee, "but Dean's a bit moody. He's in the kitchen most of the time, though, so I don't get to see much of him, thank God. Oh, and I made ten pounds in tips."

Jack smiled, his eyes radiating genuine warmth. "I'm glad you're enjoying it, it's good to see you so happy."

"I've got a lot to be happy about," she said, taking his hand and giving it a squeeze. "I've got you and now I've got a job that I love. I just wish Jemma was still here. Then everything would be perfect."

"Have you thought any more about the EVP recording?"

"I can hardly stop thinking about it. Do you know what puzzles me the most? Not that Jemma left a message for me from the spirit world, but what the hell was she doing at the Marling Hotel?"

Jack took a sip of his latte and gave Alice a thoughtful look. "I think it means she's following you. You said you've sensed her at my house, and there was that incident with the bracelet at your flat, remember? She must have heard us discussing the ghost-hunting vigil and followed us. Maybe she thought there might be a way for her to communicate with you there. She obviously wants to talk to you."

"That's what Maggie thinks as well. I just wish my psychic abilities were better. I'm obviously not as gifted as I first thought I was."

"Hey, you're very gifted. There's no doubt about that, but it takes most mediums years before they're able to communicate directly with spirits. They may see and hear them, but it's a whole new skill to interpret messages and actually converse with ghosts."

Alice sighed. "Yeah, I guess. Maggie said she would help so I'm going to call her when she gets back from her yoga retreat."

Five minutes later, when they had finished their coffee, Alice picked up her bag and got up to leave, but Jack gestured for her to sit back down.

"Erm, Alice?" He shifted in his seat and fiddled with a teaspoon as he appeared to search for the right words. "Look, I was just wondering—erm, well, it's just..." He cleared his throat, put the teaspoon down then picked it up again. "Well, it occurred to me that you're staying with me at the house practically all the time these days."

"Oh," said Alice, mortified. "I'm sorry. Am I crowding you? If you need some space, that's fine. Honestly. I can go back to my flat whenever you want, it's not a problem." Bloody hell, she'd been so content at Jack's house that she hadn't realized she had outstayed her welcome.

"No, that's not what I'm trying to say." Jack dropped the spoon then reached over and took her hand in his. "I definitely don't want space away from you. Doesn't it seem a bit silly for you to pay rent when you could move in with me?"

Whoa, has he really just asked me to move in with him? Really? "Are you sure?"

"Nah, only joking. Of course I'm sure, you silly thing. Well? What do you think?"

Alice closed her eyes and imagined living with Jack in that beautiful house with Casper and the ghosts, one of them possibly being Jemma. Christmas was only a couple of weeks away. They could get a real Christmas tree, one that reached right up to the ceiling, and they could put it up in the bay window of the living room. It would be decorated with lots of tiny little white fairy lights. They would go to John Lewis to buy all the decorations…

"Well?" asked Jack.

"Yes. Yes, I'd love to," she said and threw her arms around him.

* * * *

"Good on you, girl," exclaimed Jemma as Alice and Jack arrived home, busy discussing their plans for Alice to move in.

"She's going to put a bloody great big Christmas tree up in the window," grumbled Max, from his corner. "She'll put lights up everywhere and the whole fucking house will look ridiculous."

"Oh, for God's sake, Max. It's Christmas, the house will look great." Tom threw Max an impatient glare then turned back to Jemma. "Jack never really bothered with Christmas before. This house hasn't had a Christmas tree since his grandparents lived here and I, for one, will be really pleased to see a bit of Christmas cheer return. Alice is going to bring some life back into this old place."

"Waste of bloody time and money, if you ask me."

"Well, Max, we're not asking you," snapped Jemma. "Where's Susie?"

"Gone to see your friend Claire," replied Tom. "It's nice to see them getting on so well, although I wouldn't have thought they'd have very much in common."

"I think she sees Claire as a mother figure," said Jemma. "She really misses her mum."

Jemma glanced across the room and caught a look in Max's eye that brought back her uneasiness in an instant. She couldn't forget his hateful words when he'd sworn that, one day, he would get his revenge. As Tom was the only one left whose pain could give him the satisfaction he so desperately craved, she knew she had good reason to worry. Max's hatred had been festering for so long that it seemed to have poisoned his mind, and there was no knowing what he was capable of. However, Tom was adamant that Max would have done something a long time ago if he had intended him any harm. But he hadn't seen the uncontrolled rage in Max's eyes. Rage that was still as strong now as it had been when he had first died. With a growing sense of urgency, Jemma decided that she had to get Tom and Susie to leave as soon as possible, because if Max guessed what they were up to, it might just prompt him to carry out his threat sooner rather than later.

"Tom? Shall we go to Norfolk? I need to get away from here," she muttered with a nervous glance in Max's direction.

"Good idea. Come on, let's go."

As they manifested on the beach, they were greeted with a very different scene from their last visit. The high, white-crested waves crashed onto the shore, their deafening sound drowning out all other noise except for the howling wind. How Jemma longed to feel that wind blowing through her hair.

She searched around for Sandy and his owners, but the beach was deserted. No living creature would be daft enough to go to the beach on such a stormy day.

"I bet this beach gets packed out in the summer," she shouted as they walked over to their dune. The tall mound sheltered them from the wind and made it easier to hear Tom's reply.

"Actually, it doesn't really. It isn't a tourist attraction because there are no amusement arcades, funfairs, hotels, stuff like that. It's just the beach and nothing else. If it gets busy in the summer, it's mostly local people who want to get away from the tourist areas. When I was a child I assumed that all beaches were like this because this was all I knew."

Tom put his arm around Jemma's shoulders as they sat down then pulled her close until she was snuggled against him. She closed her eyes and savored the happiness that she knew was about to be shattered. She could never have anticipated the intensity of her feelings for Tom when she'd first met him. He had become everything to her. Her world. How was she going to exist without him? Forcing back burning tears, she took a deep breath.

"Tom?"

"Jemma?"

They both spoke at the same time.

"You first," said Jemma, wanting to put off her speech for as long as possible.

"I'm sorry I haven't been open with you about what happened when I died." Tom hesitated as he turned and looked into her eyes. She willed him to feel the unconditional love that she projected back at him and he did seem to brighten.

"It's not that I don't trust you. I do, more than I trust anyone. It's just hard for me to talk about it. But you've become very important to me and it's about time I told you the truth."

"Are you sure? You don't have to tell me right now. It can wait." *Did I really just say that?*

"No, it can't."

He pulled her closer then wrapped his other arm around her so she was enveloped in his embrace. She closed her eyes as she clung to him. How would she survive without him? A knot tightened in her stomach and she pushed the thought back. Now wasn't the time to wallow in self-pity. She had waited months for this moment and she knew it wouldn't be easy for Tom to tell her what had happened, so she needed to stay strong for them both.

Tom sighed as he stared out at the vastness of the ocean. "Oh God, where do I start? My family were always high achievers. My father and grandfather were both doctors and my brother followed in their footsteps. My mother was a successful writer before she married and it was always assumed that I would be successful too. And I was. I graduated from university with a first in business accounting and landed a job in a top city firm, working my way up to risk analyst for one of our biggest clients."

"Your parents must have been very proud," said Jemma.

"Yes, they were, but it was expected of me, there was never any doubt that I would do well. When my father died, I had just been promoted, so he went to his grave knowing that both his sons hadn't let him down — he was proud of us.

"But then a few months later I went to work as usual one morning and was called to a meeting with the CEO. That wasn't unusual so I wasn't concerned. It turned out that I had made a mistake, a big mistake that had cost our client millions. I had incorrectly valued a derivative transaction, a genuine mistake, one that anyone could make. But the client demanded that I be fired and I was." He shook his head as if he still couldn't believe what had happened.

"But you were successful and well-established in your career, surely you got another job quickly?" asked Jemma, shocked.

"No, the city is a very small place and word gets around quickly. The headhunters who had been banging on my door trying to offer me bigger and better jobs suddenly slammed the same door in my face. They didn't want to know. I was devastated. I had lost my job and I had lost our client millions. I was also worried about telling my mother. How on earth was I going to explain it to her? I knew she would be disappointed in me and I couldn't bear that."

The sound of a dog barking interrupted him. Moments later Sandy came bounding over, looking delighted to see his two invisible friends as he wagged he wet tail at them. As his owners dragged him away, once again baffled by their dog's bizarre behavior, Jemma stood up and held her hand out to Tom.

"Come on," she said, her voice soft. "The wind has died down a bit, let's walk and you can tell me what happened next."

As they strolled along the beach, hand in hand, Jemma willed Tom to stay strong. She had a feeling that his story was about to get a whole lot worse.

Chapter Thirteen

As Sandy disappeared into the distance Jemma turned her attention back to Tom. "So is that why your mother disowned you?" she asked, giving him a gentle prompt to continue with his story. "Because you got fired?"

"No, she was actually very supportive," he replied with a half-hearted laugh. "She told me she understood it was an honest mistake and that she was confident that I'd get another job in time. I couldn't bring myself to tell her that I was already finished in the city and that nobody would employ me. That's when I started to fall apart." His voice was so quiet that she could hardly hear what he said over the howling wind. "I started drinking heavily. I stopped applying for jobs because I couldn't face any more rejections, and I cut myself off more and more from my friends and family. In the end, it got so bad that I couldn't even be bothered to shave or get dressed in the mornings. I just rolled off the sofa and reached for the bottle until, one day, my mother turned up to find out why I hadn't returned any of her calls."

A bitter smile played on his lips and Jemma's heart wept for him as he struggled to tell his story.

"My mother was furious when she saw me. Honestly, she went mad. She yelled at me, poured the booze down the sink, yelled some more. We had a massive row, but I was too pissed to realize what I was saying and I said some horrible things. She ended up storming out, calling me a loser and telling me that she was ashamed of me." Tom rubbed his brow, his hand shaking, so Jemma reached out, took it and held on to it as he continued.

"After she left, I felt awful, but instead of her anger bringing me to my senses, I decided to go into Soho and get even more drunk. I grabbed my car keys and made my way down to the car. It was only after I'd started the engine that I thought about what I was about to do and realized that, whatever my problems, I wasn't going to drive while I was still pissed. So, I got out again and staggered down to the corner shop and bought another bottle of whiskey, which I planned to drink back at my flat."

Jemma stared at Tom as he spoke. Lines ran like deep crevices across his face, his eyes sunken and dark. She squeezed his hand again to let him know that he had her full support.

"The next thing I knew, the police were knocking at my door accusing me of killing someone in a hit-and-run accident," he continued.

"Why did they think it was you?" she pressed.

"Well, I was so pissed that when I'd got out of the car I'd left the key in the ignition and some kid who happened to be passing saw it, stole my car and went for a joyride. He was drunk or high on drugs or something. Several witnesses confirmed that he was driving like a maniac. He ran over a girl who was crossing with her mum at a zebra crossing…"

"Susie, right?" said Jemma, recalling what Susie had already told her.

Tom nodded. "Yeah. The thief must have panicked because he abandoned the car and ran off. Her mum survived, but Susie died and when the witnesses confirmed the description of a seemingly drunk driver along with my abandoned car, it didn't take them long to trace me. When the police arrived they had apparently banged on my door, but I had drunk myself into oblivion and didn't hear anything. They had to break it down and found me, pissed out of my head and unable to remember anything. I was found guilty of manslaughter and sent to prison and it was there, a couple of months later, that I was diagnosed with a brain tumor. My mother refused to visit me, even when I was on my deathbed, and I died alone and disgraced." His head hung low, his shoulders hunched forward as if his sorrow weighed him down. "I died believing I had killed Susie, but when I got here she told me that it wasn't me and it was only then that I was able to piece it all together."

Jemma was stunned into silence. She had imagined many stories of what could have happened to Tom, but she could never have dreamed of anything so tragic. No wonder Tom had been so reluctant to talk about it.

"I know I didn't actually kill Susie, but that doesn't stop the guilt eating away at me every time I look at her. If I hadn't left the keys in my car that day, it wouldn't have been stolen and Susie wouldn't have been killed."

Her heart broke for him as he blinked away a lone tear. She wanted to reach out and soothe the pain that seemed to be oozing from his pores, to wipe away the bitterness, but she knew there was nothing she could do or say to make it better. No matter how hard she tried to tell him that leaving his keys in the car wasn't a crime, it wasn't going to change the way he felt. He blamed himself and the only way he would ever find peace would be for Susie to go back to her family. Which brought her back to the reason she needed to talk to him.

"Tom," she said, her voice gentle. "You have to leave. You know that, don't you?"

"But, Jemma, I don't know how. You and Susie weren't meant to die, remember? But I was. I died of a brain tumor, so I'm not here for the same reasons as you. Even if I could come to terms with everything and be able to move on, it still wouldn't help Susie. What would happen to her if I left? I'm not leaving her here."

"We'll have to find a way of helping you both leave. First, we need to get as much information as we can about these wormholes. If we could find out how to use them, would you go?"

"But that would mean you'd be left here on your own."

"I know," she whispered, only too aware of that fact. "But you have to try. And you never know, maybe I could find a way out too. After all, that was the intention when I first got here."

She stared at him, growing more aware of the sacrifice they would both have to make in order to put things right. It seemed so cruel that she should finally have found love, even in death, then to lose him again so soon...

Tears pooled in her eyes as she imagined her existence without Tom. She had been so happy the last time they had been here at the beach. How could everything change so quickly?

"Hey, don't cry." Tom drew her into his arms and held her. She clung to him, terrified that if she let go he would vanish in front of her eyes. After a few moments they pulled apart and continued their walk along the beach.

"Tom? How often do you visit your grave?" asked Jemma, breaking the silence.

"My grave?" he said, his voice fueled with bitterness. "What grave?"

"You mean you don't know where you're buried?"

"No, my loving mother got rid of my ashes. Have you been to yours since your funeral?"

"No, but I've been thinking about it." She had been close to going several times, but every time she'd tried, she had changed her mind at the last minute. She knew she should go, felt that it might somehow offer some sort of comfort as she was buried near to her mother. "Have you visited your mother since you died?"

"I saw her once when I visited my father's grave. She was hunched over it, pulling weeds and arranging some fresh flowers. I turned and left again."

"Why don't you go and visit her? The fact that she's still alive means you have an opportunity to find out how she feels about you now. After all, it's been twenty years, and that's a long time for a mother to hold a grudge against her dead son."

"I don't know if I can face seeing her."

"What if I come with you? We could leave some personal things around for her to find that remind her of you and then watch her reaction. Come on, Tom, it's worth a try, isn't it?"

Tom sighed, but Jemma couldn't tell if he was irritated by her persistence or touched by her concern. "We'll see," he replied, with the same lack of commitment she had heard so many times before. She was close to pushing him for a more positive response, but managed to stop herself. If she persisted he might retreat into his protective shell and shut her out again. She would leave it for now. If he knew that his mother did love him, though, it might be a way for him to find some sort of peace. If he thought she was going to let it drop altogether he was very much mistaken.

"Do you know what?" he said, turning to her. He ran his fingers across her cheek, holding her gaze. "When you first arrived here, I thought you were beautiful but a bit shallow. I couldn't have been more wrong. You are the most genuine and unselfish person I've ever met and I love you more than you'll ever know."

Joy bubbled up inside Jemma as his words zinged to her brain. Whatever the future, nothing could take away the ecstatic memories she would have of Tom. Pulling him to her, she murmured, "Well, Hot Lips, when I first saw you I thought you were gorgeous and I still think that. Oh, and I was right — you really do know how to kiss a girl, but just remind me again."

* * * *

Alice hummed away to herself as she finished wiping the tables at the end of her shift at Glitz. Her second day had been just as much fun as her first. Now that the lunchtime rush was over and the customers had all left, she had turned the volume up on the sound system and settled down to the task of clearing away, while Oscar nipped out to pick up some supplies.

Abba's *Dancing Queen* was playing and Alice sang along in her hopelessly tone-deaf voice. She knew she sounded like a wailing cat, but she was on her own so nobody would hear her. When Frida and Agnetha erupted into the chorus she twirled and pointed her finger at an imaginary seventeen-year-old. Throwing the cloth in the air, she attempted a wobbly spin as she sang along. She landed her turn, one hand on her hip and the other pointing in the air, then closed her eyes and threw her head back just like Agnetha did in the video. She was enjoying herself so much that she wasn't taking any notice of what was going on around her, but when she opened her eyes, ready for the second verse, she found herself staring straight at Dean. *Oh crap.* He was standing in the kitchen doorway, arms crossed and with the cloth she had just thrown hanging off the top of his head.

"I'd stick to waitressing if I were you," he said, handing her the cloth before disappearing back into the kitchen, leaving Alice crimson with embarrassment. *Shit, how long has he been standing there?* When Oscar had popped out, she had assumed she was on her own. She hurried over to the counter, turned the music down then cleared away in silence. As soon as she was finished, she grabbed her jacket and rushed out of the door.

She met Jack at the top of the High Street as they'd arranged and as they walked home together, she told him about how mortified she had been when she had turned to find Dean glaring at her with the dirty cloth draped over his head.

But instead of being sympathetic, Jack laughed. "I wish I could have been there to see the look on your face."

"Jack! It's not funny," she cried and play-punched him on his arm. She had to admit, though, now that a bit of time had passed she was beginning to see the funny side.

When they got back to the house, Jack went into the kitchen to put the kettle on. "By the way, do you like

Underscore?" he asked.

"Yes, they're quite good. Why?"

"I've got four free tickets to see them on Sunday night for a one-off gig in London. The tickets include backstage passes and access to the after show party. Do you fancy it?"

"I'd love it. Wow, will we actually get to meet the band?"

"Of course. Do you know anyone else who likes them? Like I said, I've got four tickets."

"Jemma would have come. I remember her saying at your party that she quite liked their last song." Alice's mind drifted back to that night and she smiled as she recalled Jemma going on about how cute the singer was. "I could ask at work. It would be a shame to waste the other two tickets."

"Okay. Now, how do you fancy downloading a film and getting a takeaway tonight?"

"Ooh yes. Tell you what, why don't I nip down and get us a bottle of wine while you finish the washing up?" Before Jack had a chance to protest, she threw a tea towel at him and ran out of the front door. When she got to the off-license she found a bottle of Pinot Grigio that had been reduced to an affordable price. *Perfect.* As she approached the bored-looking man sitting behind the till she reached into her jacket pocket for her wallet. Damn, where was it? She tried the other pocket, but that only contained her house keys and phone. Then she remembered stuffing the tips she'd made into her wallet just before she'd left. *Shit, I've left it on the bloody table in the restaurant.* She would have to go back and get it. It would only take fifteen minutes or so to get to Glitz if she was quick. With a quick apology to the now impatient- man on the till, she hurried out and headed off to Camden. She glanced at her watch. Glitz didn't open until half past five and it was only four o'clock, but with any luck Oscar would be setting up ready for the evening shift.

When she got there, she pushed the door to see if it was unlocked. It was, although there was nobody inside. She would slip in, grab her purse and leave again without anyone seeing her. The sound system was on, playing something familiar on a low volume. She crossed the restaurant to the last table she had cleaned and saw her purse. *Thank God*. She was just about to pick it up when there was an almighty crash from the kitchen. Alice jumped back in fright and clapped her hand to her mouth to stifle a scream. The silence that followed was broken by the next song starting then by raised voices coming from the kitchen. Alice froze, not sure whether to grab her purse and run or if she should find out what the crash had been in the kitchen.

"For fuck's sake, Oscar, smashing our plates isn't going to help," Dean bellowed from the kitchen.

"Well, listen to me, then." Oscar sounded just as furious. "I'm telling you that we needed an extra waitress and Alice is perfect."

Alice had just been about to sneak out, not wanting to eavesdrop on someone else's argument, but when she heard her name, she remained rooted to the spot, not sure what to do.

"We could have rearranged some of the other shifts. You don't seem to understand, Oscar, we're not going to survive if you keep employing people and spending money as if nothing's wrong."

"Oh, come on, Dean. The reason all this is happening is because of that damned ghost. It's put a curse on us."

"Don't be so ridiculous. There's no ghost here and certainly no curse," snapped Dean. "There is a problem with the accounts, though, and it's quite simple, we're spending more than we're making. That's it, but we'll never make a success of this business if you won't accept that we have to cut back. And that includes staff."

"Well, Alice is staying." Oscar's voice was adamant. "The customers love her, she's the best waitress we've had since opening this place. She stays."

Deciding that now was probably a good time to get out, Alice grabbed her wallet and tiptoed toward the door, praying that they wouldn't hear her. Just as she reached out for the door handle, though, a noise behind her made her stop. She froze then turned slowly around and found herself face-to-face with Dean and Oscar.

Chapter Fourteen

Alice flashed a forced smile at them. If she'd ever wanted the floor to open and swallow her up, now would be a good time.

"Alice? What are you doing here?" Dean was the first to speak. Judging by the look on his face he was trying to work out how long she'd been there and how much she might have heard. An awkward silence hung in the air as she tried to think of something to say. Her flushed face must have given away the fact that she had heard everything. Dean glared at her, his face grim and unsmiling as he waited for her answer.

"Er… Hi," she faltered with a nervous laugh. "I just came to pick up my wallet. I left it here earlier."

"Look, Alice." Dean's face softened. "You must have heard our discussion out there, but please don't take any of this personally. It's not you we have a problem with, it's money."

"But that doesn't mean you don't have a job here," Oscar chipped in. He turned back to Dean with steely determination on his face. "Sadie handed in her notice last week and with some tweaking of shifts we can manage without replacing her, but I'm telling you, Dean, we need Alice. Even if Sadie wasn't leaving, we'd still be one person short. You're not here in front of house to see the rush. I can't manage the whole restaurant on my own and if people have to wait too long for service they'll go somewhere else. There are plenty of other restaurants in Camden, we can't afford to lose our customers."

"Okay." Dean sighed, finally appearing to accept defeat.

"Alice stays, but stop using that stupid ghost as an excuse. This place is not haunted, all right?"

Oscar pulled a face as Dean marched back into the kitchen. "Sorry about that. Look, are you in a hurry? I'm going to make some coffee and I could do with a chat."

"Well, I…" Alice was about to say that she needed to get back to buy the wine, but, hey, it wasn't going anywhere, so instead she smiled. "Coffee sounds great."

"I hear you did a brilliant rendition of *Dancing Queen* earlier." He grinned as he frothed some milk on the machine. "I wish I could have seen it."

"Oh no," groaned Alice, cringing as she recalled Dean's face, half covered with the dirty dishcloth. "Was Dean really cross?"

"Of course he wasn't. Actually, he'd never tell you, but he thought it was quite funny, especially the look on your face when you spotted him. Here, white, one sugar." Oscar handed her the mug and gestured for her to sit down. "I've been meaning to talk to you, I thought you may be able to offer some advice. As you're probably aware now, we have a few financial problems. I just don't understand why, we're busy every day, especially evenings. You're on tomorrow evening, right?" Oscar took a sip of his coffee as Alice nodded. "You'll see what I mean, then. We're fully booked for the next three nights yet we don't seem to be able to break even. I just don't understand it. Was the restaurant you worked at in New York successful?"

"Yes, very. The owners made a decent profit, as far as I'm aware."

"So what are we doing wrong, then? Okay, this isn't New York, but Camden's a pretty cool place. It's always busy. We get both regular customers and passing tourists. The food is good, so I've been told, and people seem to love the atmosphere we've created. We should be raking it in, or at least be making some profit. I just don't get it."

"I've never run a restaurant before, but I've worked in a few and I can quite honestly say that this is the best place

I've ever worked in. I love it and I know your customers do. I really don't know." Alice wished she could say something more positive, but she couldn't understand why Glitz wasn't thriving either.

Oscar opened his mouth as if he was going to say something then closed it again. A second later, he asked, "Do you believe in ghosts?"

"Yes, I do, as it happens. In fact, I'm psychic and have been working on developing my skills. My best friend died back in September. She was like a sister to me. I was devastated." The familiar tightening of her throat threatened the return of her tears. Quickly, she swallowed them back and continued. "I know for a fact that Jemma's ghost is with me. She's always around."

"I'm sorry to hear about your friend. I lost a very good friend to AIDS a few years ago. I still miss him terribly. The reason I asked is…" He hesitated for a second. "Well, Dean thinks I'm crazy, as you heard, but I think this place is haunted and that there's some sort of curse on it."

Alice glanced around the empty restaurant. If there was a ghost haunting it, she couldn't sense it. "Well, if it's any consolation, I don't feel anything here. Certainly nothing negative that might suggest a curse or anything. What makes you think it's haunted?"

"Well, what other explanation is there?" Oscar shrugged, throwing his hands dramatically up in the air. "You know, sometimes when I'm here on my own, I get this really creepy feeling that someone's watching me."

"I know someone who's a medium. Maggie would be able to tell you for sure if this place is haunted. Would you like me to ask her to come round?"

"Oh, would you? Thank you, Petal, it would really put my mind at rest if a medium checked this place out for me." Oscar stood and stretched. "Excuse me a sec, I'm just going to change the music, I need an Abba fix. This stuff is fine in small doses, but it doesn't half get dull after a while."

"It's Underscore, isn't it?" asked Alice, recognizing the

song that was playing.

"Yeah, Dean loves them, but I find them a bit boring."

"Really? I quite like them. In fact, I'm going to see them on Sunday. Jack, that's my boyfriend, has got free VIP tickets and we actually get to meet the band afterward."

"Oh wow, you lucky thing," exclaimed Oscar, looking impressed.

"I thought you said you found them boring?"

"I do, but as I said, Dean is a huge fan. I'd love to be able to surprise him with tickets to see them. Do you think there are any left?"

"Well, actually, this could be your lucky day. Jack's got four tickets and we were going to ask around if anyone wanted to come with us. So that's sorted then. You're coming."

"Oh, thank you, sweetie," cried Oscar as he threw his arms around her. "Dean is going to be so chuffed."

"No problem."

"All that said, I'm still going to change this CD for Abba. I don't suppose there's any chance of a repeat performance of *Dancing Queen*, is there?"

* * * *

Jemma stood motionless, not unlike one of the stone statues surrounding her, deep in thought. She bent down and touched the cold gravestone that she had been staring at for so long, the tears running freely down her face.

"Oh, mum, I thought I would see you again when I died. I miss you so much."

She closed her eyes and could almost feel her mother kissing her, brushing her hair and cuddling her as she snuggled her into bed. The memories were so fresh and yet it had been such a long time. The one consolation was that if she wasn't here, she must have been able to move on to a better place. Was her mother able to see her? Did she even know that her daughter had died? Maybe she had tried to contact her, just like she herself had tried to contact Alice? Someone had left some fresh carnations at the head of the grave. That must have been Aunt Tess. It was comforting to know that someone still came to visit her mother. Did her own grave have flowers on it? She only had to look a little to the left, as she was buried very close by, but so far she hadn't been able to summon up the courage. It was such a strange feeling to know that she was about to visit her own grave. At least she had one, unlike Tom. She couldn't imagine how painful it must be for him not to be buried next to his father. What the hell had his mother been thinking? How could anyone abandon their child when they were dying and not believe their protestations of innocence? Wouldn't they stand by their child no matter what they had done? A surge of anger toward the cold, cruel woman burned her heart.

Brushing away her tears, she vowed to visit her, to see if she had come to her senses over the many years since her son had died. If Tom wasn't going to do it then it was up to her. Maybe she should throw a few things around and bang some doors – give the bitch a fright.

She stood up again. Her throat tightened as she turned. There it was. Her grave. This was seriously weird.

The dark marble shone and the gold lettering identified it as hers. Fresh carnations lay at the head of her grave, just like at her mum's. Poor Aunt Tess, it must have been so difficult for her to have lost two family members, both so early in life. Next to the carnations lay a few white tulips bound in white ribbon. On closer inspection, she noticed that the tulips were made from silk. *Clever.* That way they would never wither and die. Next to them was a small card, laminated to protect it from the weather. *Jemma, you were like a sister to me. I miss you so much. I hope all the angels look after you in heaven and that you have found peace. All my love, Alice.*

Fresh tears fell down Jemma's face as she reread the small card. She was so glad she had managed to leave that white tulip for Alice on her first day of work. Claire had taught her how to materialize small objects into the living world and, although it took an enormous amount of will and energy, it had been worth it to see Alice's reaction when she had found it. Alice couldn't have been more wrong about the angels, though.

After a while she stood, walked across the empty graveyard and sat on an old wooden bench. The churchyard was dark and depressing in the winter light, the trees bare of their leaves, which lay rotting on the soggy ground. The old stone church threw shadows across most of the graves, some of which were hundreds of years old. A few of them had fresh flowers resting on the cold stone, most of them red poinsettias, probably where family members had come to pay their Christmas respects. Otherwise there was no color anywhere. The dim and somber atmosphere matched her mood. For some reason, she found it comforting to sit in the silence, with just her thoughts.

Those thoughts soon returned to Tom. He was everything she could have wished for in a man – handsome, funny and clever, although he could be a bit intense sometimes. She would have been happy to have stayed with him in this dimension for the rest of eternity. If only they could help Susie get back without Tom having to leave as well. But, no matter how hard she tried to think of ways around it, it was clear that if Susie hadn't been killed, Tom wouldn't have gone to prison. His mother would have buried him with his father and grieved for him the way a loving mother would. She was sure it was also Tom's feelings of guilt that kept him here because although he didn't actually kill Susie himself, if he hadn't left the key in the car that day, Susie would still be alive.

Even though she knew she had done the right thing by insisting that Tom and Susie should leave, she couldn't stop the fathomless dread from gnawing through her insides like a swarm of insects feeding off her soul. What would she do when they had gone? She would be alone. Forever.

She had told Tom that she would also leave when he did, but she could never go now because that would mean losing her memory of him. Besides, apart from her friendship with Alice, what did she have to go back for? But Tom would never leave if he knew she wasn't going as well, so she would just have to lie. She would be left with Max. A shudder ran through her as something else occurred to her. If Max knew that Tom was planning on leaving, he might not help them with the wormhole. Whether he ever intended to carry out his threat of revenge or if it was just the thought of it keeping him going, Max wasn't going to be happy if he found out. The rage that was still burning inside him with so much ferocity could resurface and make things worse.

No, Max mustn't know, but they did need his help. She would tell him that it was for her. He already believed she was planning on leaving, so she'd just let him carry on thinking that.

The one consolation was that she'd still have Claire. Thinking of her made Jemma want to go and see her, so she took a last look around the graveyard before closing her eyes and focusing on Ashdown Forest. As soon as she approached the clearing she spotted Claire waiting, as usual, for her beloved Robert. *He must be pretty special for his wife to wait for him all these years, although it's a bit strange that he has never turned up and even more odd that Claire is still waiting for him.* No matter how perfect a man was, surely there came a point when she had to admit defeat and accept that he would never come? *Maybe he isn't as perfect as Claire might like to think?*

Jemma stopped dead in her tracks when she arrived at the clearing. Claire's bench was empty. *How strange, she's always here.* Unless Robert had turned up at last, but that didn't seem very likely after all these years. Disappointed, she walked over to the bench and sat down. It didn't feel right without Claire there, though, so after a few minutes she decided to go home and come back tomorrow. Claire was impartial to the whole Tom-Susie-Max thing, so it would be good to talk it all through with her.

A split second later, she appeared back in the kitchen at Jack's house. That was empty as well. *Where the hell is everyone? Oh well, I might as well get my chat with Max out of the way.* As well as learning more about these wormholes, she needed to plant some more seeds to let him think that it was just her leaving.

Walking through the wall, she fixed a smile on her face. "Hi, Max. Oh!" She stared, open-mouthed, at Max, who was deep in conversation with Claire.

"Hello, dear," said Claire, smiling as she looked up.

"Er… I didn't know you knew Max?" blurted Jemma.

"Well, I didn't until you introduced us. I've visited him a few times and we're friends now."

"But what about Robert?"

"You said yourself that if he came back after all this time, he can wait for me for once."

"Oh, yes. Okay. Right, I must go now. Nice to see you." Jemma waved then disappeared back into the kitchen.

"Hey, what's up?" Susie was back, sitting on the kitchen table, swinging her legs.

"Did you know that Claire has been visiting Max?" asked Jemma, still reeling from her surprise.

"Yeah, she's been to see me as well. Is that a problem?"

"No, of course not. I knew that you two were friends, but I didn't know that she was mates with Max now. Don't you find that a bit strange?"

"No. Why?"

"Well, for a start he's a miserable old sod who's angry with just about everyone, and she's…well, she's *nice*."

"Opposites attract and all that," said Susie, make it clear that she didn't see what all the fuss was about.

Claire had been the only person Jemma could confide in, but now that she was friendly with Max, she couldn't trust her not to tell him about her plans. She felt strangely let down, but didn't want to look like a sulky brat, so she just smiled. "Yes, I suppose."

"Anyway, where have you been today? I came to see if you fancied playing some tricks on next door, but you weren't here."

"I went to visit my grave," replied Jemma. "And my mum's grave as well."

"Wow, how was it?"

"Very emotional. Have you seen Tom?"

"Yeah, he said he was going to visit his dad's grave earlier. He's probably still there."

"Susie? Do you know anything about his mother?"

"Yeah, I know a bit. I know that he hates her and will never go and see her."

"I don't think he hates her. He's devastated that she rejected him and he's bitter, yes, but he doesn't hate her."

"She's a right cow," snapped Susie, scowling.

Jemma smiled. She loved the way Susie always came straight to the point. "Yes, well, we'll see. I don't suppose you know where she lives?"

"I do, as it happens," said Susie, looking smug.

"Really? Are you serious?"

"Yep. I followed Tom to his dad's grave a few years ago, then I just waited until his mum came to visit. I was curious and wanted to see what she was like. I knew it was only a matter of time and, sure enough, she turned up the next day. I knew it was her from Tom's description, then I just followed her home. It was easy."

"That's great. Can you still remember where she lives?"

"Jemma, what are you up to? Tom will never go, you know."

"I know, but who said anything about Tom? I'm going. I just want to watch her, find out a bit about what she's like and, hopefully, gauge her feelings toward him now."

"He'll go mad if he finds out you went to see her," stated Susie with her usual bluntness.

"Well, he won't find out. *Will he*?" retorted Jemma, giving Susie her best 'don't you dare tell on me' look.

"Do you want me to come with you?"

"Would you?"

"Yeah, no problem. Come on, then, let's go," said Susie, jumping down from the table.

"What, now?"

"Yeah, why not? Come on." Susie grabbed Jemma's hand and, a moment later, they materialized in a dark and gloomy room. "Here we are. This is it."

Jemma stood still, taking in her surroundings. Crumpled clothes lay scattered on the floor and long-dead flowers in a cracked vase stood on a side table covered in a thick layer of dust. None of the antique lamps had been turned on, which added to the bleakness of the room. The only light, apart from the gray hue of dusk, was a faint orange glow from a dying fire. One of the advantages of being a ghost was being able to see in the dark. That was clearly going come in handy now.

"Look." Susie pointed toward the fireplace. The smoldering embers cast eerie shadows against a large, high-backed armchair that faced the hearth. An old woman sat in the chair, so still that she didn't seem real.

Jemma walked over to the woman and stared at her in disbelief. "Is that her?"

"Yep," said Susie as she threw herself onto the old sofa. "That's definitely her. She's not quite what you expected, is she?"

Chapter Fifteen

Jemma couldn't take her eyes off Tom's mother. She had been expecting a proud, immaculate woman with not a hair out of place, manicured hands and expensive designer clothes. The woman sitting here was nothing like that at all. Her long, un-brushed gray hair hung down in thin straggly wisps and her drawn, hollow face showed deep lines, aging her more than Jemma believed she was. What appeared to be dried tears stained her pale cheeks. A lump formed in Jemma's throat as she gazed at the old woman whose head was bowed as though she might be asleep. In her frail, thin hands rested a tarnished silver picture frame. Jemma gasped as she leaned over to take a closer glance.

"What?" asked Susie, who had been snooping around the room.

"Susie, look. The picture she's holding is of her and Tom." It looked like it had been taken when Tom was in his mid-twenties, and they had been at the beach in Norfolk. She recognized the tall sand dunes in the background. Tom was laughing, his eyes alive and sparkling, with his arm draped round his mother's shoulders. But the thing that moved Jemma most was the unconditional love on his mother's face as she smiled up at her youngest son.

"Come on, Susie," said Jemma. "I think we've seen all we need to see here." She looked again at Tom's mother. She had probably fallen asleep in her armchair every night while crying tears of regret over her dead son, lost in her tragic lament. Tom was so wrong about her. She may have been angry and unforgiving once, but that was a long time ago.

"Susie, do you think there's a way we can convince her to move Tom's ashes so he can lie next to his dad?"

"Dunno. How? We can't talk to her."

"I know. But there must be a way. Can you imagine what it would mean to Tom if his mother finally granted him his dying wish?"

"Yeah, but it wouldn't change anything. He'd still be here because of me."

"Yes, but it means that when he goes, he can leave with peace of mind, knowing that his mum did love him and that she did the right thing in the end."

Susie shrugged. "Yeah, I suppose, but I still don't see how you're going to manage to convince her."

Jemma drew her eyebrows together as her mind worked overtime. She wasn't going to let this drop. "Let's go."

When they got back to the house, Susie disappeared next door to catch the latest episode of *Tracy Beaker*, leaving Jemma alone. She couldn't get the image of the old woman out of her head. The happy, smiling woman in the picture bore no resemblance to the sad, rather pathetic old woman she had seen today. There had to be a way to get through to her and she knew just the person to help her. Claire had been around for a very long time. She must have seen and learned many things about this dimension. It had been her who had shown her how to leave the tulip for Alice and she had hinted then that she had a few more tricks up her sleeve. When they had first met, her impression of Claire had been that she was a weak and naïve lady. After all, she had waited all those years for a husband who was obviously not going to come. But as she had gotten to know her better Jemma had discovered that she was, in fact, a strong and intelligent woman who knew a lot more than she let on. It was as if she was hiding behind gullible innocence to block out something dark and painful from her past. Not on purpose – she was sure that Claire believed that Robert was going to come for her one day – but that didn't fit with the Claire that she was getting to know.

Walking through the wall into the living room, she was dismayed to see that Claire was still talking to Max. *Bugger*.

"Hello again, dear." Claire smiled as Jemma hesitated in front of them. "Are you all right?"

"Well, actually, I was wondering if I could have a word with you before you leave. In private," she added when Max's eyebrow twitched.

"Of course. I was just about to leave anyway. I need to get back to see if Robert has turned up, so why don't you come back to the forest with me and we can talk then?"

"Okay. Thanks." Jemma shifted under Max's glare. *Oh shit, have I just pissed him off even more?*

"That was good timing, dear," said Claire, grinning, as they arrived back at the deserted clearing and made their way to the bench. "Max is very sweet, but he can get quite intense at times."

"*Sweet?*" Jemma could think of many words to describe Max, but sweet was not one of them.

"Now, dear, what was it you wanted to talk about?"

"I went to visit Tom's mother today. Oh, it was so sad, Claire, she was nothing like I thought she would be. I went expecting to hate her for the way she's treated Tom, but she's heartbroken. Tom thinks she doesn't love him, but it's obvious that she does and I really believe that she regrets the way she treated him." Jemma paused, recalling the overwhelming sadness she had witnessed earlier. "The thing is, Claire, I want to try to make her move Tom's ashes so that he's buried next to his dad. It was his dying wish, but I don't know what to do and I was hoping that you might know of a way."

"Why, that's obvious, dear," said Claire.

"Is it?"

"Does he smell?"

"Pardon?"

"I mean, is there a smell that you associate with him? When people die, the scent they were wearing stays with them forever, just as their clothes do. Smell is far easier to

155

manifest into the living world than solid, material things. If you can manifest a tulip, you can definitely do it with a smell. Find out what smell his mother would associate with him then make sure she smells it when she's visiting her husband's grave. She would probably think of Tom and hopefully realize what she has to do."

"But Tom doesn't smell of anything. He was in prison when he died and didn't have the luxury of scents or aftershave."

"Well, find out what smell his mother would have associated with him before he went to prison. Did he paint? Or might there be a smelly food that he was partial to? There must be something. What about tobacco, did he smoke?"

Jemma shook her head as she struggled to recall something Tom had told her a while back. "There could be something, come to think of it. Tom said that he'd bought Grace, that's his mum, a honeysuckle bush once because she loved the smell of them so much. Apparently every time she caught a whiff of the bush in the summer it would remind her of him. That's it, Claire. Honeysuckle. I'll manifest some honeysuckle next time she goes to his dad's grave. Thank you." She leaned over and gave Claire a quick peck on the cheek—something that was natural for Jemma to do. But, judging by the surprise on Claire's face, it must have been a sign of affection that she hadn't seen in many years.

Brushing away a sneaky tear, Claire smiled. "Any time, dear."

* * * *

The following day, Jemma's patience was starting to wear thin as she waited for Grace to go to the cemetery. She followed her to the shops to buy some milk then home again. As it started to get dark, Jemma admitted defeat and returned to the house. The following day Grace didn't even leave her home at all, but on the third day, as Jemma was studying some dusty antiques on an equally dusty shelf,

Grace pulled herself up from her chair, shuffled into the hallway and put her coat on.

"Goodbye, my love. I'm off to see your father." Grace spoke to a photograph that was hanging in the hallway. Jemma ran up to it and studied it. It was of Tom and had been taken when he was a lot younger, probably a student judging by his long, unkempt hair and Pink Floyd T-shirt. Next to the photo hung another picture of an attractive man with the same striking green eyes as Tom's. *That must be his brother.* Grace didn't give that one quite as much attention as the one of Tom.

Jemma waited as Grace climbed into her car, an old BMW that had seen better days, then she went straight to the cemetery to wait for Grace to arrive. After about half an hour, the slow, lonely figure of Grace appeared round the bend, now carrying a bunch of colorful flowers in her arms. When she reached the grave, she knelt and placed the flowers by her husband's headstone. She stayed there for some time, removing dead leaves and rubbing some bird droppings off the gravestone with a bit of tissue. Then she closed her eyes, maybe to say a prayer, and that was when Jemma focused all her attention on her task. Using immense concentration, she managed to manifest a sprig of honeysuckle to the grave in front of her. All she could do now was wait for Grace to open her eyes and spot, or smell, the bait. She studied Grace's face, waiting for what seemed like an eternity, then the old lady's nose twitched, followed by a puzzled frown. Her eyes shot open and her gaze went straight to the honeysuckle lying in front of her. She let out a little cry and slapped her hand to her mouth. For a few seconds she just remained there, not moving at all as she stared in silence at the sweet-smelling flowers before tears welled up in her eyes. "Tom?" she whispered in a frail voice.

She started crying then, her whole body wracked with uncontrollable sobs as she let out her years of pent-up grief and guilt. Jemma felt so sorry for her that she put her arm around her. Although Jemma knew she wouldn't have felt it, Grace did seem to calm down a little. As she wiped her tears away with her coat sleeve, Grace picked up the honeysuckle and stared at it as if she couldn't quite believe what she was seeing. Jemma wished she had brought Tom along so he could see this, but she had been worried that it might not work, then he would have been furious and left even more hurt.

"Tom, was that you? Did you leave this for me? Are you really here? Oh, Tom, I'm so sorry. If you can hear me, then please, please believe me. I love you so much, and I miss you and —" She paused then rose awkwardly to stand up. "Can you forgive me, Tom? What I did was unforgivable and I'm so sorry, my love." Grace fell silent and stared at the sprig for a few more minutes, wobbling a little on her frail legs.

A veil seemed to float over her face as she withdrew again. She shuffled over to a nearby bench then lowered herself onto it, still looking overcome by her emotions. Then she buried her face in her hands as if she believed that hiding would take away the pain.

"You can help him, Grace," whispered Jemma, willing the older woman to hear her. "Come on, you know what you have to do."

Although Jemma's voice wouldn't have been audible, Grace raised her head and cocked it to one side. It was almost as if she thought she'd heard something, but wasn't quite sure. Then all of a sudden, she straightened up and burst into tears again. "How could I have been so cruel? He should be here, with his father," she cried between her sobs. "Tom, if you can hear me, I'm going to make sure you're moved here, where you belong. Do you hear me, Tom?"

"Yes, Mother, I hear you." Tom's voice was just a whisper, but Jemma jumped as though he had just shouted in her ear. She swung around. Tom stood behind her, with an expression on his face that she couldn't quite read.

"Tom! How long have you been standing there?"

"Long enough. I saw what you did," he said, his voice low.

"You're not cross, are you? I just wanted your mum to acknowledge that she loved you and hoped that she would then think to move your ashes."

Tom wrapped his arms around her. "God, Jemma, how could I be angry with you? Look what you've done for me. Did she really just say those things?"

"Yes, she did. She loves you, Tom. Really loves you. I went to visit her and she's been mourning you all these years."

Tom walked over to his mother and reached out to touch her cheek. Grace sighed, as if acknowledging the gesture, bent down and picked up the sprig of honeysuckle then stared at it in wonderment. Jemma wanted to stay and watch, but, she knew that she should leave them alone. With reluctance, she walked away, leaving mother and son to their emotional reconciliation.

* * * *

"Where the hell is she?" grumbled Alice, snapping her phone shut yet again and staring in frustration at the small purple card in her hand.

"Who?" asked Jack, glancing up from his laptop.

"Maggie. I've been trying to call her for ages, but she never picks up. She must be back from that retreat thing by now."

"Maggie is a law unto herself." Jack chuckled as he closed the laptop. "She'll be back when she's ready. Come on, we need to leave in ten minutes for the gig. Where are we meeting Oscar and Dean?"

"By the main doors. How do I look?" she asked, giving a little twirl.

"Gorgeous, as always." Jack planted a kiss on her lips then disappeared upstairs to get ready.

Alice shook her head. *Blimey, how can a man get ready to go out in less than ten minutes and still look good?* It had taken her an hour and that had felt rushed. Sure enough, ten minutes later Jack was waiting by the front door, clean-shaven, well dressed and looking as if it had taken at least forty-five minutes instead of ten. Not wanting to be outdone, Alice decided to have one last check of her makeup and ran upstairs to the bathroom, leaving Jack by the front door with his coat on and ready to go.

"Come on, Alice. We need to leave now."

"Won't be long," she called back. She finished applying her lipstick then smiled at herself in the mirror. She didn't scrub up too badly. She was about to turn the light off and go back downstairs when something made her stop and turn back to the mirror. At first she wasn't sure if it was just the light playing tricks, but when she glanced into the mirror again, her eyes were drawn to a little cloud of mist to the left of her reflection. Then the image of a face started forming in the mist, blurry and undefined at first, but becoming more distinct until she recognized the eyes staring back at her. It was the ghost-boy and he was standing right behind her, his pale features hovering just over her left shoulder. Stifling a scream, she swung around to face him, but the bathroom was empty. She was alone. Holding her breath, she turned back to the mirror, but the boy was gone. All that was left was a tiny patch of moisture on the glass. With a cry of relief she leaned against the sink and closed her eyes.

"Alice, are you coming? We'll be late," Jack called, now sounding a touch impatient.

"Er, yes. I'm coming." After sensing Jack's reaction the last time she had seen the boy, Alice wasn't sure if she should tell him what had just happened. She couldn't forget the doubt in his eyes and, although Jack had said he believed her, there was no mistaking the change in his voice when he had reassured her. Maybe he was right to doubt her? Maybe she really was losing the plot?

"You okay?" he asked as she made her way downstairs.

"Yes, fine. Let's go." She smiled and grabbed her coat.

When they arrived at the theater, they couldn't see Dean and Oscar, so they waited among the milling crowd outside. It was a beautiful old Victorian theater, grand and imposing. A thrill of excitement tickled Alice's belly as she looked through the doors into a large foyer. Chandeliers hung from the ceiling and a grand, sweeping staircase led to the upper level. It was beautiful.

A few minutes later, Oscar came rushing through the crowd and flung his arms around Alice, giving her an enormous hug. "Hi, sweetie, sorry we're late." He gave her an affectionate peck on the cheek then turned to Jack and gave him a hug, although he didn't get a kiss. "You must be Jack, I'm so pleased to meet you," he purred. He turned to Alice and gave her a wink. "He's cute." Alice laughed and introduced Jack to Dean, who extended his hand in a more formal but nevertheless friendly handshake. This time Dean was smiling, unlike the time she had first met him.

Jack led them to the front of the queue and showed the doorman his pass. The doorman studied it then gave each of them a brief glance before ushering them inside.

"Wow, this place is amazing," cried Oscar as they made their way up the grand staircase to the balcony bar, pushing their way through the crowd. When they stepped through a doorway into the bar a wall of heat and noise hit them face on. People jostled them as they rushed to get past and Alice gripped her bag tighter. Oscar linked his arm through Jack's and said something that Alice couldn't hear. Jack nodded and gestured to her that they were going to get some drinks, leaving her and Dean alone.

"Thank you for asking us to come along tonight," shouted Dean over the drone of voices and music.

"Oh, that's okay."

He said something else, but his words became lost in the bedlam.

"Pardon?" Alice strained to hear what he was saying.

He leaned closer. "Tell you what. Let's go through to the

balcony, the support band has finished and it'll be quieter there as everyone's in here. I'll just let the other two know."

When he returned, he grabbed her hand and led her through some doors and into the dress circle. He was right. The support band were packing away and most of the crowd had disappeared into the bar. Downstairs in the stalls, the determined crowd stayed put so they could get as close to the stage as possible when Underscore came on. Alice grimaced. *Rather them than me.* When they had found some free seats and sat down, Alice sighed with relief, thankful to get away from the crowds. Although there was music playing in the background, it wasn't as loud as it had been in the bar area. She glanced at Dean, not sure what to say to him. She still couldn't help being wary of him after their initial meeting, and the knowledge that he had wanted to sack her wasn't easy to forget. She racked her brain to think of something funny or clever to say, but it had gone to sleep, so instead she pretended to be interested in a patch of chewing gum on the seat in front.

"So do we really get to meet the band afterward or was that just Oscar exaggerating?" asked Dean, ending the awkwardness.

"Oh no. I mean, Oscar wasn't exaggerating. After the concert has finished we have to make our way to Danny's Bar for the after show party. We're on the guest list."

Dean looked impressed. Danny's Bar was one of the trendiest wine bars in London, frequented by pop stars, actors and rich VIPs. Jack had told her earlier that the door policy was so strict that mere mortals like themselves didn't make it inside very often, and if they did, a single glass of champagne cost over twenty pounds. But, for tonight at least, they were on the guest list and the champagne would be free.

Not sure what else to say to Dean, Alice glanced around the theater. Although it was mainly used for rock and pop concerts now, it still retained some of its original features, like the cute golden cherubs grinning down at them from the ceiling. It would have been striking when it had first been built. The shows would have been spectacular and the audience elegant and probably affluent—the men dressed in their dinner jackets and the ladies parading in their beautiful long evening dresses, carrying fans and miniature jewel-encrusted binoculars. She could almost smell the men's heavy cigar smoke and sweet scent of ladies' perfumes. She became drawn into a different world, where the faint images of people in period costume paraded around her. In her trance-like state she could even hear their voices, talking and laughing. Then, out of the corner of her eye, she noticed the silhouette of a man in a top hat coming toward her, waving some sort of cane. He was angry, very angry, yelling at someone. The force of his fury grew stronger as he came closer and a shiver ran through Alice as he seemed to stare directly at her. It was as though the man was shouting at her, but that was silly. Why would a complete stranger be so mad at her? But there was no mistaking the tirade of abuse that was being targeted at her and, although she couldn't hear what he was saying, fear chilled her as she recoiled when she thought he was going to hit her with the cane.

"What's up?" Dean's voice snapped her back to the present and the man vanished.

"Oh, nothing," she stuttered, shaken. "I just thought I saw something." She drew in a deep breath, relieved that she had only been daydreaming, although she could have sworn the man had been there.

"He doesn't want us here," said Dean, just as Jack and Oscar headed toward them with their drinks.

"Who?"

"You didn't imagine the man in the hat. He's a ghost. He's haunting this theater and he's seriously pissed off. He resents this intrusion every night—the noise, the crowds. It's his theater and he's desperate to get rid of all these noisy, common delinquents who are invading his space."

Alice stared opened-mouthed at Dean. That was what she

had seen and felt. *How the hell does he know?*

"How do you know there's a ghost here?"

"Because I've been seeing ghosts all my life, Alice. It's not something I enjoy and it's certainly not something I normally like to talk about, but I know you understand." He smiled his thanks to Jack as he handed him his drink. "We'll talk about it later," he whispered, before he turned back to Jack and asked him about his job.

Chapter Sixteen

Underscore were fantastic on stage and the crowd seemed to adore them. It was great to see Dean, who was normally so serious, let his hair down as he danced and cheered along to the up-tempo music. Even Oscar, who claimed not to like the band, seemed to know the words to most of the songs. Then, about ten minutes before it was due to finish, Jack led them down to the main foyer, where he showed a security guard his pass.

As they were shown through a door that led to the backstage area, Oscar turned to her and grinned. "Look," he whispered, nodding toward Dean. "He's like an excited child."

Alice smiled. She was beginning to see Dean in a very different light. He was much nicer than she had thought when she'd first met him. They made their way through a series of corridors, their footsteps echoing against the muffled sound of the music on stage, until they got to the green room. Inside was a small group of people lounging on tatty sofas, some with beers in their hands and all chatting. One of them stood up when he spotted Jack and came over to them with a big smile on his face.

"Hey, mate, good to see you." He embraced Jack then gave him a friendly slap on the back.

"Hi, Rick. This is my girlfriend, Alice, and this is Oscar and Dean."

They all shook hands as Jack said, "Rick is Underscore's manager. It's thanks to him that they're so big now."

Rick laughed. "I'd say that some of your great reviews have helped. Anyway, you're all very welcome. The boys are just about finished. They'll be off stage in a minute. I'll introduce you all then you can come with us to Danny's on the tour bus. That okay?"

Alice couldn't help noticing Dean's face flush with excitement. It was quite sweet, really. He looked like a star-struck teenager. This was so cool—Jack's reviews must have been pretty amazing to warrant a ride on the tour bus.

Ten minutes later, the band came off stage and greeted Jack like an old friend. Alice watched in disbelief. He seemed to know the band personally.

The short journey on the tour bus was a revelation. Alice had never dreamed that a vehicle that resembled an ordinary coach from the outside could be so lavish on the inside. There were plush sofas, a music system, a plasma screen TV and a very well-stocked bar, which was attended by a discreet barman. As Alice sipped a glass of chilled champagne Jack explained that he and Rick knew each other from their university days. She learned that Jack had been Rick's advisor when he was putting the band together. "I didn't tell you because I wanted to see your face when I introduced you," said Jack, grinning.

Danny's Bar was every bit as impressive as Alice had imagined it would be. On arrival they were ushered into the private party area where a waiter handed them another glass of champagne. The club had been decorated to look like the ice hotels in Scandinavia, with nearly everything appearing as if it was made of ice. The ice-effect bar itself was lit by stunning purple-colored lights and the whole mirrored wall behind it was covered in tiny LED lights that resembled twinkling stars in a clear, dark blue sky. At first glance she thought the tables were made of ice—until she touched one of them and found it wasn't cold. Each one had a hidden bulb at the base that shimmered through the acrylic, creating a spectacular lightshow that changed from one shade of blue to another. A hidden projector in the ceiling threw streaks of green waves weaving through the air, mimicking the Northern Lights. It was breathtaking.

While Jack excused himself and left to greet some acquaintances, Alice stood still for a few seconds, taking it all in, until Oscar flipped her chin to close her mouth. "Careful, Petal, you're looking like you've never been here before," he whispered.

"But I haven't."

"I know, but you don't want anyone else to think that, do you? Pretend that you come here all the time and that you're not in the least bit impressed and... *Oh my God,*" he gasped, "*there's Boy George.*" Without another word, Oscar glided over to the singer and greeted him with an enormous hug. "George, *darling,* how lovely to see you," he gushed, sounding so convincing that Alice actually wondered if he really did know him.

"He's never met Boy George in his life," said Dean, as if reading her mind. "He gets a bit excited when he sees a famous face, bless him."

Feeling a little star-struck herself, Alice, who wasn't that bothered with celebrities, poked Dean in excitement when Adele smiled a friendly greeting as she brushed past them. Then Rob, the singer of Underscore, wandered over and started chatting to them.

"Well, hello," he purred, kissing the palm of Alice's hand. "How the hell did Jack get such a gorgeous lady?"

Alice giggled and tried her hardest not to blush as Rob flashed his famous smile at her.

"When you get tired of him, give me a call," he said with a wink.

Even though she was well aware that he was famous for flirting with just about every female he met, Alice couldn't help but feel just a little flattered that she was on the receiving end. She peered at him through her lashes then leaned forward as if she was going to kiss him. "Don't hold your breath," she replied, laughing in his ear.

When he gave her a quick kiss on the cheek before disappearing again, she almost had to scrape Dean up off the floor.

"Bloody hell, Alice. Rob from Underscore just flirted with you. And you flirted back, you little hussy."

She giggled and took a sip of her champagne. "Are you having a good time?" she asked, surprised to find herself warming to Dean more and more.

"Too right I am," he said with a broad grin. He put his arm around her shoulder and gave her a squeeze. "For one night only we're partying with the stars and I'm loving every minute."

They wandered over to a free table and sat down. Alice sighed with relief as she took the weight off her feet. Those new high-heeled strappy sandals might look good but, God, they hurt.

"So, how long have you been seeing ghosts, then?" she asked, unable to hold her curiosity back any longer.

"Like I said, all my life. I didn't realize they were ghosts at first, I just assumed they were normal living people, like myself." He took a sip of his drink then continued. "I used to play with a little girl, when I was about six years old. Her name was Janet and she was the same age as me. We played hide and seek for hours. I never questioned the fact that nobody ever spoke about her. She lived in the attic and she was my secret friend. One day, though, I mentioned her to my mum and she got really upset. Apparently the people who lived in the house before us had a daughter called Janet who had died of meningitis when she was six years old. My mum thought I knew and was making it all up, which of course I wasn't, and got really cross with me, so I decided not to tell her anymore. As I got older, I realized that it was best not to mention my invisible friends to anyone, as they invariably thought I was crazy and took the piss out of me. So I never spoke about it again."

"What about Oscar? Does he know?"

"Yes. I didn't tell him at first, but when he started getting this stupid idea that Glitz is haunted *and* cursed, I told him so I could put his mind at rest that there's nothing there. Trouble is Oscar, being Oscar, thought I was making it up to shut him up. I can't win."

"I'm psychic too," confided Alice.

"I know. I could tell from your reaction to the man in the top hat at the theater. And Oscar told me."

"I don't see ghosts as easily as you do, but I feel them and I'm learning how to develop my skills. I've got a long way to go yet, though."

"I wouldn't say that. The fact that you saw what you did earlier suggests that you're very sensitive to spirits' presences. What do you think about Oscar's wild claims about Glitz?"

"Well, I must admit I haven't felt anything either." She slipped her sandals off for a moment and rubbed her aching feet. "I can't help wonder if he might be using it as an excuse for the way things are right now."

"Exactly! That's what I think. And Darren isn't helping either," he grumbled.

"Who's Darren?"

"Oh, he's a nice enough guy. He's a friend of Oscar's and is always popping in for a coffee. You'll undoubtedly get to meet him soon. Anyway, he claims to be psychic and is the one who has fueled Oscar's beliefs about the restaurant being haunted. He keeps going on about these bad vibes affecting the energy of the place and that we need to exorcise it to get rid of the curse. Utter bullshit, of course, but Oscar believes it."

The first glimmer of an idea started forming in Alice's head then and she grinned as it became clearer. "I think I might know of a way to nip this silly curse in the bud."

"Tell me more," said Dean, leaning across the table, looking as though he relished the idea of hatching a conspiracy.

"Well, you need to make up a story about a ghost with a grudge. Tell Oscar that you sense an angry man, use the man in the top hat as a model if you like. You could say that he cursed Glitz because of a debt a previous proprietor owed him before he died. Invent a name and sow lots of fake seeds about this so-called curse. You then wait for Oscar to tell Darren all this information, and Darren will hopefully offer to come in and do a reading or whatever it is he does."

"Ooh, Alice. Are you saying that we set Darren up?" Dean asked with a glint in his eye.

"Yes. If all goes to plan, Darren will come out with all this fake information and we can then tell Oscar that we made it up. Then, to finally drill the message into his head, we tell him that I'll get Maggie, who's a real medium, to come in and give you her opinion. In fact, I've already mentioned her to Oscar, so he won't think anything of it. She'll confirm what we're saying and hopefully that'll be enough to convince Oscar that there's no curse or ghost at Glitz. You can then get on with dealing with the real problem by seeking professional advice from a business advisor."

"You're a genius," said Dean, looking as if a huge weight had been lifted from his shoulders.

"Why, thank you. There's only one snag."

"What's that?"

"Maggie seems to have vanished off the face of the planet. Jack says she often does this and that it's just a matter of waiting for her to turn up again, but it's so annoying. I really need to talk to her myself."

"Anything I can help with?"

Without really intending to, Alice found herself telling Dean all about Jemma, right from the day she died, including the message on the EVP recording and ending with the strange ghostly boy she had been seeing ever since Jemma had died. "The thing is, Dean, I'm beginning to doubt my own sanity. He seems so real and yet nobody else has seen him. He just disappears into thin air right in front of me. So, apart from helping me talk to Jemma, I'm hoping that Maggie will tell me I'm not going mad and that she can help me understand who he is and what he wants."

"Have you considered the possibility that he could be an angel?" asked Dean.

Suddenly the music, voices, celebrities and bright lights all faded into the background as Dean's words reverberated in her ears. "An angel?"

"Well, some people, including myself, believe there are angels around us who are here for various reasons. I've heard about people encountering them and that there's usually a reason for their presence, like the angel needs to deliver a message or something. The trouble is, your natural reaction when you see something like that is fear, but the fear drives them away. They can't communicate effectively unless you're calm. I'm not saying that this boy is an angel, but the next time you see him, try not to be afraid of him. Remain calm and ask him if he needs to talk to you. Just remember, if he wanted to hurt you, he would probably have done so by now."

"It never occurred to me that—"

"What never occurred to you?" Jack's voice made them jump and a spark of irritation flashed through Alice at the interruption.

"Oh, nothing. Is there any more champagne?"

As Jack tried to grab the attention of a waiter, Dean leaned over and whispered, "Why didn't you tell Jack? I thought he was helping you with all this?"

"He is, but he's started doubting me and that's made me feel insecure about telling him anymore. Can you imagine what he'd say if I told him the boy could be an angel trying to deliver a message? He'd have me carted off to the nearest mental hospital."

"Be careful not to shut him out, Alice."

"Hmm." She frowned as Jack came over with the waiter in tow. "Where's Oscar?" she asked, keen to change the subject.

"Chatting to his new best mate, Boy George," replied Jack, laughing.

The rest of the night flew by, and at two o'clock they made their way out to a waiting taxi. By this time they were more than a little merry with all the champagne. They sang Abba songs at the top of their voices all the way home, much to the bemusement of the poor taxi driver. Once they'd dropped Oscar and Dean off at their flat above Glitz, Alice stared out of the window in silence as the cab made its way back to Swiss Cottage.

"You're quiet," said Jack. "Are you okay?"

"Fine," she replied, knowing that she was doing what Dean had told her not to do. She was shutting Jack out and, as much as she wanted to tell him what Dean had said, she just didn't trust his reaction anymore. With a sinking feeling, she hoped it wasn't the beginning of the end for them.

* * * *

"Ohh, my head hurts!"

Jemma glanced up as Alice walked into the kitchen with her hand on her forehead.

"Sorry, you won't get any sympathy here." Jack grinned, looking pretty fresh considering their late night. "Not when it's self-inflicted."

"She's got a hangover," said Susie, who was lying across the kitchen table. "Lucky cow, I never got to find out what a hangover feels like."

"Well, count yourself lucky," said Tom in a grim voice. "Trust me, they're not worth it."

"My last hangover was when we woke up here after Jack's party," recalled Jemma with fondness. "Now that was a hell of a hangover."

"You were still beautiful, even with puffy red eyes and old makeup smeared all over your face," said Tom, ruffling her hair.

"Ah, you're so romantic." Jemma laughed and play-punched him on his arm. Tom grabbed her hand and pulled her closer then kissed her on the lips. Despite the impending devastation she knew was just around the corner, Jemma's heart swelled with happiness as Tom nipped her lower lip.

When he released her, he gave her a long, hard stare that made her knees weaken.

"You'd still be beautiful no matter what state you were in. You're even gorgeous as a corpse."

"God, you two are soppy. I think I preferred it when you pretended not to fancy each other," said Susie, pulling a face of disgust.

Tom chuckled then squeezed Jemma's hand before turning back to see what the mortals were up to.

They watched as Jack made Alice a cup of tea and some toast. While Alice struggled to get the toast down, Jack washed up yesterday's dishes.

"How come you're so bloody chirpy today? You had just as much to drink last night as I did." Alice groaned as she rubbed her eyes.

"Ah, but I drank water in between the glasses of champagne."

"Cheat."

"Have they had an argument or something?" asked Jemma.

"Not that I'm aware of. Why?" asked Tom.

"It's just that when they got back last night, Jack went to make them both a drink and when he brought it up to Alice he found her passed out on the bed, so he went back downstairs. But she wasn't asleep. I was watching her. She was awake for ages, looking as if something was bothering her."

"Oh, she was probably just thinking about the concert and trying to stop the room from spinning."

"Maybe."

The three ghosts watched in silence as Alice fumbled with a packet of paracetamol. Suddenly the doorbell shrilled, making them all jump.

"Who the hell is that at this time on a Sunday morning?" grumbled Alice.

"Alice. It's half past eleven," said Jack, laughing as he went into the hall to answer the door.

They heard Jack pull the bolt across and open the door. "Hello. Can I help you?"

"Hello. I'm sorry to bother you," said an apologetic voice.

"Who is it?" called Alice.

"*Grace?*" cried Jemma and Susie in unison, glancing at Tom, who now looked as if he'd seen a ghost. They rushed out into the hallway and, sure enough, there was Grace, standing on the doorstep, looking frail and cold.

"My name is Grace Cresswell. I used to live here." She sounded nervous and awkward, as if she had rehearsed what she was going to say, but couldn't quite remember all the words. "I...I was wondering if I could possibly talk to you about something. It's important."

"Oh. Yes, of course. You'd better come in," said Jack, holding the door open for her.

"Thank you," said Grace, stepping into her old home and peering around the hallway with curiosity.

"This is Alice," he said as she appeared from the kitchen.

"Hello," said Alice with a welcoming smile. "Would you like a cup of tea?"

"Oh, thank you. That would be lovely."

Jack led Grace into the living room and offered her a seat, while Alice disappeared into the kitchen to put the kettle on.

Jemma, Tom and Susie had followed Grace and Jack into the living room and now Tom was watching his mother as if he couldn't quite believe his own eyes.

"Why is she here?" asked Jemma.

"I've no idea," said Tom. "It's so strange to see her back here after all this time."

"What the hell is that woman doing here?" They all turned towards the voice from the corner. Max was glaring at Grace, his eyes blazing with hatred.

"That's my mother," said Tom, with anger edging into his voice. "What's it got to do with you?"

"She was married to *him*," he spat.

"Yes, she was, but my father had nothing to do with what

happened on the Titanic. You can't possibly blame my mother for something that happened before she was even born."

"George Cresswell got away and then your bloody pa died. You all got away with it, but I'm the one who's fucking dead because of *your* family." Max's face was, once again, filled with the same anger and bitterness Jemma had seen before. A shiver of unease rippled through her as she remembered Max's threat, but Tom stood his ground and faced Max head-on.

"Max. Whatever your issues are with my family, now is *not* the time to discuss them. My mother's visit today has nothing to do with you, so why don't you crawl back into your corner and keep your mouth shut." Tom's voice trembled with anger and for an awful moment, Jemma thought Max was going to retaliate. They glared at each other with equal hostility, like two cats about to fight for dominance of a territory.

"Here we are." Alice's cheery voice broke the silence as she walked into the living room carrying a tray with three mugs of steaming tea.

"Thank you. It's very kind of you." Grace took her mug of tea and smiled at Jack and Alice. As if sensing her discomfort, Alice asked her what they could do for her.

"Sit down, Max," ordered Tom and, to Jemma's surprise, Max turned and shuffled back to his chair in the corner without another word. Tom sat next to his mother and waited expectantly for her to tell Jack and Alice why she was there.

"I'm not sure where to start." Grace took a sip of her tea. "I sold this house about twenty years ago to a couple called Mr. and Mrs. Burns. My husband had died the year before, and my son, Tom, died a few months after him."

"They were my grandparents," said Jack. "I inherited this house from them a few years ago."

"They were very decent people. I was glad the house had gone to such a nice couple. It was where my sons grew up and their father before them. Well, something awful happened just before my son died. As a consequence we had an argument, a terrible argument, and it resulted in us not being on speaking terms when he died. I did something that no good mother would ever do. I turned my back on my son when he needed me. He died alone." Grace's eyes clouded over with pain and the torment she had been going through all those years showed clearly on her face.

"Mrs. Cresswell, you don't have to explain this to us," said Jack.

"Yes, I do." Grace took another sip of tea and continued. "When Tom died I was angry with him. I blamed him for something he hadn't done and refused to grant him his dying wish, which was to be buried next to his father. I was so angry and hurt, I just wanted to hurt him back. So I gave Tom's brother, Luke, his ashes after he had been cremated and told him to get rid of them and that I never wanted to hear Tom's name mentioned again." A tear ran down Grace's cheek. Susie must have felt sorry for her because she ran over and put an invisible arm around her. Grace was struggling to remain composed and fiddled with her mug as she tried to continue. "Something strange happened yesterday. It was as if someone shook me hard and woke me up from a bad dream. Everything was suddenly so clear and all it took was a bit of honeysuckle. I swear I could feel Tom's presence. I know it sounds mad, but I just knew he was there and that it was him who had left the honeysuckle for me."

Grace wiped a tear away then she put her mug down. "Of course I don't blame Tom for what happened. I know he would never have done what he'd been accused of. I should have believed him, I should have stood by him, but I let him down and now I have to make it up to him."

"How can we help?" asked Jack.

"Well, I called Luke last night and told him what had happened yesterday and that I had to make it up to Tom somehow. And that's when he told me that when I'd ordered him to get rid of Tom's ashes, he knew I would regret it one day, so he hid the urn and told me he had scattered the ashes in the park."

"Where did he hide it?" asked Alice.

Grace cleared her throat. "Here, in this house."

Chapter Seventeen

There were gasps from both dimensions as Grace continued. "They're in the attic, tucked away in a little alcove under the eaves. That's why I'm here. To ask if I could have my son's ashes back."

"Oh my God," muttered Tom. "I was in this house all along."

"Course you fucking were," spat Max from his corner.

"You knew?" Tom turned toward Max in disbelief. "You knew my ashes were here all these years and you never said a word. Why?"

"Why would I help you?" Max growled. "After what your family did to me."

That was the last straw for Tom. He jumped up and banged his fist so hard on the table that the empty mugs shook. One of them actually toppled over. Jack, who was already making his way upstairs to the attic, didn't see it, but Alice and Grace did and they looked at each other in surprise.

Jemma jumped up to hold Tom back. He was on the brink of losing his temper with Max and it was up to her to stop him from making an already difficult situation even worse. "Tom, stop!" she cried. "This is not the time. Go with Jack up to the attic and see where Luke left your ashes. Don't let Max spoil this."

"You're right. I'll deal with him later," growled Tom, throwing Max a warning glance before disappearing after Jack.

"Did you see that?" asked Grace while Jack was upstairs. "The mugs just moved by themselves."

"Yes, Grace. That was your son Tom," shouted Susie, as if she expected Grace to hear her.

"It was probably the resident ghosts trying to get our attention," joked Alice. "So what are you going to do with the ashes?"

"I'm going to do what I should have done twenty years ago. I'm going to reunite Tom with his father," said Grace, brightening up. "Unfortunately the graveyard is full so I won't be able to bury him, so instead I'm going to scatter the ashes by his father's grave. I'm also going to order a bench to be placed near the grave with a memorial plaque to commemorate them both."

"That sounds lovely. I'm sure your son would be very happy with that."

"I do hope so." Grace sighed as Jack and Tom reappeared with Jack holding a small bronze urn.

"Oh," cried Grace, reaching out for the urn. "Thank you so much. You've no idea how much this means to me."

"I'm glad we could help," said Jack.

Grace rose and looked around the room. Jemma guessed she might be remembering it the way it was when it had been her living room. "Does that corner still feel a bit creepy?" she asked, nodding toward Max's corner.

"Why, yes," exclaimed Alice. "Has it always been like that?"

"My husband's parents said it was fine until about 1912, then suddenly strange things started happening. They used to say there was a ghost haunting this room."

"It's funny you should say that, because we believe this house is haunted as well. Maybe that was your old ghost paying his respects to you when those mugs moved," said Alice, laughing.

"Respects?" growled Max, as Susie and Jemma giggled.

"Hey, Max," taunted Susie. "Grace thinks you're pleased to see her."

"Piss off!"

"I must go now," said Grace. "Thank you again for your

kindness. And thank you for the tea." She smiled at Alice as Jack helped her with her coat. "You're a lovely couple and I'm so pleased that you're living in my old house." As she left, Grace took one last glance back at her old home before hugging the urn close to her and making her way back to her car.

"Goodbye, Mother," said Tom quietly as he watched her from the window.

"Wow, who would have thought that your ashes were here all along," said Susie once they had returned to the kitchen, leaving Max alone in his dark corner.

"I can't believe that Max knew all this time and never said anything," said Jemma, swallowing a surge of anger.

"Forget about it," said Tom. "He really isn't worth it. Do you mind if I disappear for a while? I'd like to follow Mother home and spend some time with her."

"Of course not. I was thinking of paying Claire a visit anyway."

"And I've got an appointment with *Tracy Beaker* next door so I'll see you later," said Susie before disappearing through the wall.

Tom put his arms around Jemma and held her. "Thank you," he whispered. "Thank you for being such a persistent busybody and for not listening to me. This is all because of you, you know. I love you so much."

"I love you too. Now go after your mother. I'll see you later."

When she was alone, Jemma reflected on Grace's visit. She was thrilled for Tom that her plan had worked, but Tom's reaction to her arrival had left her thinking about her own mum. It made her want to be near her so, instead of going to find Claire, she decided to visit her mum's grave. First, though, she should ask Max if he could tell her what he knew about wormholes. The sooner she had the information she needed, the sooner they could start to make plans.

Adrenaline rushed through her as she returned to the

living room while trying to work out what she was going to say. She had seen the way Max had backed down with Tom before, so maybe he wasn't as scary as she had first thought?

"Max?" She tried to make her voice sound friendly.

"Get lost."

Standing face-to-face with him, she wondered if he was as dangerous as Susie had made him out to be. "You wouldn't really hurt Tom, would you?"

His lips curled into a smile of sorts. Jemma smiled back. Maybe she had finally made some sort of breakthrough with him? Relief flooded her. Once this whole Tom issue was cleared up, they could get on with their discussion about wormholes and everything would be fine. But then his smile turned into a laugh — a dark and sinister rumble that sent prickly shivers all the way down her spine.

"What do you think?" he sneered, his eyes flashing with danger

"I don't think you would harm him, actually. In fact, I don't think you can." *Shit, did I really just said that?*

"What?"

"I think if you really wanted to hurt Tom you would have done so a long time ago, so you either don't really mean it or you can't actually hurt him at all." And she was either being very brave or downright stupid confronting him like that. She just couldn't help herself. She glared defiantly at him, waiting for his response, but he remained silent. Then, like a flash of lightning, he vanished from his chair and reappeared in front of her, towering over her like a giant, ferocious wolf. His eyes now burned with rage, making her recoil in fright. Before she could retreat she was lifted into the air by some sort of invisible force and hurled across the room, landing on the floor by the window. The force that had thrown her was more powerful than anything she had ever experienced. Unable to move from stunned disbelief, she could only stare at him in terror. He took a step closer. She squeezed her eyes shut in the hope that he'd disappear if she couldn't see him.

"So you don't think I can hurt him? Well, we'll see about that." He laughed again, the ugly sound taunting her and reminding her of the power he had just shown against her. "I know Tom thinks I'm just a harmless old spook, so don't bother warning him because he won't believe you. I've been waiting a long time for my moment and it seems it has finally come. I will get him, you can be sure of that, and if you get in my way I'll destroy you as well. Now, *get out!*" He nodded at her and the same force that had thrown her now pushed her toward the wall until she disappeared through it back to the kitchen. At last the force released her, leaving her alone and crumpled on the floor. At first she nearly cried with relief, but then the implications of her impulsiveness started to become clearer.

What have I done? She had pushed Max too far this time. She'd been wrong in assuming that he might be harmless after all. She should have listened to Susie. Max was more than capable of hurting Tom, and her for that matter. If he did anything to harm Tom before he was able to leave it would be her fault. She glanced around as her skin prickled with unease. She thought she had seen a movement across the kitchen, but the room was empty. What if Max followed her and attacked her again? She was alone in the house with him and he could come through that wall any minute. Fear gripped her throat. If she'd been alive she was pretty sure she wouldn't have been able to breathe. She needed to get away. Should she go to Grace's house and find Tom? No, she didn't want to spoil his time with his mum. She needed to be alone. Alice was out with Jack so the old flat would be empty. She would go there and decide what to do next.

A moment later, she walked across her old bedroom and threw herself onto her bed. At least she would be safe there.

"You stupid, stupid idiot," she cursed. Her ordeal flashed across her mind over and over. The fury in Max's eyes, her complete helplessness as she was thrown across the room and the deadly threat in his words. She vowed never to be alone in the house with him again. The next time Tom and Susie both went out she would go out too — anywhere, as long as it was as far away from Max as possible. She shuddered as she recalled the moment she had crashed onto the floor. It was a miracle she hadn't broken any bones. Now that she thought about it, she hadn't been hurt at all. She waved her arms and stretched her legs as if to prove it to herself, and sure enough, she was fine. No pain. Did that mean that, although Max had the power to move her, he couldn't physically hurt her? There was some comfort in that thought. But she still hadn't gotten around to asking for Max's help with finding a wormhole. There was no way he was going to help her now. *Well, I don't want his help, anyway.*

She remained in the quiet safety of her old room for what must have been a couple of hours in the living world. She wished she could feel her mother's arms hold her as she reassured her that everything would be fine. She needed her mum right now. If she couldn't have that, she would do the next best thing and visit her mum's grave. She closed her eyes and transported herself to the graveyard in Stenhurst.

"Hi, Mum," she said softly as she approached the grave and sat down. Aunt Tess had left a huge red poinsettia at the head of the grave and it looked beautiful against the black marble gravestone. A quick glance to the left showed her that Aunt Tess had also left one on her grave. "I've fallen in love, Mum," she said out loud. "His name is Tom and he's the most amazing man I've ever met in my life." She smiled to herself at the irony of using the words 'my life'. "He'll be leaving soon, though, and I don't know what I'm going to do when he's gone." Her voice trembled, the pain of what was to come almost too unbearable to contemplate. It was at times like this that mothers would put their arms around their daughters and hug them, comforting them with words of love and wisdom. That was what she needed now. She ran her finger along the marble as if she expected her mum's face to smile at her in the shiny reflection, but the gravestone stared back, cold and silent.

She remained by the grave until it was dark, deep in thought and losing all sense of her own reality. Her mind flooded with memories, good and bad — memories of idyllic picnics, happy, tender moments. Then there were the angry arguments, rows about homework, bedtime and the length of her skirts. They were all as fresh as they had been back then. Painful too, because now they were just memories, nothing more.

Much later, Jemma jumped when a hand touched her on the shoulder, snapping her out of her lament. Her instinct told her that it was Tom's hand and she put her own up to meet his. "Hi," she said.

"I was worried about you." He sat down beside her and drew her close.

"I'm fine. How did you know where I was?"

"It wasn't too hard to work out where you'd gone. You know, with all this stuff about my mother…"

"I've been telling my mum all about you. I wish she could have met you, she would have liked you." They sat in silence for a while, each of them giving the other quiet reassurance.

"Tom? What do you think will happen to you when you leave?"

"I don't know. I suppose, if it works, I'll become a free spirit and my energy will become part of the universe."

Her heart splintered. "I'll miss you so much," she croaked, barely able to get the words out.

He tightened his grip around her. "I'm going to miss you too, my love. When you've gone back yourself, you won't miss me, because you won't remember me. But I'll be able to watch you. Keep an eye on you."

She almost made the mistake of telling him that she wouldn't be going back, but stopped herself in time. "I hate the fact that I'll forget all about you, that I won't ever know you're there." She hated herself for lying to him, but there was no other way.

"I know." His voice was heavy. "But I promise you, Jemma, I'll never forget you and I'll always be there with you. I'll never leave you."

Jemma turned to him and gazed at him through blurry tears. "I don't want to lose you," she said, choking on her words. "I'm not sure I can—"

"Shh," he murmured, his expression mirroring Jemma's pain. He cradled her face in his hands and locked eyes with her. When a tear rolled down her cheek, he brushed it away with his thumb. "I love you so much."

"I love you too."

"Jemma—"

She knew what he was about to say, but shook her head. "We have to do this."

He sighed. "Yeah, I know. I just wish there was another way to help Susie."

"Me too. When are you going to do it?" asked Jemma, already dreading the answer.

"Well, providing I don't have any problems finding a wormhole, it could be any time. I do know that it's no use trying to create a wormhole, it's far too difficult and dangerous. We'll need to find an existing one."

"Oh."

"But I'll need some help. I've no idea what to do with it even if I do find one. I was going to ask Max, but after today I'm not so sure."

"No," snapped Jemma. "Not Max, no way. I know you don't think Max is dangerous, but I do and I'm afraid of what he might do if he knows you're going to leave. I'll talk to Claire, she may be able to help, although the fact that she's become friends with the miserable old sod does complicate things a bit."

"Why?"

"Because she might feel obliged to tell him that you're leaving. We must tell her it's just for me. Promise me that you won't tell her it's for you. Please, she must think that it's just me leaving. It's the only way we can be sure that

Max won't find out."

"Okay. But one thing is for sure, I'm not doing anything until after Christmas."

"Why?"

"Both you and Susie will be going back in time to your lives and will have all your Christmases before you. One more Christmas here won't hurt Susie, so let's enjoy the time we've got left together. You and I are going to have the best Christmas ever. We won't be sad, we won't talk about what's to come. We're going to spend Christmas Day together somewhere really special. Just you and I."

"That sounds wonderful, but what about Susie? We can't leave her on her own on Christmas Day."

"Susie always goes to be with her parents on Christmas Day. She prefers it that way. I'm the one who's normally alone. Let's enjoy the day, then I can start looking on Boxing Day."

"So when are you going to tell Susie that you've decided to go?"

Tom shrugged. "I don't think we should say anything until the last minute. You know what she's like, she'll blab and Max might overhear."

"Yes, I agree. How long does it take? To find a wormhole and use it?" asked Jemma, hoping he would say it would take days, maybe even weeks, before he would be ready to leave.

"Once we locate it, I'll have to use it immediately, otherwise it'll collapse and we'll have to start searching again. If we find one straightaway and it works, I could be gone on Boxing Day."

Jemma's heart crashed with a thud. Boxing Day was only four days away. With a renewed sense of dread, she knew that it was only a matter of time, very little time, before Tom and Susie would be gone and she would be left on her own with Max's wrath. Yes, she could leave as well, but she couldn't face going back to her empty life, where she would have no memories of Tom.

A couple of months ago she would have done anything to get back. *How ironic*.

"So, when is your mum going to scatter your ashes?" asked Jemma.

"Tomorrow. She rang Luke when she got back from Jack's and he's driving down tonight. It'll just be the two of them. Will you come?"

"Of course I will. And Susie. We'll both be there for you."

A mist was moving across the dark and silent graveyard, making it appear like an image from a horror film. Jemma imagined a vampire rising out of one of the graves, searching for his next victim, and shuddered. She had always been a bit scared of the idea of vampires, although she had insisted that she didn't believe in all that rubbish. The only movement, though, was the odd ghost wandering aimlessly across the graves, each with their own tragic reason for being there. A living person might have caught a glimpse of them, their energy barely visible as a faint transparent light in the form of a blurry figure. If she had walked through this graveyard on her own in the dead of night while she had been alive, she would have been terrified. It was odd, but she was at ease here, somehow comforted by the fact that she was a part of this surreal supernatural scene.

Tom lay down on his back then pulled Jemma down next to him. Although the grass would have been damp and cold to a living person, Jemma only felt Tom's warmth as she snuggled up to him. There were advantages to being dead, like not getting wet or catching pneumonia from lying on the freezing ground in December.

"I still can't get my head around the fact that I can feel heat and air from you," she mused.

Tom chuckled. "I know. One of Susie's friends once said it has something to do with the energy that is left within us the moment we die. Apparently it never leaves us. Sometimes you can even hear the distant echo of a ghost's heartbeat."

Jemma lifted her head off his shoulder and placed it on

his chest. Sure enough, the distant drumming that beat against her ear was unmistakable. "I can both hear and feel your heart."

"It's not real, but it is kind of comforting, isn't it?"

"Mmm," she murmured as she closed her eyes.

"Did you believe in ghosts before you died?" he asked, as he stroked her arm.

"No. Alice did and I always used to tease her about it. How about you?"

"No, I didn't either. Even after I'd died I was skeptical. It took quite a lot of persuasion from Susie before I finally accepted I was one. And if someone had told me I would fall in love here, I definitely wouldn't have believed them."

Although it was too dark to see his face, Jemma could hear the smile in his voice. "Have you ever been in love before?" she asked.

"No. I'd had girlfriends of course, but I'd never met anyone that was special. Like you," he whispered. "When did I last tell you that I love you?"

"About five minutes ago," replied Jemma, giggling. "But tell me again."

"I love you."

"Pardon? I didn't hear you."

Tom raised himself onto his elbow then took a handful of Jemma's hair and held her head in place as he stared down at her. "I love you, Jemma Haley." Then he smashed his lips against hers and kissed her with a new urgency.

When he pulled away Jemma was ready for more. Much more. "Tom? Can we… I mean, is it possible for us to…you know…make love?"

He took her lower lip between his teeth and nipped it before releasing it again. "Oh yeah, it's definitely possible, but not here. I want our first time to be special."

"So when can we –?"

He silenced her with another kiss, exploring her with his tongue and sending little shots of joy bursting through her. When he stopped, he grinned. "Soon, my love. Be patient."

"Patience never was one of my strong points."

"Well, if you don't mind an audience…" he said, grinning. "We aren't exactly alone here."

Jemma had been so caught up in the moment that she had forgotten about the other lost souls wafting through the graveyard. "Ah, okay. I guess we'd better get back anyway. You've got a big day ahead tomorrow, one that you've waited over twenty years for, and I'm going to make sure you enjoy it."

* * * *

The following morning dawned cold and crisp, but at least it didn't rain. An air of anticipation, almost excitement, surrounded the small crowd that was gathered around Adam Cresswell's grave. To a living person it would have looked rather sad, just two people shivering in the freezing cold, but in Jemma's world there was quite a decent crowd in attendance. Apart from Tom and herself, Susie and Claire had come along, as well as a couple of other ghosts that Tom had become friends with over the years. Max was absent, of course, but that was just as well.

"I can't believe that Luke came," muttered Tom. "He's always so busy." Tom had once told her that he and his brother had been close when they were growing up, but as they'd left home to go to university, then gone on to build their respective careers, they had drifted apart and only saw each other on special occasions, like Christmas. He'd said there had been a quiet rivalry between them, borne out of the need to seek their parents' approval, but it had never stopped them getting along when they did see each other.

"Hey, Tom?" said Susie. "Do you think your dad is here? Not in the grave there. I mean here, watching with us now?"

"I really don't know," said Tom. "It would be nice to think that he is."

"Well, if he's a free spirit then it might be possible. Although we can't communicate with them, they could very well be able to observe us," mused Claire.

"Wow," said Susie. "How cool is that? A whole family reunited across different dimensions."

Tom smiled. "Thanks for coming, Susie. I know you don't like graveyards so I appreciate you being here."

"Yeah, well, you've waited a long time for this."

"I'm glad you're here," he said, giving her a hug.

They watched as Grace unscrewed the lid of the urn and cleared her throat, ready to speak.

"Tom, I know you're here. I can feel you," she said, shivering. "This is for you, my dear. I know this was what you wanted and I'm sorry, so very sorry, that it's taken me so long to honor your wish. I also want to say how sorry I am for the way I treated you. It was unforgivable and it grieves me greatly that you died believing that I didn't love you. But Tom, I do love you. I've always loved you and I want you to know that I do believe you about what happened. I should never have doubted you and I will never forgive myself for that. All I can do now is hope and pray that moving you here will go some way toward making things right—" Her voice broke into a sob at that point and Luke put a comforting arm around her.

She tipped the urn and emptied the contents over her dead husband's grave, then she and Luke bent their heads to say a quiet prayer.

"Do you think he's here, Luke?" she asked.

"I know he is," Luke replied. "Come on, Mother, let's get you home before you catch your death. It's freezing."

"Goodbye, Mother," said Tom as he watched Grace and Luke walk away, with Grace still clutching the empty urn. "Thank you."

Jemma reached out and took Tom's hand. "There's nothing stopping you from leaving now."

"Except you," he replied.

* * * *

Alice was alone in the kitchen, sipping tea and listening to the radio. Jack had left early to attend a press conference for some major band who were splitting up and she was due to be at Glitz at eleven o'clock to help set up for lunch. Now that a bit of time had passed since Saturday, guilt had set in for being so snappy with Jack. She should have told him what Dean had said about the boy possibly being an angel. She had been about to tell him yesterday, but then that poor old lady had turned up asking for her son's ashes. She should have trusted him. Of all people, he would be the last person not to believe her. He had seemed a bit cool toward her yesterday, but she couldn't blame him. Tonight she would tell him and ask him what he thought. Maybe they could search for information about angels on the Internet together. Casper, who was sitting on her lap, nudged her arm with his nose and she snapped out of her thoughts and glanced up at the clock.

"Shit!" It was half past ten, she had to be at work in half an hour and she wasn't even dressed yet. With lightning speed she flew up the stairs, grabbed some clothes and was ready in record time. She was only two minutes late as she rushed through the doors of Glitz.

"Good morning, Petal," called Oscar. "Come and have a coffee before you start."

Alice made her way over to the little private alcove where the staff had their coffee breaks and found Oscar chatting with a man she didn't recognize. He was handsome in a very classical way and was wearing an expensive-looking designer suit. He looked a bit like a 1950s film star.

"Sweetie, this is Darren."

Darren smiled and gave her a little wave. "So you're the Dancing Queen of Glitz."

"Oh God, Oscar, have you told the whole of London?"

"No, Sweetie, just the whole of Camden."

"Hmm. Anyone want another coffee?"

"Ooh, yes please, Petal. Darren will have one too. Oh, and would you stick *Voulez Vous* on for me please? I need another Abba fix."

"Yes of course. I do a mean rendition of *Kisses of Fire*." She laughed as she made her way to the espresso machine.

Alice had found the right CD, popped it in the player then started frothing milk for the cappuccinos, when Dean popped his head through the kitchen door. "Psst," he whispered. "In here, quick."

Alice glanced over her shoulder toward the alcove. Oscar and Darren were busy chatting, so she left the milk on the side and slid silently into the kitchen, where Dean was waiting.

"Thanks again for Saturday night." He smiled, giving her a friendly peck on the cheek.

"That's okay. I really enjoyed it too. So, is that the same Darren that you were telling me about?" she whispered, nodding in the direction of the restaurant.

"Yes, that's him. Just so you know, I pretended to be on the phone when he arrived and I made sure that he would overhear what I was saying." Dean lowered his voice, even though the crystal-clear voices of Frida and Agnetha were blaring from the restaurant. "I told this bogus caller that I had just found out that in the late 1800s a rich man called James Salisbury owned this building. He ran a tobacco business from here and was very powerful and revered. One night, when he was working late, someone broke in and murdered him. Shot him right through the heart with a rifle and stole his money, watch and other valuables. I then said that it has been rumored over the years that this James Salisbury has been haunting the building ever since and has cursed every business that's ever operated from here." Dean grinned. "What do you think?"

"Very good. But why would he curse this place?"

"Who cares? Darren won't think of that. I was watching him while I was saying it and he was definitely listening. So now I need you to prompt Oscar so he starts talking about the ghost or curse while you're drinking your coffee and then we'll see if he takes the bait. Is that okay?"

"No problem." Alice giggled. With a quick nod at Dean she slipped back into the restaurant.

"What happened to you?" called Oscar as she approached the coffee machine.

"Oh, nothing. I was just looking for some more milk."

"It's in the fridge under the counter where it always is, silly."

"Oh yes, so it is." Alice made three cappuccinos, took them over to the alcove and joined Oscar and Darren. "So, Darren, you're a friend of Oscar's?"

"We've been friends for over ten years," said Darren, with a fond nod at Oscar.

Alice smiled and racked her brain to find a way of bringing up the subject of ghosts. Darren seemed nice and she couldn't help feeling a twinge of guilt at what she was about to do.

"Darren, did you know that Alice is also psychic? You two should get together to compare notes."

"Really?" Darren beamed. "I'd love to have a chat with you some time. Did you know that this place is haunted?"

"Well, Oscar did mention something," replied Alice. This was too easy. She hadn't even needed to bring the subject up herself. Had Oscar set this up in the hope that maybe he could get them both to convince Dean that he was right? Her gut feeling about Darren, though, was that he wasn't deliberately acting as a fraudulent psychic, but did seem to believe what he was feeling. It was a shame that it was having such a negative effect on Oscar, otherwise she would have preferred to leave Darren to his deluded belief that he was a gifted psychic. She hoped he wouldn't be too upset when they exposed his shortcomings, but it needed to be done. Oscar needed a wake-up call so he could concentrate on getting the business back on its feet.

"Well, I've just suggested to Oscar that we hold a séance. Will you join us?"

Alice made sure she looked enthusiastic and agreed to taking part in the séance.

"I'm a bit busy with work right now so how about we do it on Christmas Eve?" asked Darren.

"Okay but it's probably best not to tell Dean," whispered Oscar. "He's such a non-believer that his negative energy could keep the spirits away. We'll do it after we've closed and spring it on him at the last minute."

"I'm not meant to be working on Christmas Eve," said Alice, as she got up to set the tables. "Shall I come in anyway and give you a hand?"

"That would be great," said Oscar. "I can arrange for you to swap shifts if you like. And remember, mum's the word." He tapped his nose dramatically.

"Okay." Alice grinned. As soon as she turned away from Oscar and Darren, though, her smile vanished as more guilt set in. She hated lying to Oscar, who she now considered a friend as well as her boss. But it was for his own good. *He'll understand, won't he?* Excitement buzzed through her as she wondered what her first séance would be like. It was just a shame that it was all based on a lie.

Chapter Eighteen

The lunchtime shift was busy and Alice was rushed off her feet so she didn't have a chance to tell Dean about the planned séance. By three o'clock she had finished clearing away and was ready to leave. Jack wouldn't be home until late, so she planned to pop round to the old flat to start packing up. She had left a lot of stuff there when she'd moved into Jack's, especially Jemma's things. She wouldn't have coped with the task of sorting through them before now. Jack had offered to do it, but she'd felt it was something she had to do herself — eventually. But now her parents wanted to rent the flat out to someone else, which was fair enough, and she had promised them that she would have the flat cleared and vacant by the new year.

She held her breath as the let herself in through the door, still half expecting to hear Jemma's voice call out a welcoming greeting. But the silence was more intense than she'd remembered and a shiver of apprehension ran through her as she closed the door and walked into the small living room. She stood still for a moment, looking around, letting the memories flow back. With a deep sigh, she made her way into Jemma's room and took in the task that lay ahead of her. Everything was pretty much the way it had been before her friend had died. Jemma's clothes were everywhere, strewn across the chair and hanging out of drawers. Several stacks of various things were dotted around the room, comprising a mixture of magazines, shoes, clothes and cosmetics. Alice never had been able to understand how Jemma could live in such a mess, but Jemma had always insisted that she knew which stack contained what and, oddly enough, she did always seem to know where to find whatever she was searching for.

Where do I start? No matter how organized the mess is, it's going to take ages to get through this lot. The best thing would be to sort it into three piles, one for rubbish, one for charity and one to keep. She had to be ruthless. She would only keep things that had special memories for her or that Jemma's aunt might want. After plugging her phone into some speakers, she began sifting through the mess as the dark tones of The Sisters of Mercy kept her company.

* * * *

Alice lost track of time as she became caught up in the music. As the piles became smaller and the bin bags filled, memories flooded back, bringing a kind of therapeutic calm with them. It was as if packing Jemma's things away was putting a finality on her grief, somehow helping her come to terms with what had happened. She would always miss Jemma and she was well aware that some days would be easier than others, but it was time to move on and let Jemma's memory be a happy and positive one. Her spirits lifted as she made progress and the carpet became more visible. But then she remembered Jemma's message on the voice recorder and her heart sank again. Every time she tried to move on, the message echoed in her head. *What is Jemma trying to tell me? Where is she? If I can hear Jemma's voice on a recorder, why haven't I been able to talk to her?* She had so many questions she needed to ask. She couldn't wait for Maggie to get back from that retreat so she could talk to her some more. Right now Maggie seemed to be her only chance of making contact with Jemma and until she returned Alice was powerless to do anything. Jack had tried to teach her how to reach a deep meditative state in the hope that that might help, but nothing had happened. She sighed and stuffed a pair of Jemma's old shoes into the charity bag. She wasn't going to get any answers today so there was no point dwelling on it.

When the floor was clear Alice sat back with satisfaction and admired her progress. She couldn't allow herself to relax, though. She still had the wardrobe to do. She had already filled six bin liners, three of which were for the charity shop and only one that was rubbish. The other two contained the things that either she or Aunt Tess would keep. Surveying the room, she decided to move the bags out into the hallway to give her some more space.

"Hey now, hey now now," she sang as she dragged a heavy bag through the doorway.

All of a sudden the music stopped and the flat was thrown into silence. "Shit," she grumbled under her breath and made her way back into Jemma's room to switch the music back on. But before she reached the speakers she froze. Something wasn't right. Goose bumps shimmied up her arms as if someone was blowing cool air on them and making the tiny hairs stand on end. The silence grew from a mere lack of sound to an intense heaviness. It was as though she had been covered with a thick blanket, making it hard to breathe. She tried taking a step forward, but couldn't move. Then, with sudden clarity, she remembered that she had experienced this sensation before, the day the boy had appeared in her kitchen.

"Don't panic," she whispered to herself. She needed to stay calm like Dean had told her to, but it was bloody hard when her heart was beating so hard it hurt her chest. But she did manage to get her ragged breaths under control and the frantic haze in her head began to clear. She waited, still and silent, until the boy appeared in front of her, looking as enigmatic and ethereal as before.

"Alice. Do not be afraid, I mean you no harm." The voice was clear, although the boy had not moved his mouth.

"I know that now. Are you an angel?" Her voice was small but steady.

The boy remained silent, although there was a very slight hint of a smile on his lips. Alice knew that he was indeed an angel. Dean had been right. Now that she wasn't in a state of terror, she was able to study the boy more closely. His eyes shone as if they were made of the most brilliant diamonds and his whole being radiated warmth and light that contrasted with the cold, dark atmosphere she was standing in. She was mesmerized and could only stare in wonderment at the vision in front of her.

"I am sorry that I frightened you. I have been trying to talk to you since Jemma died, but your fear kept me from making contact with you." The voice was soft, gentle, and Alice was soothed by the melodic tone. His words danced in front of her, wrapping themselves around her body before seeping through to her inner consciousness.

"Every living person has an angel and I am Jemma's. But I let her down, Alice, because she was not meant to die that day. She is trapped in a place for lost souls – somewhere I cannot reach her or help her."

"That's awful," whispered Alice, tears flooding her eyes. Her heart shattered at the knowledge that Jemma wasn't at peace after all.

"You have a special gift, Alice, and you need to use that gift to pass on a message to Jemma for me. I cannot communicate with the lost souls, but you have the ability to talk to her. You must tell her to leave the eleventh dimension and return to the living. It was not her time to die and she will never be able to move on and find peace if she stays where she is. You must tell her this, Alice. She will know what to do, but tell her also that she must beware of Max."

"Max?" asked Alice, trying to recall if Jemma had ever known anyone called Max.

But the angel was starting to fade. She knew his work was done and that it was now up to her to do as he had asked. As the last particles of light faded, Alice just managed to catch a smile from him before he disappeared. She knew that that would be the last time she would see him.

Then the music started playing again, just as suddenly as it had stopped, making Alice jump. She hurried over to turn it off, now resenting the intrusion. She needed the quiet because she knew that she would never hear or feel silence in quite the same way again. She wanted to remember every last detail of what had just happened. There had been something so captivating about the presence of the angel that she needed to preserve her memory of him. She would never experience anything so overwhelming and powerful again.

As the euphoria of the angel's appearance started to wear off, the implications of what he had said started to dawn on her. Jemma was trapped and possibly in danger from this Max. The angel had said that she must return, but how could that happen? She was dead. This was all way beyond her modest psychic knowledge. What should she do? Then she remembered her chat with Dean. She needed to talk to him. *Now!* She grabbed her coat and ran out of the flat, leaving the bin liners lying on the floor.

It didn't take long to get to Glitz. She just hoped Dean was still there. The melodic tones of Underscore greeted her as she pushed open the door and she sighed in relief that he hadn't left yet.

"Hello there," said Dean, looking up from his paperwork. "I wasn't expecting you back again so soon."

"Dean, I'm so glad you're still here. You were right. It was an angel. He came back. I've just seen him."

"Whoa, slow down," said Dean laughing. "Come and sit down."

Alice flopped onto the seat opposite Dean. "He was beautiful, Dean," she cried. "I've never been so moved by anything in my life."

"You're very lucky. Few people ever get to see an angel, let alone talk to one. What did he say?"

"Well, that's what's worrying me. He said that Jemma wasn't meant to have died and that I've got to pass on a message to her to tell her to come back. But how can you come back from the dead? Oh, and I've got to warn her about someone called Max. He said that I can use my gift, but I don't know what to do. How the hell am I going to do this?"

At that moment, Oscar burst through the doors. "Hello, sweetie. Are you telling Dean about the séance?"

"That's it," exclaimed Alice. "A séance, of course. Why didn't I think of that before?"

* * * *

"Jemma?"

"Huh?" Jemma glanced up from the computer screen that Jack was using and smiled at Susie.

"Are you homesick? Do you still want to leave?"

"Er…" Jemma hesitated as Susie jumped onto the kitchen table and sat cross-legged in front of her. This was when she should be telling Susie that she wasn't going home, but her and Tom. But Tom was right. There was no way Susie could keep her mouth shut, so instead she smiled. "Yes. I plan to leave just after Christmas."

"But why? I don't get it. You've been so happy lately, what with your thing with Tom and all. Why do you want to leave him?"

"It's not Tom, or you, that I want to leave, Susie. I just feel that it's the right thing to do." She hated lying to Susie, but what else could she do?

"Bollocks!"

"Susie!"

"Well, it is. The right thing to do? For who, exactly?"

Oh shit, this is going to be lot harder than I'd thought. Susie was a lot of things, but she wasn't stupid. But Jemma had no choice — they just couldn't risk Susie blabbing to Max — so she strengthened her resolve to keep quiet.

"Susie, will you stop going on about it? I've got a headache."

"Ghosts don't get headaches."

"Oh for God's sake, Susie, will you just leave me alone," snapped Jemma. She needed to get away from the questions so, leaving Susie looking bewildered and a little hurt, she stormed out of the kitchen.

Jemma found herself at the forest, not far from Claire's bench. For a moment she considered going somewhere else to be alone. There must have been hundreds of forests. She should try somewhere different for once, where nobody would know her. But now that she was there she might as well find Claire and ask her what she knew about the wormholes. She was beginning to wish she'd never tried so hard to persuade Tom to go back. It would have been so easy just to leave things as they were, and she would have had her happy ending.

Claire was in her usual place. Jemma frowned as a hint of irritation niggled at her. When was Claire going to realize that Robert was never going to come for her?

"Hi," she said as she approached the bench. "No sign of him yet, then?"

"Hello, dear," said Claire, her smile revealing that she was pleased to see Jemma. "No, dear. Not yet."

"Oh." Jemma wasn't sure what else to say, other than 'get real, woman, the bastard has deserted you'. But she liked Claire and didn't want to hurt her feelings, so she kept quiet.

Claire studied her for a moment. "Are you all right? You seem a bit distracted."

"Oh, Claire. I've just upset Susie and I feel awful. I told her that I'm leaving after Christmas and now she thinks I don't care about her."

"Are you leaving? Why? I thought you were happy now that you've found love with Tom."

Jemma shrugged. This was getting harder. "I am, but there are reasons why I have to go back. I wish I hadn't been so abrupt with Susie, though. It's not her fault."

"Why were you abrupt with her?" probed Claire.

"Because she wouldn't stop asking about it." That sounded so lame, but she couldn't think of anything else to say. Claire seemed to agree.

"But why shouldn't she ask about it? It's a big thing for her, she's very fond of you, so it's only natural that she would be upset."

"Oh, don't you start," said Jemma. The truth was that she was happy, very happy. She had Tom, Susie and Claire and, now that she had gotten used to being a ghost, she quite enjoyed the freedom that came with it. But she knew she sounded pathetic right now. No wonder Claire didn't believe her.

"Jemma?" asked Claire. "What's wrong?"

"Nothing. I can't say…" Jemma felt herself weakening. She so wanted to tell Claire everything, to share her grief at losing Tom in a few days' time. If only it wasn't for bloody Max.

"Jemma, if there's anything you want to talk about, you can trust me." Claire spoke with such sincerity that Jemma felt even worse.

"It's not you, Claire. I do trust you, it's just… Well, it's Max, actually. I know you're his friend, but…"

"Jemma. Max is my friend, yes, but so are you. Whatever you tell me would be in strict confidence. I wouldn't betray your trust. Not even to Max," she said, smiling.

A wave of relief washed over Jemma. It would be so good to talk to someone else and get an unbiased opinion. Of course she could trust Claire.

"I'm not going back, Claire. Tom and Susie are. I found out that Susie is desperately unhappy and that she misses her mum really badly so I resolved to help her get back. But then I found out that due to the accident that killed her, Tom would have to go back as well. I finally managed to convince Tom that he has to go back for Susie's sake, but the trouble is I can't tell Susie because she'll blab. If Max finds out that Tom is planning on leaving, he might just decide to take that revenge that he's been planning for so long. Please, Claire, you mustn't say anything to either of them."

"Of course I won't, dear, I gave you my word. So does

that mean you'll be leaving as well? I suppose that once Tom has gone, there'll be nothing to keep you here."

Jemma stared at Claire. Suddenly she understood why Claire might have been waiting for Robert all these years. "I'm not leaving, Claire. If I go back, I'll forget about Tom. It will be as if he never existed, but I need to remember him because he's the only truly good thing that's ever happened to me." Jemma fought to keep the tears looming behind her eyes at bay. "Is that why you're still waiting for Robert? Because you're worried that you might forget him?"

Claire's face clouded over and she shook her head. "To be honest, dear, I don't know why I'm here. When I first arrived, all I knew was that I had to wait for Robert, but now... I don't know, Jemma. I just don't know."

Jemma reached out, took Claire's thin, delicate hand and gave it a squeeze. "Well, whatever happens with Robert, I'll still be here for you. We can help each other."

"Thank you, dear. But I think you're making a mistake by not going back. Nobody in this dimension is meant to be here, that's exactly why we're here." Claire shook her head as if acknowledging the absurdity of her words. "We're in the wrong dimension."

"Well, wrong or not, I'm staying, so you're stuck with me. We do need your help though, Claire."

"Oh?"

"You mentioned a while ago that you knew a bit about wormholes and stuff. Well, I was going to ask Max, but I don't think that would be a good idea."

Claire chuckled. "You're right about that, dear. We must keep this from Max at all costs, so we'll discuss this as though it's you going back. Max isn't a bad person, Jemma, but he has got a lot of bitterness in him and he's looking for someone to take it out on."

"I still don't understand how you two can be friends," said Jemma, frowning.

"Like I said, dear, he's not a bad person. We're helping each other and I suppose you could say that we've established a mutual respect. Now, let's not talk about Max. You need to find a wormhole. Do you know what a wormhole actually is?"

"Er, something to do with space-time?"

"That's right, dear. As you know, space and time are actually the same thing. It is possible to go back in time through space, but it's impossible to go into the future. A wormhole is a tear in space-time that links one point with another. A bit like a tunnel linking two islands together. The problem with wormholes is...well, there are several. First, they're very small, which is why solid matter can't pass through them. This also makes them very hard for us to locate. Another problem is that they are very unstable and can collapse at any time. And of course, you then have to find one that links our point in space-time to the point where you were before you died."

Jemma's head spun with every word Claire was saying. This was going to be a lot harder than she had imagined. It had never occurred to her that it might not be possible to find a wormhole for Tom. She couldn't help but feel a guilty flicker of hope that if it wasn't possible, then Tom would have to stay.

"But," continued Claire, "it is possible to manipulate an existing wormhole enough for you to get to your specific destination, or even create a wormhole yourself."

The flicker of hope vanished. While there was any chance that they could do this, they had to give it a go. "What do you mean, create a wormhole?" she asked. She had a vague memory of Tom also mentioning something about this.

"It's very hard, dear. You need to use enormous amounts of energy, best taken from the sun, and focus it on one particle, compressing it until it collapses and forms a mini black hole. The weight of that black hole will then cause a small tear in the fabric of space-time, thereby creating a mini wormhole. The trouble with creating your own wormhole is that you need such a huge amount of energy that most people who try don't succeed. No, I think you're better off finding an existing one and manipulating it to go where you want."

Jemma gazed at Claire as she spoke. She made it sound so straightforward. Jemma had clearly underestimated her.

"Now, it's important to know a couple more things about them. Firstly, you can only travel one way through a wormhole, so there's no going back. Secondly, while it remains open, you will be in full control of your memory, even once you're out the other side. But as soon as it collapses you will forget everything."

"Oh," said Jemma, brightening up. "Does that mean that I could go back and somehow stop the wormhole from collapsing so that I don't forget Tom?"

"No, dear. I'm afraid it's impossible to keep a wormhole open for more than a few seconds. What it does mean, though, is that the moment Tom is through, he'll have to stop the accident that killed Susie from happening again. If he's not quick enough the wormhole could collapse and he won't remember what to do. Then the same thing will happen again and he'll be back where he started."

"Right, so he needs to be quick once he's back. So how do we actually locate an existing wormhole and manipulate it to go where we want?"

"I can show you that when the time comes. I know we all believed that it was near impossible to leave this place, but since getting to know Max, I've learnt that it's not as difficult as we had first thought. Max just isn't very keen to share his knowledge, for obvious reasons."

"But how does Max know all this stuff?" asked Jemma.

"Apparently he tried to leave himself once, years ago, but because of his bitterness over his death, as soon as he tried, he found himself back here. It really is only possible to leave if it's for the right reasons, it seems."

"Well, I think Tom has cleared the way for him to leave. He now knows that his mother regretted her actions before he died. Also, the fact that his ashes are now with his father has given him peace. And I think that the fact that he doesn't feel the burden of guilt over Susie's death anymore will also help."

"Jemma." Claire reached out and took Jemma's hand. "It's important that Tom knows there are risks involved with traveling in wormholes. They're very unstable and, like I said before, they can collapse at any moment. If one were to collapse while Tom was still inside, he would be trapped. There's no escape...ever!"

Chapter Nineteen

Jemma wandered along the sandy beach in Norfolk searching for Tom. They had arranged to meet by their sand dune later that day and, although time didn't exist where they were, they still used references such as mid-afternoon or late morning when making arrangements. It was now late afternoon and she had been the first to arrive at their rendezvous point. They had hoped to watch the sunset, but it was a gray, dark and cloudy day, so there would be no orange and red sky tonight. Making the most of the time she had alone, she lay back on the dune, closed her eyes and thought about what Claire had said earlier. There were risks, big risks. What if Tom did get trapped in an unstable wormhole? Not only would he be stuck there forever, but Susie wouldn't get back either. Both Susie and herself would have to remain where they were without Tom, knowing that he would have met his terrible fate because of them.

She didn't know how long she lay there, but she became aware of movement next to her. Then a wet tongue started licking her face.

"Sandy," she cried as she sat up and stroked the dog's soft head. He gave a yelp of delight and did a little dance for her, chasing his tail round and round. She laughed as he barked in excitement then sighed when his owners called his name. "Better go back, gorgeous boy. Bye bye."

"Gorgeous boy?" Tom's voice greeted her as Sandy bounded away. "Have you replaced me already?"

"Did anyone ever tell you that you look a bit like Johnny Depp?" she asked, gazing up at him as he towered over her.

"Who?"

"You know, Jack Sparrow… Oh, of course not, he wasn't famous when you were alive."

"So is this Johnny guy good-looking, then?"

"Hmm," she replied, smiling. "Just a bit. You look like him, especially your smile. You have the most gorgeous smile."

He laughed and sat down next to her. "Don't stop. So tell me what else you like about me."

"Oh, that's about it," she joked and planted a kiss on his divine lips.

"I think you've pissed Susie off," he said as soon as his lips were free to talk again. "She was stomping around the house earlier calling you all sorts of names."

"She's not pissed off as much as she's hurt," said Jemma. "She asked me if I was going to stay and I told her that I was still planning on going back. So she started questioning me about it, understandably, but I got defensive and shouted at her. I didn't mean to, but I just didn't know what to say. I feel awful now."

"I know, but you did the right thing by not telling her the truth."

"Yeah, I know. I went to see Claire afterward and I told her everything. She told me some stuff about wormholes, but Tom, there are risks. If the wormhole collapses…mmm." Tom cut her off mid-sentence by kissing her on the mouth.

"Let's not talk about wormholes right now," he said when he drew away. "I just want to enjoy being here with you. Alone."

"We're not alone very often, are we? We never have the house to ourselves because the OMG is always there," she said, staring out to the ocean.

"OMG?"

"Old Misery Guts," replied Jemma, grinning. "This is the only place where we are truly alone. I don't even see other ghosts here."

"I know. That's why I love it, apart from the scenery, of

course. And now I love it even more because you're here."

Jemma turned back to Tom. A shot of electricity charged through her when the love in his eyes shone as he stared at her. "I love you so much," she whispered. Her mouth was so close to his that their lips were almost touching.

"I love you too." His voice was husky, sexy.

When his lips brushed hers her body melted. Even before she had died Jemma had never felt so alive. Despite the fact that she didn't need blood to pump around her body anymore, she swore she could feel it pulsing through her veins now. If she could feel these things, how would more intimate sensations feel? Heat seared through to her core as her heart hammered in her chest. Not bad considering that her heart didn't beat anymore.

"Tom, I want you to make love to me," she whispered.

"I can do better than that," he murmured. "I want to show you something so intimate and magical that it'll make even the hottest sex seem tame." He grinned then took her chin in his hand and held her gaze. "Would you like that?"

"Yes," she whispered. The hot sex would suffice, but if he could better that, then bring it on.

He let go of her chin then kissed her. She closed her eyes and savored his taste.

When he finally released her, he murmured, "Remember that barrier of energy I taught you to use for protection?"

"Uh-huh." He was tracing his hand across her cheek now. When he reached her hairline, he ran it through her thick mane before bunching her auburn locks into his fist so he held her head captive. She couldn't suppress the strong shudder that rocked through her.

"You need to let it go now," he ordered. "You have to trust me. I will be in control of you, but don't be scared. Relax and let me in."

She did as he said and mentally removed the cloak of energy that had been protecting her. As it dissolved, Jemma became aware of just how vulnerable she was, but she knew she was safe with Tom. He kissed her again, and this time his lips passed through her own. The shock made her jump as sensations she had never experienced before swept through her. It was as if every molecule in her body fizzed like bubbles in champagne. Her soul floated on a cloud of sparkling fairy dust. *Hang on, it isn't my soul, it's Tom's.* They had become one. He explored her mind, her heart and other parts of her body that hadn't been reached in a very long time. It was so much more intense than mere physical touch was capable of—this was lovemaking on a different plane altogether.

A myriad of emotions danced inside her as Tom's energy possessed her—pure hot desire flooded her, followed by delirious happiness, then desperate urgency, but above all, love that was so intense it was almost overwhelming. Their bodies were truly united now. Every one of Tom's atoms were a part of her and still the sensations grew stronger. She could feel Tom's emotions, his love for her. She knew that he would be feeling her love for him as well. They were connected on the deepest level and she never wanted it to end.

She had no idea how long they were joined together, but when Tom started to withdraw, she took control back of her body with reluctance. Once they had erected the barriers of energy around themselves again, Jemma found that night had fallen. The sea splashed onto the sand as the tide crept in, the dim crescent moon adding specks of pale light bouncing off the white crests.

Tears stung Jemma's eyes as Tom pulled her into his arms. "Thank you," she whispered as she clung to him.

"It beats sex, doesn't it?" he murmured as he covered her face with soft, light kisses.

"I never knew that was possible. I felt you, Tom, your emotions, your love."

"And I felt yours." He traced the outline of her lips with his fingertips and smiled when she pretended to bite the tip of his finger.

"How did you know what to do?"

He shrugged. "I didn't. I just guessed what would happen and I was right. Although it was even better than I could have imagined."

She smiled as the moon lit his face. "I feel as though you gave me ten orgasms in a row. I've never felt pleasure like that."

"Me neither." His face grew serious at the same time as a cloud cloaked the moonlight.

"What?"

"I'm sorry to spoil the moment, but we have to talk about Susie. If she makes too much of a fuss she'll attract Max's attention."

"We'll have to lie. When we get back, I'll tell her that I've changed my mind and have decided that I can't leave either of you. She'll be so pleased that she won't think it odd that I changed my mind so easily."

"Okay, but what about Claire? You said that you told her everything. Are you sure we can trust her?"

"Yes, she gave me her word. She said she'll help us find a wormhole, but she also said there was a chance the wormhole could collapse while you're inside and if that happens—"

"Yes, I know," interrupted Tom, "but it's a chance I have to take. You'll face the same risk, you know."

For a moment Jemma came close to telling him she wasn't leaving, but if she was going to lie to Susie to keep the peace, then extending it a little for Tom wouldn't do any harm. So instead she sighed. "I'm only too aware of it. I'm just trying not to think about my journey, it's easier to focus on yours."

"Right. We'd better get back, then. The sooner you make your peace with Susie the better."

"Tom?" Jemma reached out for Tom's arm as he stood up. He took hold of her hand and pulled her up, putting his arms around her as soon as she was within reach. Jemma held on to him, not wanting to leave. "Can we do this again?"

"What, come here?"

"No, you know... What we did. Can we do that again?"

Tom smiled and whispered into her ear. "If you thought that was good, just wait until next time."

They were giggling like a pair of lovestruck teenagers when they materialized in Jack's kitchen. Alice and Jack were preparing dinner and, at first, Jemma wasn't interested in what they were talking about. She was too busy trying to snap back to reality so she could find Susie. But something in Alice's voice made her stop and take notice.

"I've got to find Maggie, Jack," cried Alice, her voice sounding desperate. "It's really important, I've got an urgent message for Jemma and I need Maggie's help to get in touch with her."

Jack's frown deepened as Alice told him about her encounter with the angel. "Oh, Jack, I wish you could have seen him. He was the most incredible thing I've ever seen. Thank God Dean had told me that he might be an angel, otherwise I would have freaked out again. He wouldn't have been able to communicate with me in that case and I wouldn't have got the message for Jemma. I'm so relieved that the boy was real, Jack. I was beginning to think I was going mad. You were beginning to think that as well, weren't you?"

The question must have caught Jack off guard because he averted his gaze and looked uncomfortable. "I never thought you were going mad, Alice, but you had been under an enormous amount of strain, and when you're stressed, the mind can sometimes play tricks on you."

"In other words, you thought I was going mad. I knew you didn't believe me." She couldn't hide the hint of accusation in her voice.

"I did believe you," he snapped. "But you were becoming more and more hysterical every time you had an encounter with him and I was worried about you. You were the only one who ever saw him, so it could very well have been a figment of your imagination. Anyway, at least your precious Dean believed you."

Alice stared at him in shock. There was a new hostility in his tone that hadn't been there before. It had never occurred to her that he didn't like Dean. In fact, they had seemed to get on well at the concert. They were similar in so many ways—like their love of music, and they were also both very spiritual. The only reason she could imagine why Jack wouldn't like Dean was because he was jealous of her friendship with him. *How ridiculous.*

"Yes, Jack. He believed me and he was right, so what's your problem?" Her temper was beginning to flare, but the last thing she wanted right now was an argument. *Damn!* She had been so sure that Jack would be as pleased for her as Dean had been and that he would want to hear every last detail. He hadn't even asked her what the message for Jemma was. She had been on such a high after her encounter, but now she felt deflated and even more pissed off with Jack for spoiling her moment. "Anyway," she muttered, "if you hear from Maggie I'd appreciate it if you would let me know."

"Fine. I'm going out. I'll be back later." With that, Jack grabbed his jacket and left, banging the front door behind him.

Alice stared at the door in bewilderment. *What the hell had that been all about?* "Screw you, Jack!" she shouted, waking Casper, who had been asleep on one of the chairs. He looked up at her and gave a little grunt to show his annoyance at being woken up, before curling himself back up to resume his lazy slumber.

By the time Jack got home, it was gone eleven o'clock and Alice had been in bed for twenty minutes.

"Alice?" he whispered.

But she was still angry with him so she pretended that she was asleep. If she spoke with him now she'd only say something she would later regret.

* * * *

213

The following morning she woke feeling tired and groggy. She reached out to Jack, but his side of the bed was cold and empty, and last night's argument came flooding back. With a sigh, she dragged herself out of bed and went downstairs to put the kettle on. The house seemed so empty without Jack. He would usually be sitting at the table now, drinking tea and reading the morning papers. Normally, she would sneak up behind him, kiss the back of his head and steal his tea. She missed him and she hoped that this wasn't a sign of things to come.

In the end she didn't bother making any tea. If she couldn't have Jack's, she'd do without. She wished now that she hadn't swapped her shift for tomorrow. It would have been a relief to go to work now and get out of the atmosphere of this house. She showered and got dressed, but when she was ready, she still didn't know what to do with herself. When she'd changed her days at work, her first thought had been to ask Jack to go Christmas shopping with her. That didn't seem very likely now. She might as well go back to the flat and get some packing done. She stiffened as an uncomfortable thought struck her. What if Jack regretted asking her to move in and that was why he was being so stroppy with her? Maybe she shouldn't be in such a hurry to pack the rest of her stuff.

By the time she reached the flat she had convinced herself that Jack had gone off her and that he was going to tell her tonight that he didn't want her to move in after all. As she unlocked the door she was in tears and on the verge of returning to the house to move her stuff back before Jack told her to. *What's happening to me?* It wasn't like her to fall apart because of a stupid argument. But she loved Jack with all her heart and the thought that she might lose him struck a cold rod of fear into her soul.

She sighed. She couldn't face going into Jemma's room, so she would concentrate on her own stuff today. She would have to move no matter what, as her parents had a new tenant lined up for the new year, so she might as well make a start. With a heavy heart, she pulled her clothes out of the wardrobe then stuffed them into some bin liners. When that was done she reached under her bed for the flattened storage boxes that had been there since they'd moved in. It was as she tugged at the boxes that she noticed something on top of one of them. She took a closer look. Bloody hell, it was the green top that she had planned on wearing on the day of her interview at Glitz. How the hell had it gotten there? She knew with absolute certainty that she had put it on the chair before she had gone to bed. On reflection, she was glad now that she hadn't worn it. What had she been thinking? She would have looked hideous in it. Jemma would have hated it. In fact, Jemma would have told her not to wear it. Then she remembered the incident with the bangle. Jemma had been there that night.

"Oh God. Jemma must have hidden it to stop me wearing it." With that she burst into fresh tears, allowing all the grief and frustration to come flooding out. She cried like she hadn't done since Jemma had died. She sobbed for her dead friend and for the possible loss of her beautiful lover. How could her life have gone so wrong in such a short time?

She didn't know how long she sat on the floor clutching onto the green top, but all of a sudden she became aware of a hand on her shoulder, a hand giving her comfort and gentle reassurance. She suddenly noticed that the atmosphere had changed, that there was another presence in the room. Her skin tingled as she turned around, expecting to see Jemma standing behind her, but the room remained empty. Even so, she knew Jemma had been there and, through her tears, she laughed aloud. "You were right about the top, hun. Thanks."

With renewed optimism, she continued packing. As she emptied the contents of her dressing table, though, something occurred to her. "Jemma?" But the atmosphere had returned to normal and the presence was gone. "Shit, Jemma. I forgot to tell you something. Jemma?" But the room remained silent and empty and Alice knew that she had missed an opportunity to give her friend the message from the angel.

Alice buckled down after that and, with the help of *Abba Gold* blaring from her speakers, managed to finish packing up most of her things in the bedroom. The living room and kitchen were next and Alice worked tirelessly, focusing only on the job in hand. It was nearly dark by the time she taped up the last box and it was only then that she realized that she hadn't had anything to eat or drink all day. It was time to head home. Was the word 'home' still relevant? Home to her didn't mean the actual house and without Jack it was just a house. No, home meant Jack, his pleasure at seeing her walk through the front door, her nicking his tea and him her toast, and Casper jumping up onto the bed for a snooze just as she and Jack were getting intimate.

When she pushed open the front door a short time later, she was greeted by the delicious smell of cooking. "Hi," she called.

Jack appeared from the kitchen with two glasses of wine in his hands. "Hi, beautiful," he said, handing her a glass of ice-cold Pinot Grigio. Alice smiled her thanks and took a sip of the crisp, cold wine. It was delicious. The tension eased out of her muscles as she took another sip. *Mmm, I needed that*. She put the glass down and put her arms around him, hugging him close to her. The faint smell of his aftershave mixed with a strong smell of chopped onions. She loved it nonetheless.

"Sorry about yesterday," he said and kissed her. "I wanted to say sorry last night when I got in, but you were asleep."

"That's okay. I was a bit grumpy myself," she said, close to tears with relief that he didn't hate her. "I thought you were really pissed off with me when I saw that you weren't there this morning."

Jack smiled. "I was at work. I moved tomorrow's interview to today so that we could spend the day together tomorrow. It's Christmas Eve and I thought we could go shopping. How was work?"

"Oh." Shit, he had changed his interview so that he could spend the day with her tomorrow. She had swapped her shift thinking that he wasn't going to be around. "Actually, I didn't go to work today. I swapped shifts so I'm going in tomorrow instead. I thought you were here today and that we could go shopping together. I didn't know where you were this morning, so I went to the flat to finish packing up. Sorry." She watched Jack's smile fade. *Shit, talk about crossed wires.* When he didn't say anything, she started babbling about Oscar's silly belief about Glitz being cursed and Dean's plan to set their friend, Darren, up at the fake séance. The more she said, the deeper Jack's frown became.

"So you didn't change your shift to be with me then. You changed it to go to this séance."

"No. Yes. I mean I wouldn't have agreed to swap if I had known you were going to be here tomorrow." She waited for a sign of a smile, but his expression remained stony. "I know, why don't you come with me? You could chat to the customers while I work. The atmosphere will be really festive and you could drink loads of mulled wine and then join the séance when the restaurant closes."

"No, thank you. I'll have last-minute shopping to do. I need to wrap presents and will be busy preparing for Christmas Day. Basically, all the things I thought we'd be doing together." With that he turned and headed back into the kitchen, leaving Alice alone, with the bitter smell of burned onions hanging in the air.

Chapter Twenty

"Happy Christmas Eve," said Alice, leaning over in the bed to give Jack a kiss. They had gone to bed in silence last night, their unresolved argument hanging over them. Any attempt by Alice to make conversation had been met with curt answers. It was now morning and the air between them was still chilly.

"Yeah, you too," Jack replied. He didn't kiss her back. "What time are you going to work?"

"My shift starts at eleven o'clock. Why don't you walk me to work and we could stop off for breakfast at Belsize Park?" *Take the bloody olive branch, Jack.*

"Sorry, I won't have time. I've decided to go into the West End, so I'll need to leave early before it gets too busy." He didn't sound sorry. It sounded more like an excuse to get away as fast as possible. With a sigh she slid out of bed and made her way to the bathroom. After a hurried shower, she applied a touch of makeup, dried her hair and found a clean jumper from the ironing pile before making her way downstairs.

During her shower she had made a decision. If it was so important to Jack that she didn't go to work today, then she would ring Glitz and tell them she wasn't coming in. They'd be furious as they were expecting to be busy today, but Jack came first.

"Hey, I'm coming with you," she called as she hurried into the kitchen. But the room was empty, except for the sound of Casper slurping his breakfast. Alice sighed and dropped her handbag onto a chair. He hadn't even waited for her to come down so they could say goodbye. "Well, fuck you," she growled, then stomped back upstairs to change into her Glitz T-shirt. Why the hell was he behaving like a spoiled two-year-old? She was tempted to stay at Glitz overnight and gatecrash Oscar and Dean's Christmas tomorrow. *Ha, that would serve Jack right.*

Half an hour later she arrived at Glitz. The door was locked, but that was no surprise as she was nearly an hour early. She hadn't felt like hanging around at the house and had thought that she might as well come in early and make herself useful. She rang the doorbell and waited. Dean opened the door after only a couple of seconds.

"Hello there," he said, looking surprised to see her. "You're early, is everything all right?"

"Fine." She gave him her best smile and tried to appear as if nothing was wrong.

"Okay. Well, now you're here, you might as well join us for a coffee."

"Thanks." Alice was close to tears, but she didn't want Dean to see her upset, so she mumbled something about needing the loo and hurried into the Ladies. She took a deep breath and willed herself not to cry, but just as she was pulling herself together Oscar popped his head through the door.

"Are you all right, Petal? Dean told me that you seemed a bit down." The genuine kindness in his voice was the last straw and Alice burst into tears. "Hey, sweetie, what's wrong?" Oscar came all the way in and put his arms round her, letting her cry on his shoulder.

When she had no tears left, she grabbed a bit of tissue and wiped her eyes. "Sorry about that."

"That's all right, sweetie. I hate to see you so upset."

"No, I mean about the black mascara I've just smudged all over your lovely white shirt," she said and managed a smile of sorts.

"Never mind about that. So are you going to tell me what's wrong?" asked Oscar.

"Me and Jack had a row. He's pissed off with me for

changing my shift today because he had plans for us, but I thought he was working. He hadn't told me that he had changed an appointment, so how the hell was I supposed to know?" She wouldn't tell him about Jack's remark about Dean or that she had been about to leave them in the lurch today. Instead she splashed cold water on her face and looked up at Oscar through the mirror. "Don't worry about me, I'm fine now."

"Well, any time you want to talk, we're here for you." Oscar gave her a hug, took her hand and led her back into the restaurant where Dean was waiting.

"You okay?" he asked, handing her a latte.

"Yes, thanks. I'm fine now. So what's the plan for today?" she asked, eager to change the subject away from her.

"Well, first we need an Abba fix." Oscar grinned and ran over to the CD player before Dean could get there first. As the first notes of *Super Trouper* filled the room, Oscar came back over and sat next to Alice. "We're fully booked today so that'll keep you occupied," he said. "Wow, imagine being able to say that we're fully booked. Anyway, we'll play lots of Christmas music and have a good laugh, just you see. We've decided to remain open all day and close a bit earlier than usual. We'll play it by ear, but I'm hoping we can close by nine o'clock, which is when Darren's coming. He really liked you, by the way." That made Alice feel even worse. Darren seemed like a really sweet guy and she and Dean were about to reveal him as a fake psychic. She glanced over at Dean, who shrugged but didn't say anything.

* * * *

Oscar had been right—the restaurant was packed and the atmosphere was warm, friendly and noisy. Oscar had produced a huge jug of hot homemade mulled wine and mince pies for anyone who wanted them, and some of the regular customers had brought cards and little gifts for them all. There was a slight lull at around four o'clock, but by five it was busy again and it remained busy until they closed the door to the last customer at half past nine. Darren had arrived early and had chipped in, helping to clear the tables and entertaining the customers with exaggerated ghost stories.

"Phew, what a day." Dean sighed as he poured them a large glass of wine each when the last customers had finally left. "Happy Christmas, guys."

"So, Darren, are you going to do this séance for us then?" asked Oscar, his eyes glowing with anticipation.

Darren appeared thoughtful for a minute before replying. "Yes, but this isn't the right atmosphere for a séance. There's been so much noise and positive energy here today that I don't think a séance would work. How about I just do a reading? You know, I walk around and listen to what the soul of the place tells me, then I'll feed it back to you."

"Sounds good," said Dean, looking serious. "Make yourself at home."

Alice swallowed her disappointment. Damn, she had really needed that séance. Even though she knew there was a chance that Darren wasn't a genuine psychic and that the séance would most likely have been pointless, she had hoped that it might have been an opportunity for other spirits to voice their presence. *Spirits like Jemma, perhaps?* Forcing a smile, she nodded with Oscar and Dean. She needed Maggie to come home more than ever if she was going to have any hope of talking to Jemma.

They all watched as Darren wandered around, every now and then closing his eyes as if he was concentrating on something specific. He went from the restaurant into the kitchen and even upstairs to the flat for a while. Oscar followed him around like an eager puppy, waiting for his conviction about the curse to be confirmed. Dean and Alice watched from their table. At one point Dean winked at her as Darren raised his face to the ceiling and made a strange noise, his eyes shut and arms outstretched. Alice had to admit it did look rather comical, and smiled back at Dean.

"Right," said Darren as he headed back toward the table.

"Here we go," whispered Dean.

When they were all seated again, Darren glanced at each one of them in turn before settling his gaze on Oscar. "I've been looking out for any signs of a businessman who may have been murdered here and possibly the smell of tobacco." Dean and Alice exchanged a quick glance. "But I'm afraid I haven't been able to come up with anything."

Oscar gasped and Alice raised her eyebrows at Dean. That was not what they'd been expecting him to say.

"I have to be honest, Dean. I did overhear something you said on the phone the other day and I was really excited by it, but I didn't sense anything at all just now. I'm really sorry, but I couldn't find anything to suggest that this James Salisbury ever existed. I guess I'm not as gifted as I thought I was."

Alice grinned at the shock on Dean's face. It was such a relief that Darren hadn't fallen into their trap and that he had been honest enough to come clean about not sensing anything. She liked Darren and this stupid plan of hers had long since lost its appeal. She stood, went over to Darren and gave him a hug. "Thank you for trying," she said. "And for being honest."

"Well," exclaimed Oscar, "I wasn't expecting that. I was so sure you would find something. But that doesn't mean that this place isn't haunted."

Alice squeezed Oscar's shoulder and picked up her bag. "When Maggie gets back, you know, the medium I told you about, I'll ask her to come round if you like. If there's anything here at all, she'll find it. Now, I think I'd better get back to Jack and see if he's talking to me yet."

"I'll call you a cab," said Dean, reaching for his phone. "I'd offer you a lift, but I've had too much to drink."

"That's okay, I can walk."

"No way," objected Dean. But a minute later he hung up with a worried frown. "Shit, there are no cabs for two hours, at least. I'd forgotten it's Christmas Eve."

Oscar jumped up and grabbed his coat. "I'll walk you home, Petal. It's not far, but there's no way we're going to let you walk back on your own."

Both Dean and Darren got up too. "We're coming as well."

It was fun walking home with her three friends. They linked arms and chatted about the joys of Christmas until they reached Jack's house. "Would you like to come in for a drink?" she asked as she reached for her key.

"Better not," said Oscar. "Why don't you and Jack come over on Boxing Day? We're having a few friends around for drinks and a bite to eat."

"Thanks, I'll let you know tomorrow. Happy Christmas, guys, and thanks for walking me back."

As she closed the door behind her, Alice heard the sound of quiet voices coming from the kitchen. How strange, she hadn't been aware that anyone was coming tonight. She pushed the kitchen door open and gasped. There, sitting at the kitchen table and sharing a bottle of wine with Jack, was Maggie.

"Maggie!" Alice dropped her bag and rushed over to hug her. "Where the hell have you been?"

"Nice to see you, too." Maggie chuckled. "I've been at the most incredible retreat in Thailand. You should come with me one day. Anyway, I'm back now. Jack has told me that you've been trying to get hold of me. Is everything okay?"

Alice, still with her coat on, flopped down next to Maggie and told her all about her encounter with the angel. "He gave me a message to pass onto Jemma, a really important message, but I haven't been able to give it to her yet. I realize now that the best way is probably to hold a séance, but I don't know what to do, so I really need your help. Would you hold a séance for me, Maggie? Please?"

"Of course, love. Just let me know when you want to do it and–"

"Now, it's got to be now. Please, can we do it now? It's really important."

Maggie shrugged and glanced over at Jack, who nodded. "All right, we'll do it now, but I don't want to do it here."

"Why?" asked Alice and Jack, at the same time.

"There's a bad vibe in this house. I can't quite put my finger on it, but something doesn't feel right and I don't want to risk unwelcome spirits trying to come through. Is there somewhere else we could go to that Jemma has a connection with?"

"We could go to the old flat," said Alice. "I've still got the key."

Maggie nodded and finished her wine before reaching for her coat. Alice couldn't stop smiling as they all left the house. If all went well tonight, she was going to talk to Jemma.

* * * *

When Alice, Jack and Maggie had left through the front door, Jemma and Tom transported themselves to the flat. They had been at the house when Alice had come home and had heard their conversation.

"That Maggie must be good," mused Tom as they waited for the mortals to arrive. "She picked up on the negative energy from Max, which is just as well because if they had held the séance at the house, Max could have spoilt it."

"I'm so excited," cried Jemma for the fourth time. "I can't believe I'm finally going to talk to Alice."

"Hopefully you'll get to find out what this mysterious message is."

"Ooh, I can't wait. What a shame Susie was out. She would have enjoyed this."

"She's gone to her parents' house. She goes every year on Christmas Eve and stays with them all night and all Christmas Day. They always hold a vigil for her and she's never missed it. This will be the last time she does it. She'll be leaving the day after tomorrow and she doesn't even know it."

"It's best that way," said Jemma, putting her arms around him. "I think she's still avoiding me, even though I told her that I'd changed my mind about going back. I'm not sure if she believes me."

"It's not for much longer," said Tom.

"No," she whispered. "Not long now." She wasn't referring to Susie, though. She had been thinking about Tom's departure, which was creeping ever closer. "Here they are," she said as she heard the sound of keys in the front door downstairs, followed by voices coming up the stairs, accompanied by the sound of Maggie's bangles.

Seconds later Alice, Jack and Maggie walked into the flat. Maggie stood still for a moment as if assessing the atmosphere. "Yes, this is better." She ordered Jack to pull the kitchen table into the middle of the room. She then took a few white candles out of her huge canvas bag and placed one on the table and the rest around the room.

While Maggie was busy setting everything up, Jemma walked over to Alice and touched her gently on the arm.

"She's here," cried Alice. "I just know she's here, I can sense her."

"Wow, we've both come a long way, haven't we?" said Jemma. "She didn't even hesitate."

Tom chuckled. "I remember that first night when you tried so hard to get her attention. You practically screamed in her ear and she still didn't react."

"And then I screamed at poor Susie thinking she was one of the mortals."

"You were so angry and frightened then."

"And naïve."

"You were determined not to accept your fate. You also forced me to address some of my own issues and I'm grateful to you for that. I needed a kick up the backside and you didn't half give me one." He kissed her on the lips. "And now we've come full circle. You're about to talk to Alice and then we're both leaving the day after tomorrow."

"Let's not talk about that now," said Jemma. "I just want

to enjoy the time we have left."

"You really should go first," said Tom. They had talked on several occasions about who would enter their wormhole first, but Jemma had always been adamant that it had to be him. After all, she wasn't going anywhere.

"No, you need to go first, because if you don't make it, then Susie won't get back and she'll need me to look after her." This was true and Tom couldn't argue with it. "Look, Tom, they're about to sit down."

The table was ready. Maggie had placed a white tablecloth on it and had lit all the candles. Once Alice and Jack were seated, she switched off the ceiling light, which was now just a bright naked bulb hanging without its shade. As soon as it was off, the room softened with the combination of the orange streetlights from outside mixed with the flickering glow of the candles.

"I'd like you to place your hands on the table and loosely touch the fingertips of the person next to you. There's no need to hold hands. I'll start with a short prayer of protection before we begin." Maggie smiled at Alice. "There's no need to look so scared, love, it's perfectly normal to ask for protection. Now, sometimes other spirits will try to make themselves known and I will be very firm in telling them that they are not welcome. I will act as the leader and medium, but as you're gifted yourself, Alice, you may find that Jemma makes direct contact with you. If that's the case, just relax and enjoy the experience. Jack and I will look after you. Now, before we start I've got two very important questions. Firstly, are your phones switched off? And secondly, does anyone need the loo?"

Jemma giggled as she watched Alice fiddle with her phone. This was all in aid of her and she was enjoying it. She watched Maggie perform the prayer before they started. Then Maggie said, "Are there any spirits present with us today?"

"Yes," cried Jemma. "I'm here. Alice?"

"Jemma Haley, if you are here, we respectfully ask that

you let your presence be known to us this evening."

"Cut the crap," said Jemma. "Just get on with it. I'm here."

"Jemma, if you are present, please give us a sign. Maybe a knock on the table, or you could try to touch one of us." Maggie's voice remained calm and soothing, trying to lure the spirit in.

"Bloody hell, can't you hear me? *I'm here!*"

"What was that I just said about you coming a long way?" said Tom, laughing. "You can't just barge in like that. You need to do what I taught you when you first got here. Relax and concentrate. Start with a knock on the table, use some of the energy from the candle if you need to."

Jemma forced herself to calm down then focused all her thoughts on the table, borrowing a little warmth from the candle as she did so. The candle flickered and, when the time was right, the sound of her knock could be clearly heard.

"Thank you," said Maggie. "If that was you, Jemma, please knock twice for yes and once for no."

"This is so cool." Jemma giggled as she gave the table two small knocks.

"Thank you, Jemma. Your friend Alice is here. She would like to communicate with you."

"Yes, I know. So talk to me, Alice."

Tom chuckled. "Be patient. You'll need to use Maggie as a medium if you can't communicate directly with Alice, but try Alice first. Focus on her, will her to hear your thoughts. You don't have to say anything out loud. If she's as gifted as I think she is, she should be able to tune in to you."

Jemma did as Tom said and focused in on Alice with every last bit of energy she possessed. She watched as Alice closed her eyes, then she tried to direct her thoughts through Alice's closed eyelids and into her soul. Damn, she was struggling. She couldn't seem to summon enough energy and kept losing her concentration. This was a lot harder than she had imagined, but there was no way she was going to give up. Taking some more energy from the candle, she tried again and directed her thoughts right through to the core of Alice's body. Then she felt something. She felt Alice, her thoughts, her feelings, everything. She had made contact with Alice!

Chapter Twenty-One

"Jemma," cried Alice. "I'm here, Jemma."

Jemma's throat tightened as tears welled in her eyes. Alice was talking to her. The voice hadn't come from Alice's mouth, though, it had come from inside her.

"Yes, hun. It's me." Then they were face-to-face, seeing each other as though they were both holograms.

"Oh, Jemma, I've missed you so much," cried Alice. She tried to reach out to Jemma, but her hand went straight through her. "I'd love to give you a hug."

"I know. Me too. I've been watching you. I've tried to talk to you so many times, but I couldn't do it."

"I heard you on that voice recorder and I've felt you around me many times. By the way, thanks for helping me find the bangle the night before my interview."

"That's okay." Jemma stared at Alice, still not quite able to believe they were communicating. But now that the moment had finally come, her brain froze and she didn't know what to say. She searched for something meaningful, but her mind had gone blank. "I'm glad you didn't find that horrible green jumper I had hidden. You would have looked like an anemic elf."

"So it was you. I *knew* it." Alice smiled, but soon grew serious again. "So, how are you?" They both laughed at the strangeness of such a normal question. "Apart from being dead, of course."

"I'm okay. I've met this guy, he's dead as well. He's here with me now. His name is Tom and he's gorgeous."

"Oh wow. Are you in love? Do ghosts fall in love?"

"Oh yes, absolutely definitely. He's wonderful." She

decided not to go into detail about Tom's imminent departure and so instead she told Alice that she was living in Jack's house with Tom and a girl called Susie who had both been there for twenty years. She didn't mention Max.

"I knew there were ghosts in that house. I miss you so much, Jemma."

"I miss you too. I'm always around you. I'll always be with you. Oh shit…"

"Jemma?"

Jemma could feel her energy beginning to dissipate and had to work extra hard to refocus before she completely lost her connection with Alice. She drew more energy from the candle and the heat from the three people sitting around the table, then, at last, she became aware of Alice's presence again. "Sorry about that, hun. It's actually quite hard, remaining focused enough to communicate like this." The candle was flickering like mad now and Maggie and Jack had shivered as Jemma had drawn the heat from them.

"I'd love to ask you loads about the afterlife, but I don't want to risk you slipping away before I've had a chance to pass on a message."

"Oh yes. I heard that you had a message for me. From an angel or something?" In her excitement at finally talking to Alice, Jemma had forgotten about the message.

"Yes, that's right. He said that it's really important that you return to the living. You weren't meant to die, Jemma, and you'll never be able to move on if you don't come back."

"I can't go back," whispered Jemma. "I would lose all my memories of Tom and he's the only good thing that's ever happened to me. Why would I give that up in order to return to the useless life I led before?"

"Jemma, for God's sake. Your life was never useless. You were the most wonderful, funny and kind person I ever knew, and you were just getting your life back on track the day you died."

Jemma was about to protest and tell Alice that she wasn't going to change her mind, when Alice continued. "Oh, and the angel said something else. He said that you have to beware of someone called Max."

Jemma gasped. She was so shocked to hear Max's name that her brain tumbled and she lost the concentration that had given her the connection to Alice. She blinked and found herself staring at Tom.

"Jemma? Jemma?" Alice was calling for her, but Jemma was exhausted and could only watch as Alice came out of the trance-like state she had been in while they had been communicating.

"Are you all right?" asked Tom, putting his arms around her to steady her.

"Yes. Tom, she knows about Max. How can that be? She said that the angel had said that I had to beware of Max. Why? Why should I be worried about Max? It's you that he's got issues with, not me." It didn't make sense. The reason he had attacked her that time in the living room had been because she had provoked him, not because he held a grudge against her. Then, like a slap in the face, she realized there was only one thing the message could have meant. The angel was warning her that if she stayed behind after Tom left, Max would be so mad that he would turn all his fury on her, and she would be the one in danger from him. Instead of being left alone with her memories of Tom, she would forever be worrying that Max might harm her. If the angel had gone to all this trouble to warn her, then the threat must indeed be very real.

"Hey, don't look so worried. You'll be gone in a couple of days and Max will cease to exist in your world," reassured Tom.

Jemma had almost forgotten that she had lied to him about going back. She wanted so much to take comfort from his words, secure in the knowledge that she was leaving soon. Was she doing the right thing? For the first time since she'd made the decision to stay, she doubted herself.

"Oh look, it's just gone midnight. Happy Christmas, gorgeous," said Tom and he gave her a kiss.

"Tom, there's something I've got to tell you."

"That sounds ominous. Don't tell me, you've fallen in love with Max," he said, grinning.

"I lied to you about going back. After you've gone, I was going to stay here on my own." There, she'd said it.

Tom's face grew serious again as he took in what she had just told him. "But why? Why on earth would you stay behind?"

"Because you said yourself that when I go back I would lose all my memories of you. It would be as if all this never happened. I'd go back to being the lonely, pathetic person I was before I died—no job, no boyfriend and no family. You, Susie and Claire are my family, Tom. For the first time since my mum died I feel as if I belong. Even after you and Susie have left, I'll always have the memory of you to keep me going."

"But what about Alice? You said she's like a sister to you. A sister is family, you know."

"Yes, but she's met Jack now. Even if I went back, they'd still fall in love with each other all over again, which is great, but I don't want to be a wallflower."

"Jemma, you weren't meant to die, you just heard Alice tell you that. You'll never be able to move on if you stay here. You'd be stuck here forever. You'd never see your mum again and even when Alice gets old and dies, it's unlikely she'll end up here. You'll always be alone."

Jemma sighed. He was right. Alice was right. She had no idea why she had just told Tom about her plan—she hadn't intended to, but she was glad that she had unburdened herself. Maybe she had been secretly hoping he'd talk her out of it.

As if on cue, Tom raised his brows and fixed his eyes on her. "Why are you telling me this now?"

"I'm not sure, to be honest. When Alice told me about Max just now, it finally dawned on me that I would never be at peace here. I'd be forever looking over my shoulder and that would spoil the memories that I have. I suppose it's made me think a bit more about it. I also hated lying to you. What kind of person would I be if I let you go under such a cloud of lies?"

"So what are you going to do?"

"I'm going to listen to you and Alice. The fact that Alice knew about Max is the final straw. I'll go back straight after you."

"Good. Maybe I should make you go first just to make sure you really do go," he growled, his eyes narrowing.

"No," snapped Jemma. "Because if there's any chance that you don't make it, Susie will need me. But you have my word, Tom, I will leave if you and Susie are successful."

When Jemma conceded that she wouldn't have the strength to make contact with Alice a second time, she agreed to leave the mortals as they chatted about what had just happened.

Voices greeted them as they materialized back in Jack's kitchen. *Claire must be visiting Max again.*

Jemma popped her head through the wall, grinning. She was met with a smile from Claire and a scowl from Max.

"Happy Christmas."

"Piss off!"

The season of goodwill hadn't rubbed off on Max, then. "Claire? Is there any chance of a quick word?"

"Of course, dear." Claire smiled, much to Max's annoyance, judging by the furious glare he threw at Jemma.

"Sorry, Max, you're going to have to share her, so tough," she taunted. For once, Max's hostile glower didn't bother her. She stuck her tongue out and stepped back through the wall.

"You shouldn't wind him up," said Claire when they were alone. They had gone to a quiet place in the forest where they could talk in private.

"He's such a miserable old sod, I just couldn't help it," said Jemma, already regretting her impulsive mini-rebellion.

"That may be so, but it really isn't advisable to aggravate him. Now, what can I do for you, dear?"

"I wanted to let you know that I've changed my mind about going back. I managed to talk to Alice during a séance just now, and she and Tom have convinced me that I shouldn't stay here. Would you help me find a wormhole after Tom and Susie have gone?"

"Of course I will, dear. It's probably a good idea, as Max is going to be very cross when he finds out that Tom has gone."

"Alice said that an angel told her to warn me about Max. Is he really that dangerous?"

"Let me tell you something about Max, Jemma. The reason he was on the Titanic was because he was on the run from the police. They were going to charge him with attempted murder because he had tried to kill someone whilst he was in a rage. Make no mistake, Jemma, Max can be very dangerous."

"Shit. Perhaps I shouldn't be so quick to wind him up," mumbled Jemma.

"Hmm, that would be advisable, dear."

"Claire? Is it possible for a ghost to actually harm another ghost?"

"Yes, it is, dear. Let me put it this way, can you feel it when Tom touches you? Have you been intimate with him?"

A cold shiver ran through Jemma as the realization hit her. If she could feel pleasure through Tom's touch, then she would also be able to feel pain, and even though Max could never kill her, he would be able to hurt her. She couldn't let the barrier of energy around her down, though, as that would be even more dangerous. It would be a disaster if Max could see into her soul and read her thoughts. It was obvious that Max hadn't intended to hurt her the day he had thrown her across the room—that must have been a warning. If he had the power to do that to her, then what else could he be capable of?

* * * *

"It was amazing," cried Alice as they arrived back at the house. "Not only could I see and hear her, I could actually *feel* what she was feeling."

Alice hadn't stopped talking about the séance all the way home, and she was still bubbling with excitement. "She said that this Tom guy is gorgeous and that she's in love with him. Isn't that so romantic?"

"You're very lucky," said Maggie, shaking her wild red hair out of a ponytail. "Most people never get to the deep meditative state you were in just now. You should learn to develop that, you really do have a special gift."

"She said there's also a girl called Susie who lives here with them, in this house. You were right, Jack, they've been here for over twenty years."

"Didn't that woman who came for her son's ashes, what was her name, Grace... Didn't she say that her son's name was Tom, and that he died twenty years ago?" asked Jack.

"Oh my God, you're right. It must be the same person. Wow, we met Jemma's future mother-in-law."

They made their way into the kitchen and Jack pulled a bottle of champagne out of the fridge. "As it's officially Christmas Day, I think we should have a Christmas drink. Anyone for a glass of bubbly?"

"Well, seeing that you're so insistent, it would be rude to say no." Maggie chuckled, her warm laughter breaking the underlying chill between Alice and Jack. As Jack struggled with the cork, Alice found herself wishing that Maggie was staying for Christmas. Apart from the fact that she enjoyed her company, it also meant that she wouldn't be alone with Jack. They still hadn't resolved their argument and Alice, still on a high from her encounter with Jemma, didn't want Jack to spoil it by being grumpy again as soon as Maggie left. On impulse she threw Maggie a warm smile. "Maggie, would you like to stay and spend Christmas with us?"

"That's very sweet of you, love, but I wouldn't want to intrude on your first Christmas together," replied Maggie.

"Oh, you wouldn't be, would she, Jack?"

"No, of course not. You're more than welcome to stay, Maggie." Jack's expression looked genuine and Alice couldn't tell if he was just being polite or if he, like her, was glad of a distraction from their argument.

"Thank you. I'd love to stay, then. So, tell me more about Grace."

Alice and Jack filled Maggie in on all the details of the old woman who had once lived in their house. They drank champagne, sitting around the kitchen table and chatting about the night's events. Christmas candles threw warm shadows across the room and Casper, who adored Maggie, had curled up on her lap, purring. As Alice became more relaxed she allowed her mind to drift back to her reunion with Jemma. Would the warning be enough to make Jemma come back? She shuddered as she thought about what might have happened if Dean hadn't told her about the possibility that the boy could be an angel. She would probably have become more and more frightened every time she saw him, driving him away and never managing to actually talk to him. What would have happened to Jemma if she hadn't been able to deliver the message? Had it worked? She wanted so much to talk about it with Jack, to share her thoughts with him, but his doubt still niggled at her, as well as his recent abruptness, so she remained silent.

"And what about this Dean fella?" asked Maggie, snapping Alice out of her thoughts. The conversation had moved on from Grace and they were now talking about her encounter with the angel. "How did he know that the boy was an angel?"

"He didn't, really. He just said he had heard about them and suggested that I remain calm next time. He said that if the boy had wanted to harm me, he would have done so by then, and that made sense. At least Dean believed me," she added, throwing a dark look at Jack.

"Oh, for God's sake, Alice," he snapped. "Will you stop making Dean out to be some sort of saint and making me look like I don't give a shit?"

"I'm beginning to wonder if you do. You made it clear that you thought I was imagining it all and you've been really stroppy ever since. You obviously don't like Dean and I can only imagine that it's because you're jealous." Alice pushed back her chair, scraping it against the floor and waking Casper from his sleep. He jumped off Maggie's lap then stormed out of the kitchen. *Bloody Jack. Why does he have to be so fucking stroppy? I'm the one who should be pissed off with him for not believing me in the first place, so why is he having a go at me?* She stormed into the bedroom, slamming the door behind her, and threw herself down on the bed. A wave of despair washed over her as she lay staring up at the ceiling. She hated arguing with Jack. The tears came then, running down her cheeks and falling onto the bed. She knew that she should try to forget his doubt in her and just let it blow over, but she couldn't. Meeting the angel had been the most phenomenal thing she had ever experienced, along with her earlier encounter with Jemma. If the most important person in her life wasn't happy for her, then what was the point?

A few minutes later there was a light knock on the door. "Alice, can I come in?" called Maggie softly.

Alice sat up and wiped away her tears. *Poor Maggie. Some Christmas this is turning out to be.*

"Of course," she called, trying to sound as cheerful as possible. She dragged herself off the bed and fixed a smile on her face.

"Oh, look at you," cried Maggie as she burst into the room. Maggie marched over to her and gave her a hug. When she pulled away, she wiped a stray tear away from Alice's check and walked her over to the bed.

"Sit down," she ordered. "You two need your heads banged together. I've never met a couple more destined to be together, so what on earth is going on?" She plonked herself next to Alice and glared at her.

"Oh, Maggie," cried Alice. "Jack doubted me when I kept seeing the boy, and I don't think he believed me and when

I found out he was an angel, he was even more weird with me. Then he was angry because I swapped my day off and now it seems he hates Dean." As it all came pouring out, Alice felt a bit like a wronged child telling the grown-up all about it.

"He did believe you, you know," said Maggie.

"Well, you would say that."

"No, seriously, he did. Why do you think I'm here now? Do you really think that I would turn up out of the blue on Christmas Eve if there wasn't a reason?"

Alice blinked. *Yes, I did, actually.*

Maggie smiled. "I came because Jack asked me to. He'd left about a dozen messages on my voicemail, along with all yours, but I'd left my phone at home, which is why I never got any of them. Eventually he got hold of me through a mutual friend who was at the same retreat as me. Apparently it took several long phone calls to track this guy down and he was the one who told me that Jack needed to talk to me."

"Why was Jack trying to get hold of you?"

"Duh! Because he knew that you were desperate to pass on the angel's message to Jemma and that you needed my help to do it. Jack is very gifted, but he's never performed a séance before. He wanted to make sure it was done properly. That doesn't sound like someone who didn't believe you, does it?"

"Well, no, but why didn't he tell me this?"

"You didn't exactly give him a chance, did you? I don't know what else is going on with you two, but you needed to know that. Now, go down and sort it out with him."

"But what about you?" asked Alice, numb from Maggie's revelation.

"I'm going to go into the spare bedroom and go to bed, so don't you worry about me. Now, *scoot!*" she said, shoving Alice out of the door.

Alice made her way downstairs, listening out for any movement to give away Jack's whereabouts, but the house was still and silent. The kitchen was empty, so she poked her head through the door to the living room and saw Jack sitting on the sofa, a glass of something in his hand, staring at the Christmas tree. The room was dark except for the tiny white lights on the tree and she could only see his outline. She padded over to him and put a hand on his shoulder. "Sorry," she said.

He pulled her down to sit next to him and put his arms around her. "I'm sorry, too. I've been a pain in the ass, haven't I?"

"Let's call it quits, shall we?"

"Alice, it wasn't that I didn't believe you. I was worried about you, because I could see the strain it was having on you. I love you so much and I was worried I was going to lose you." The worry lines on his face tore at Alice's conscience.

"Why would you think that?"

"Because you became so distant with me and then you became friends with Dean and he was able to help you in a way that I couldn't. I felt that I'd let you down."

"Is that why you don't like him?"

"Actually, I do like him, he's a good guy. You were right, I was jealous of him, because he was the one who guessed the boy could be an angel. That had never occurred to me and I suppose it made me feel a bit insecure about my own psychic skills. And when you changed your shift, I took it the wrong way and blamed it on you not wanting to spend any time with me. I was stupid, I know that now, and I'm sorry for giving you such a hard time."

"Jack, you will always be the most important person in my life. It's thanks to you that I was able to get into that deep meditative state so I could talk to Jemma. Without being able to do that, the message would have been useless. I'd be lost without you, so don't ever doubt yourself like that again. I mean it, Jack, you've helped me more than anyone, and I love you more than you could ever imagine."

When Jack kissed her she closed her eyes and snuggled

deeper into his arms. Everything was going to be all right. She had Jack, she had talked to Jemma and she had a job she loved. She was truly happy and, for the first time since Jemma had died, she felt as if she was able to lay her grief to rest and move on with her life. "By the way," she murmured. "We've been invited to Glitz on Boxing Day. Maggie's going to lay this ghost crap to rest once and for all. Do you fancy going?"

"Why not?" he replied, nuzzling her neck. "If we can't sort that ghost out then nobody can."

Chapter Twenty-Two

"I'm so glad they've made up," said Jemma, sighing as she and Tom watched Alice sleeping in Jack's arms in front of the Christmas tree. "It's a bit weird that we know everything about her life with Jack, but she doesn't know anything about us."

"I wouldn't say that. She now knows that we live here with her and Jack, and that you're in love with a gorgeous ghost."

"Mmm. Isn't it funny how both Alice and I found love because of my death?"

"Fucking sentimental shit," growled Max from his corner. They had forgotten about him and had been enjoying the romantic atmosphere. Now the moment was ruined. They needed to get away.

"Take my hand," whispered Tom. "I want to take you somewhere special." Jemma grabbed his hand and closed her eyes. A rush of anticipation surged through her. Where was he taking her? A second later, she opened them again and found herself on a beach similar to the one in Norfolk.

"Wow, this place is gorgeous. Where are we this time?" Like the beach in Norfolk, this one had miles of soft white sand stretching out before them. The sea was the clearest deep blue and glistened in what was obviously hot sunshine. The sky was as blue as the sea and cloudless – in fact she could barely see the horizon. Instead of the grassy sand dunes, tall palm trees swayed in a very subtle sea breeze.

"Right, let me guess, palm trees, warm sunshine and a clear sky," she observed. "We're clearly not in England. So where is this?"

"Do you remember the first time I took you to Norfolk?"

She nodded. *So this is Norfolk after all?*

"Do you remember where you thought I had brought you?"

She gasped. "Oh my God, is this the Seychelles?"

"Yep," said Tom, looking pleased with himself. "After you said you wanted to go to the Seychelles, I came straight here and have been searching for the best beach. And this is it."

"Wow," cried Jemma as she ran down to the water's edge. When Tom caught up with her she threw her arms around his neck. "Christmas Day on a deserted beach in the Seychelles with you. This has to be the most perfect place ever. When you said we would go somewhere special at Christmas, I thought you were going to take me to Lapland or something equally wintery."

Tom laughed. "Actually, I was planning on taking you to Norway later to see the Northern Lights, then I thought we could go for a stroll under Niagara Falls."

"Really?"

"Yes, if you want to. We can go anywhere we like."

Jemma wrapped her arms around his waist and pulled him as close to her as possible. "That sounds wonderful, but do you know what I'd really like?"

"What?"

"To stay here, just you and me. It's our last day together, and the only thing I want is to be alone with you."

"Then that's what we'll do. Here, take my hand." Tom held out his hand and she took it without hesitation. "Remember when we did this in Norfolk?" he asked and waded into the water. This time, instead of slightly cloudy water filled with jellyfish, the water was crystal clear with thousands of tiny, colorful fish swimming around them. Jemma held on to Tom's hand and let him lead her farther into the sea. They walked until they came across some coral swaying in the current. As the water got deeper, the fish became more exotic and beautiful. When they ventured even deeper, sharks swam around them, not in the slightest bit interested in them as they weren't potential meals. They explored the alien underwater world until they had seen just about every species of marine life then decided to head back to the sandy beach. As they got closer they spotted giant turtles, soaking up the sun by some shallow rocks. Jemma had never seen anything so lovely.

"This is the most amazing place I've ever been to. Thank you for bringing me here." They made their way around to another part of the island, strolling hand in hand along the beach, just like the living couples, who were mostly honeymooners by the look of it. They found a quiet patch of sand under a palm tree and sat down. Jemma snuggled up to Tom and sighed in contentment. "Tom?"

"Hmm?" He kissed her head and pulled her closer.

"Can we do that thing again? You know…"

"Have you ever made love on a beach?" he asked, his voice husky.

A thrill ran through her as his words registered. "No, I can't say I have."

"There are huge advantages to being invisible, you know," he murmured into her ear. His breath tickled, sending little shivers coursing through her. "Like making love on an exotic beach without anyone seeing."

Jemma closed her eyes. Her heart was thumping again, at least that was what it felt like, and a film of sweat seemed to have coated her skin.

"Undress for me. I want to see you naked."

"What? Here?" Heat burned Jemma's cheeks as she gaped at him.

He cradled her head in his large hands, forcing her to meet his smoldering gaze. "There are no other ghosts here, Jemma. Nobody will see you except for me."

He was right. What the hell did it matter even if someone did see her? She didn't belong in this world and she'd be gone tomorrow anyway. She grinned and Tom released her.

"Okay." She rose to her feet then slowly started to remove her clothes, teasing Tom by keeping her breasts hidden until he growled with impatience. When she was naked, she turned and wriggled her bottom at him. She gasped when he gave it a light smack then giggled as she stuck it out for more. But instead he pulled her back to him and held her close.

"Lie down and do not move," he ordered.

By now Jemma was so aroused she would have done anything he'd asked, so obeying such a simple instruction wasn't hard.

"Close your eyes and enjoy."

She snapped her eyelids shut, closing out the sunshine. Waves rolling onto the sand and distant voices were the only sounds, but they soon became muted as Tom started covering her body with light kisses. He flicked his tongue over her breasts, sending a current of excitement sizzling through her veins, but it was when he moved farther down that Jemma stopped thinking altogether and lost herself as Tom explored every part of her. His lips took her to a new level of pleasure that she had never thought possible, causing every nerve ending to burst back to life. Soon after he brought her to a screaming climax he climbed on top of her and showed her that ghosts could indeed make love. It was everything she could have dreamed of and more. Never had she responded with such passion and never had she been taken to such heights that she was left floating on a cloud of glorious euphoria.

Afterward she lay in his arms, spent and happier than she'd ever been in her life. Her body glowed from Tom's touch and her heart fluttered with the afterglow of his love. *Wow, sex was never this good when I was alive.*

"Let your barrier down."

Tom's voice edged its way to her brain. *Really?* She raised her head off his chest and looked at him to check if she had heard right.

"It's okay. I'll keep you safe."

She smiled. Of course he would. As soon as her protective shield of energy had evaporated, Tom's soul seeped into hers the way it had last time. She felt his pleasure from their lovemaking and he felt hers. His love for her was as powerful as a furnace roaring with red-hot flames and she was able to show him the depth of her own feelings without needing to do or say anything. They were connected on a level where no words or actions were necessary. She wasn't sure that she wouldn't have felt like this in the living world. Her love was so deep that even the supernatural forces that allowed them to become one like this might have united them as mortals. She was sure that her body would have tingled just as much and her heart would have shone just as bright if she had been alive. As long as she had Tom, anything was possible.

By the time they had erected their protective barriers again Jemma's body was buzzing both inside and out. She had never known such intimacy or utter contentment. If there was a heaven, then surely this was it. She was now lying with her head across Tom's lap. He was leaning against a palm tree and stroking her hair. "I wish we could stay here forever."

"Me too. Imagine if we could manipulate time," he mused. "I'd relive this day over and over."

"I just wish I could save the memory of today and keep it forever," said Jemma, feeling wistful.

"Jemma, this may be the last time we're completely alone, and I want you to know how much you mean to me." Reality was catching up with them again and Tom's voice was subdued. "I love you, Jemma. More than I've ever loved anyone. I love you so much that I'd be willing to forget going back and stay here with you, so if you really want, I'll say to hell with it and we can stay here together. Forever."

Jemma was so moved by Tom's words that she was speechless for a second—a rare event for her. Her head spun. He would rather stay with her than become a free spirit. *Wow, this must be equivalent to a marriage proposal.* For a moment she was so overwhelmed that she nearly cried *yes, yes, yes.* But her conscience stopped her and reminded her of Susie's distraught tears when she had told her how much she missed her family. She had promised Susie that she would try to make things right. Even though they could have bought a bit more time by telling her that the plans were on hold for now, what was the point of delaying the heartbreak? If Tom stayed Susie would remain as well, then it would be her and Tom's fault that she cried every day. Susie hadn't been meant to die, just like herself, and keeping her here, no matter what the reason, would be wrong.

So Jemma took a deep breath, a habit from her mortal days, and squeezed Tom's hand. "Thank you for saying that, but you know that we can't stay. It wouldn't be right, we'd be together at someone else's expense and neither of us would be able to live with that. I'd like nothing more than to stay here with you forever, but we can't. We just can't..." She trailed off into a sob. This time tomorrow she would be alive again and would have no idea that Tom had ever existed. Determined not to break down, she jumped up then reached for Tom's hand. "We should go now and find Claire to make the final arrangements. We'd better not put it off any longer."

Tom's eyes glistened as he took her hand and together they vanished from their private paradise and made their way back to find Claire.

A split second later they approached Claire's bench in the forest. "Hi, Claire," said Jemma, with more enthusiasm than she felt.

Claire jumped and turned around too fast. "Hello, you two." She smiled, but it didn't reach her eyes, which were red and swollen as if she had been crying.

Jemma rushed over to her and put her arms around her. "Claire, are you okay? Whatever's wrong?"

Claire sniffed and stared out over the stunning view. "It's

Max. He's just…"

"Max?" cried Jemma, anger flaring through her at the thought that he'd upset her friend. "What the hell has that bastard done?"

"Jemma, let her talk," said Tom, sitting down next to them on the bench.

"Max hasn't done anything except help me. He's talked me through some things relating to my death and made me face up to a few home truths. He's just helped me to remember what happened when I died and why Robert hasn't turned up."

"Really?" Jemma had never managed to get Claire to reveal very much about her death, so the fact that Max had had such a breakthrough was incredible. She found it hard to imagine being able to open up to Max, to trust him with her deepest, darkest secrets. *You just never can tell.* "So what happened to Robert, then? Did he run off with another woman?" she joked.

"Yes," said Claire, her voice heavy. "Just after he murdered me."

Jemma's shock stole any words she might have spoken. That was *so* not what she had been expecting.

"That's awful," said Tom, taking Claire's hand and giving it a comforting squeeze. "What happened?"

"He had been poisoning me, making me think that I was ill. It was deliberate and carefully planned. He had been seeing another woman for a while and one day I found out. By this time I was quite poorly, he'd been poisoning me for a while by then, and I was weak. Only two days before he had told me how devastated he was by my illness and, if I were to die, he would come and find me by our special bench when his time came. It was all part of his plan to make me think I was dying of a natural illness. The day I found him with *her*, he told me that he despised me and had only married me for my money, but he wasn't going to leave me, because he wouldn't get any of my fortune. He then injected me with a lethal dose of whatever it was he was giving me. Max told me that Robert wouldn't have become a free spirit and that he would have gone to what the living call hell. Wherever that is." Claire's voice was filled with bitterness as she poured out her story. "I can't believe I was so stupid. I always had a feeling that he didn't truly love me, but I never thought he'd do anything like that. To think I've been waiting all these years for that murderous swine."

"Oh my God," muttered Jemma, stunned. "And you didn't remember any of this?"

"No. Max said I must have been so traumatized by what happened that I lost my memory. It was him who helped me to remember."

"I can't believe it's the same Max we're talking about here," said Jemma, frowning. "He's such a mean, nasty creature to us and yet you clearly have a strong bond with him."

"Like I said before, we've been helping each other."

"We came to talk about the plans for tomorrow, but I don't suppose you're in the mood right now?" said Jemma, hoping that it might delay Tom's departure.

"Actually, I could do with the distraction. I'd be happy to help. In fact, I've been giving it some thought. Can I tell you what I think is best?"

"Yes, please," said Jemma and Tom at the same time.

Claire closed her eyes, as if reining in her emotions for now, then opened them again. "Well, first, I still don't think you should tell Susie anything. As soon as you've gone back, Tom, she will disappear and will never know anything about it. There's always a risk that she'll talk about it around Max, so it's best to keep quiet. Now, Jemma, you should stay at home with Susie tomorrow to keep an eye on her. You'll only know for sure that it's worked when she disappears. And besides, Tom will need to focus on the wormhole and he might be distracted if you're there." Claire stood up and started pacing in front of the bench. "Now, Tom. I'll help you locate the wormhole, then you must use all your powers of thought to direct that wormhole to the time and place you need to get to. I think it's best that you go back to the point where you leave your car with the keys in the ignition. If there are no keys, the thief won't be able to drive it and Susie won't get killed. The trouble is, if the wormhole collapses before you have a chance to remove the keys, you won't remember what to do and everything will happen again. So it's vital that you keep your mind focused on holding on to the wormhole and removing those keys as quickly as possible."

Claire paused for a moment, but continued pacing. "Now, Jemma. You should try and stay with Susie so you actually see her disappear. Then you must come and find me here as quickly as possible, because we need to get you away before Max finds out that Tom's gone. You need to think about what you're going to do to stop the accident from happening again."

Jemma had already considered this. "I have to make sure that I don't get my cigarettes out, because it was on my way out for a quick smoke that I slipped. I thought that maybe I can distract myself before the wormhole collapses so that I forget about the ciggies."

"How?" asked Claire. "What will you do to cause that distraction? Remember, you will only have a fraction of a second."

"The girl sitting next to me, Kirsten I think her name was, had just bought a large glass of Coke. I thought I'd knock the glass over so it spills everywhere. That's quick and it should distract me enough to forget about the cigarettes, as I'll be too busy helping Kirsten clean the mess up."

"All right. As long as you're both absolutely sure about what you need to do, then I suppose that's it. Come early, Tom, before Susie starts to wander off. I'll see you in the morning. Good night."

Tom and Jemma had their orders and knew they'd been dismissed. But Jemma felt bad about leaving Claire on her own after her gruesome discovery. "Claire?" she said. "Would you like me to stay with you tonight? You know, to keep you company if you get too upset about Robert?"

"No, thank you, dear. I've got a lot to think about and I need to work through it by myself. You go and enjoy your last night together."

Tom and Jemma left Claire alone and made their way to the beach in Norfolk.

"I can't believe what that Robert did to Claire," cried Jemma as they walked along the sandy beach. The waves lapped against the sandy shore, but that didn't calm her. "And what about Max? Who would have thought he could have won Claire's trust like that?"

They strolled for about a mile or so then back again. They talked about Claire, Max, Susie, Alice—everything except what lay ahead the next day. They found their favorite sand dune and sat down, ready to spend their last night in the privacy of their beautiful sanctuary.

"Is there anywhere you'd like to go tonight?" asked Tom, pulling Jemma in to his side and resting his arm on her shoulder.

"No. I just want to be with you. This is perfect." She sighed as Tom turned and kissed the top of her head. "What will you do once you're a free spirit?" she asked.

"Follow you everywhere. I'll be your spiritual stalker," he said, chuckling.

"I wish I wouldn't forget you. Do you think I might sense you?"

"I suppose it might be possible, but you wouldn't know what you were seeing or hearing and that might freak you out. More importantly, what do you think you'll do?"

Jemma shrugged. "Dunno. My life was pretty pathetic before I died, and as I won't remember any of this, I guess I'll just go back to being a hopeless loser."

Tom tensed at her words. "Don't ever say that about yourself," he scolded. "You're the most incredible woman I've ever met. You're strong, feisty, funny, clever, beautiful and loving all rolled into one. You've just got to believe in yourself."

"That's easy to say now, but you didn't know me when I was alive. When I go back tomorrow all this will never have happened and I'll be the same lost cause I was then," said Jemma, fighting back tears. She wished with all her heart she could just stay here with Tom for all eternity. She didn't want to go back to her sad and lonely existence that had been born out of a deep lack of self-confidence. Here Tom had shown her she was special, but back in the real world, what did she have to look forward to?

"Shh, don't upset yourself," said Tom, giving her a squeeze. "Right now, just remember that I'll always be with you."

"I don't— *Mmm.*"

Tom silenced her with a kiss that forced back her words of despair. His lips were demanding and banished some of the uncertainty buried deep inside her core. When he pulled away, he took her chin in his hand and said, "I don't want to hear any more negative words from you tonight. Okay?" Although he was smiling, the firm tone of his voice told her that he meant it.

"Yes," she murmured, melting under his unwavering gaze. She grabbed his head and pulled him back in for another kiss. This time it was she who took control, and she didn't hold back as she explored his mouth with hungry urgency. When she'd had her fill, she nibbled his lower lip before pulling away.

"Wow," he murmured. He grinned, then before she knew what was happening he'd flipped her onto her back and straddled her, holding her in place as she tried to stop laughing. He grabbed her wrists and raised them over her head then he bent down and smashed his lips against hers, leaving her shaking with a burning need for more. When Tom ended the kiss, he hovered over her, grinning down at her with a devilish glint in his eye. He still had her trapped beneath him and he hadn't released her hands from his grip. Heat sizzled through her veins as she waited for his next move. She laughed as she tried to wriggle out of his hold, and her excitement grew when she found she was deliciously trapped.

"I'm going to show you, young lady, just how special you are," he said, his voice now edged with a low, sexy rumble. "I'm going to worship your body the whole night long so, by morning, you will be in no doubt ever again how fucking amazing you are."

Tom was true to his word. He took her to heights she'd never thought was possible, and just when she thought he was done, he asked her to lower her shield so they could explore each other with the spectacular intimacy that mortals would never know. They talked a lot, cried a little, then made love again until the first orange hues of morning peeped over the horizon.

But as the sun rose, Jemma's heart sank, despite the night of delirious pleasure she'd just spent with Tom. This was it. This was the moment they had both been dreading.

"Let's go for one last walk before we say goodbye," she said, wanting to delay the inevitable for as long as possible.

Tom nodded, his eyes no longer shining the way they had during the night. He took her hand and helped her up then they both stood and gazed at each other for several minutes without speaking.

"Come on," she whispered and squeezed his hand.

They strolled in silence, neither wanting to voice what lay just around the corner. Suddenly, the four-legged shape of a dog appeared along the water's edge, and within seconds Sandy came bounding over to them, his tail wagging in a happy greeting. He was out on his early morning walk with his owners, who now seemed to have grown used to their dog acting so strange every day. He was a welcome distraction, but after a while his owners dragged him away, leaving Jemma and Tom alone again.

She turned to him and gazed at him through the blur of tears pooling in her eyes. "Well, I suppose this is it," she said, trying not to let the pain slicing through her heart show too much. She fell into his arms, desperate to feel his embrace one more time.

"Goodbye, my beautiful ghost," he whispered, not quite able to hide his distress. He held her so tightly that he might have squeezed all the air out of her if she had been alive.

"I'm going to miss you so much," cried Jemma. "I love you."

She clung to him, desperate to keep him with her for as long as possible, but eventually he pulled away and kissed her one final time. "Go to Susie now and remember, as soon as she disappears, go straight to Claire. I'll always be with you, my love. Goodbye." And without another word, he vanished out of her life forever.

She was alone and could only stand still as she tried to hold on to the feeling of Tom's last kiss. She could never have stayed here without him, she acknowledged to herself. The pain would have been unbearable.

Brushing away her tears, Jemma remembered that she had a job to do. She took a last look around then returned to the house to find Susie, who was watching Jack's small television in the kitchen while Alice and Jack were busy getting ready to go to Oscar and Dean's house.

"Hi," she mumbled to Susie, who barely acknowledged her. She felt numb. She couldn't quite believe that she would never see Tom again. Another wave of despair washed over her. Fresh tears welled in her eyes so she turned away from Susie so she wouldn't see. The last thing she needed now was Susie demanding to know why she was crying.

"How was Christmas Day at your parents' house?" she asked, putting on a bright voice. A little too bright, it seemed, as Susie swung around to face her.

"Okay. What's with you?"

"Nothing." What else could she say?

"Where's Tom?"

"I don't know. Maybe he's at his dad's grave."

"Uh-huh." She had lost Susie's interest again. Jemma glared at the young girl. She had no idea what they had just given up for her. But Susie remained silent and Jemma sat down on one of the chairs to wait for her to vanish.

"What?" asked Susie, glancing up from the television again.

"Huh? Oh, nothing." Shit, how come Susie was so bloody intuitive? She didn't think she was looking or acting any different from normal.

"Jemma, you're sitting in the kitchen and staring into space without speaking. You don't do silent, Jemma, so tell me what's up. Have you and Tom been arguing again?"

"Something like that."

That got Susie's attention. "Okay, tell Aunty Susie what's wrong. What's he done?"

"It doesn't matter, it doesn't concern you." *Yes, it does, actually, but I can't tell you.*

"Well, now that you're here and I've got you to myself, there's something I wanted to talk to you about." Susie's voice had grown serious.

"Oh?"

"You know you said that you would try and talk to Tom about him leaving so I can go home? Well, I was thinking yesterday while I was at my mum's that I really want to go back now. I know of a way. I've been talking to a few people I know and they said it's not as hard as we thought. All you need to do is find a wormhole…"

"There are big risks using wormholes, it's not as simple as it sounds."

"I know that, but I'm prepared to take that risk. I just want to go home, Jemma. Please."

"Susie, can we please talk about this another time? I'm feeling really shitty right now…"

"It's always about you, isn't it?" snapped Susie as angry tears welled in her eyes. "Now that you and Tom are an item, you don't give a damn about me. You promised you would talk to him, Jemma. You *promised*."

"Susie…"

"Go away, Jemma. You're not my friend at all, are you?" Susie jumped up from the chair.

"Susie, please. I do care about you and so does Tom."

"Oh yeah, you really care, don't you? That's why Tom's never here anymore and you won't talk to me." Susie paced around the room, but then stormed through the wall, clearly to get away from Jemma. Jemma followed, determined that their last words wouldn't be ones of such anger. This was so frustrating. Susie couldn't be more wrong.

"Susie," she shouted. "If we don't care about you, then why is Tom about to go back through a wormhole any minute now?" She was so upset that she didn't care any longer if Susie found out. She was about to leave anyway, so what did it matter? Susie stopped in her tracks and turned back to Jemma with an astonished expression on her face, but as she did so, she vanished in front of her eyes.

It had worked, Tom had been successful and Jemma was left alone in the living room.

Only she wasn't alone. She had forgotten, when she had rushed after Susie, that Max was also in that room. She filled with a chilling dread as she turned slowly around and came face-to-face with Max. The rage flaring out of his eyes told her that he had heard everything she had just said.

Chapter Twenty-Three

Alice and Jack decided to walk to Glitz. It was Boxing Day and a fine dusting of snow had settled over London. This was Alice's favorite kind of weather, cold with a cloudless blue sky and bright sunshine reflecting off the fresh, white snow. She'd rather have a day like this than a hot, stuffy heat wave. Taking in a lungful of the crisp, fresh air, she smiled. She and Jack had had the most wonderful Christmas together. Maggie had stayed for lunch yesterday, which Jack had cooked. He'd gone to so much trouble making sure it was perfect, and it had been.

When they'd finished their dinner Maggie had said her goodbyes after arranging to meet them at Glitz for the Boxing Day party. She and Jack had then fallen asleep on the sofa with full stomachs and happy smiles on their faces. When they woke a couple of hours later, they had made love and afterward opened their presents. Jack had gone mad, buying more presents for her than she had for him, which had made her feel guilty, but very touched at the trouble he had gone to for her. She had bought him a watch, a book on the paranormal and some expensive fragrance, but he had bought her at least twice as many presents, including the most beautiful amethyst and crystal necklace she had ever seen. He had explained that amethyst was her birthstone.

When it had grown dark, they had lit the candles in the living room and snuggled up again on the sofa with a bottle of Baileys and watched *It's A Wonderful Life* on TV. Casper had purred softly on Jack's lap, his belly full of turkey, and the three of them had been content as they had drifted off to sleep.

"What time did you tell Maggie to get to Glitz?" asked Alice as they approached the entrance to the restaurant.

"I told her to come at eleven o'clock."

"But that's nearly an hour ago, and they're not expecting us until twelve."

"Exactly. I've known Maggie for long enough to know that if I tell her to be here for eleven, then she'll arrive at twelve."

"Oh, right." Alice laughed and pushed open the door. "Wow, doesn't it look amazing?" she exclaimed as they entered. Oscar and Dean had moved all the tables to one end of the restaurant and had put up a huge dining table in the middle. It was laid for twelve people with a large selection of plates, cutlery and glasses at each place setting. The table, which was stunning, had been decorated with natural green pine, gold stars and little red hearts, all wound around thick, tall, silver candlesticks. It all resembled something from one of those posh lifestyle magazines.

"Hello, sweetie," called Oscar as he pushed through the kitchen door, his arms laden with serving dishes.

"Here, let me help you with those," said Alice, reaching for a platter balanced rather precariously on Oscar's arm. The tray was full of different types of meat—ham, salami, sausage, sliced roast beef—and was decorated with tomatoes and cucumbers carefully cut into little flower shapes. She glanced at the other two platters Oscar was carrying. One was piled with a delicious-looking selection of seafood. Alice's stomach rumbled—she loved seafood. The other contained warm bowls of homemade pâté decorated with crispy bacon and pickled cucumber. Alice had never seen such a perfect and varied selection of food.

"This looks fantastic." She eyed up some small breaded plaice fillets decorated with a yellow relish, prawns, caviar and lemon.

"This, my dear, is a traditional Danish Christmas cold table," said Oscar. "My mum's Danish and we have this every year. Normally you would have this on Christmas Day in Denmark, but Dean and I like to do the whole turkey thing, so we usually have it on Boxing Day. I hope you're hungry."

"Hello?" The voice came from the entrance and they all glanced round to see Maggie's smiling face peeking round the door.

"Hi, Maggie," said Alice. She rushed over and gave her a warm hug. "This is Oscar. Oscar, this is the woman who is going to tell you, one way or the other, if there's anything spooky going on here."

"Thank you so much for coming," said Oscar, looking like an excited child. "Finally, I'll be able prove to Dean that I was right all along. Now, before we start, who would like a glass of ice-cold Danish snaps, straight from the freezer?"

"Do you mind if I have a look around first?" asked Maggie. "It's probably best, so I don't get my spirits mixed up."

Oscar laughed and led Maggie through to the kitchen to meet Dean. Alice and Jack waited in the restaurant while Maggie walked through the premises, taking in every trace of energy she came across. She wandered around for what seemed like ages, sometimes muttering the odd, 'hmm hmm' to herself and, when she was finished, she summoned Oscar and Dean back into the restaurant, where they joined Alice and Jack.

"Right," said Maggie, in her usual brisk manner. "I've been into every room and I didn't sense anything out of the ordinary. This building is not haunted. There are no ghosts or curses here."

Oscar's jaw dropped. "But—" he started.

"No, love. I know for a fact that there is nothing here. If you've been having problems, then I'm afraid it's probably down to bad management, not ghosts."

"Ouch," said Dean, giving Oscar a look that said 'I told you so'.

"It's nothing that can't be fixed," continued Maggie. "You need to find better suppliers, rework your menu, open for longer, find an accountant, but you can't blame it on a curse, because there isn't one."

"If it's any help," interjected Jack, "my parents used to run a restaurant when I was a kid and I helped them out at weekends. When I was older I did a bit of bookkeeping for them as well. I'd be happy to help out if you'd like."

Alice beamed at him. She couldn't believe that a couple of days ago, Jack had acted as though he hated Dean and now here he was offering to help them with their business.

"Cooee!" They all glanced up to see Darren had arrived and was making his way over to them. "Sorry I'm late. Have I missed anything?"

"Yes," said Dean. "Maggie has just confirmed what I've been saying all along. There are no ghosts or curses here."

Darren looked crestfallen. "Oh, guys. I'm so sorry for feeding you all that bullshit, then. I really thought I had felt something before."

"That may be so, but at least you were honest when you were here last time and I really appreciate that," replied Dean.

"Tell you what," said Jack to Dean and Darren. "Why don't you both join the psychic group I run? We meet every second Wednesday at my house and work on tuning into our spiritual side. It'll help you develop any psychic skills that you might have."

"Thanks," said Dean, looking pleased. "That would be great."

Darren nodded. "Yeah, I'd love to come too."

They drank a toast just as the rest of the guests started arriving, and soon the party was well and truly underway.

The food was out of this world, served with huge amounts of cold beer and even more snaps. They all remained seated around the table for most of the afternoon, eating and drinking. The room was filled with the sound of laughter and lively chatter and Alice was humbled to be a part of such a warm and friendly group of people. Sometimes she and Jack would join the smokers outside for a bit of fresh air. She didn't approve of smoking, but today she couldn't care less. Several hours later the guests started staggering home and, after a lot of festive hugs and kisses, Alice and Jack left as well. Maggie had declined to come back with them and had managed to get a cab home.

They decided to walk off some of the food and alcohol and made their way back to Swiss Cottage, hand in hand and giggling like a couple of teenagers. When they climbed the steps up to the doorway, Jack kissed Alice and murmured, "I can't wait to get you into bed."

She giggled as he dropped the keys on the ground. They both bent down and fumbled for them then burst into laughter as they grabbed the keys at the same time. After several attempts Jack managed to get the front door open. They stumbled inside, banging the door behind them. Then they froze. Something was wrong, very wrong. The atmosphere was heavy with malevolence. Alice shivered as her skin tingled and the hairs on the back of her neck stood on end. She glanced at Jack, who had also stopped, and she knew that he felt it too.

"What is it?" she whispered. "Jack, what's happened?"

"I don't know," he answered, frowning. "The atmosphere is charged with negative energy. Whatever it is, it's evil. Something really bad is going on."

Terrified, Jemma stood frozen to the spot, literally. When Max had learned of Tom's departure, he had imprisoned her in some sort of force field that stopped her from moving or even speaking. She could only watch as Max paced around her, muttering to himself and acting like a bomb about to explode. Jemma had often wondered what would happen when Max's fury erupted, and it seemed like she was about to find out.

Fear paralyzed her. She was trapped, couldn't move, there was no escape. How long had she been frozen like this? She didn't know, but it seemed like hours, and with every minute that had passed Max had become angrier.

She had tried to talk to Max, to reason with him, but her voice had evaporated into muffled, incomprehensible sound waves. There was no point in denying that Tom had left because Max had seen Susie disappear, and there could only be one explanation for that. She didn't know what to do. How long would Max keep her like this? And what about Claire? She must be wondering where she was. Would she come searching for her and unwittingly let Max know that she had helped Tom? Would Max harm Claire? If only she could get away and warn her, but she was powerless to do anything. She could only watch as Max worked himself into more and more of a temper, and her fear grew.

Without warning, he started shouting an obscene and foul torrent of words at her, storming around the room and lashing his arms out as if smashing everything in it to pieces. His fury created such a strong force that a couple of ornaments actually did fall off a shelf, crashing to the floor, and Jemma closed her eyes, trying to block out what was happening. Just as she opened them again Claire materialized in front of her, facing her and with her back to Max. Claire wouldn't be able to see him. She tried to give her friend some sort of signal to warn her, but Jemma remained frozen.

"Where did you get to? I've been waiting for hours. Tom managed to remove the keys and he and Susie have successfully left. Come on, what are you waiting for?" From the frustration on Claire's face, she couldn't see the invisible field of energy holding Jemma prisoner, and had no idea either that Max was right behind her. Jemma watched, horrified, as Max's face took on a new kind of fury, something even darker and more thunderous than before.

"You did this?" he spat. His voice was quiet, dark, and his eyes had the look of madness about them. Claire jumped and swung round in shock.

"Max?"

"You helped him?"

"Max, listen—"

"Nooo…" howled Max. It had been scary enough before Claire had arrived, but now that he knew of her involvement, he lost all control. His cry sounded like that of a tortured animal and was so loud it drowned the room, the force of it sending Claire flying backward.

"I'll kill you. I'll kill you both," he roared.

"Max, we're already dead. Calm down, *please*." Claire's voice showed no sign of fear. How on earth could she appear so unafraid?

"You betrayed me." Max sounded like an evil demon from a horror film.

"No. All I did was help a friend. I never promised you that I wouldn't help them. Max, what have you done to Jemma? Why can't she move?"

"She's not going anywhere." He hissed, turning his eyes toward Jemma. If she could have moved, she would have recoiled from the glare he gave her and, for a minute, she thought he was going to throw her across the room again. Claire's warning about Max's ability to hurt her rang in her ears but still she remained frozen, unable to defend herself.

"Max, your argument was never with her. Nor was it with Tom, or even Tom's father. Please don't take it out on her. Let her go." Claire remained calm and didn't give away any of the anxiety that she must have been feeling.

"Never," he shouted. "She's not going anywhere. She won't get away again."

Some sort of realization passed across Claire's face then and she put her hand on Max's arm. "Oh, Max. Does Jemma look like her? Pauline?"

Max's face darkened even more. With another roar, he picked up a chair and hurled it at Jemma, sending it flying across the room and just missing her by about a millimeter. The fact that he was able to throw something as large and physical as a chair was testament to his fury. "Don't mention that whore's name, *ever*," he shouted.

"Max, that happened over a hundred years ago. Isn't

it about time you let go?" Although Claire was being sympathetic, Jemma was still terrified of Max's reaction to her insistent questions.

"She betrayed me, Claire. How could she do that?" Something changed in Max's voice. The anger was being replaced with what sounded like grief. Jemma was beginning to feel like she was watching a film in 3D. It was all so surreal.

"Yes, Max. Pauline betrayed you. Not Jemma or Tom and not me. It was Pauline and Joe. They are the ones you're angry with."

"Why?" he asked, sounding almost pitiful. "Why did they do it? I trusted them. Joe was going to be my best man. I was going to ask him to be godfather to our baby."

"Only it wasn't your baby, was it, Max?" Claire was trying to encourage Max to open up about his past, but he was becoming agitated again and Jemma prayed that Claire wasn't going to push him over the edge.

"No, it was *his*. I never suspected a thing. Fuck, how could I not have noticed what was going on under my nose?"

"They were obviously clever, sneaky. What happened, Max? How did you find out?" Max glared at Claire with wild eyes. *Oh shit, she's pushed him too far. He's going to explode.* Jemma braced herself for the fallout. But Max seemed to be thinking about what Claire had said. Instead of ranting in rage, his eyes filled with tears and there was genuine heartbreak in his voice as he finally told Claire the full story.

"It was the day I decided to ask Joe to be godfather. I wanted to ask him in private, before we got to the pub, so I went round to his house on the way." Max seemed to have forgotten all about Jemma's presence for now. He seemed to be consumed with the pain he had experienced on that fateful day. He walked over to his armchair and sat down, Claire following behind him, waiting for him to continue.

"I thought he was probably upstairs getting ready, so I went up. Nothing unusual in that, we were always popping in and out of each other's houses. I heard them first. I should have stopped and gone back downstairs there and then, but she laughed and I knew it was Pauline. So I opened the door and there they were, naked on the bed. He was fucking her and she was loving it. He kept saying how much he loved her and she was calling out his name."

He screwed his eyes up and rubbed them then he looked up at Claire with fresh tears in his eyes. "Why, Claire? Why did they do it?"

"What happened next?" she probed.

"I didn't know what I was doing, all I knew was that I wanted them to stop. When I pulled Joe off her, he laughed at me, he fucking laughed. He told me that she was leaving me and that the baby was his. That was when I lost my rag. I punched him, it was only meant to be one punch, but once I started, I couldn't stop. I wanted to kill him, so I kept hitting him, over and over. It was only when Pauline started screaming that I realized what I was doing and stopped. I thought he was dead, so I turned and ran. I had to get away from her and from what I had just done to him." Max buried his head in his hands and wept.

Claire held him, letting him unburden his grief on her. She stroked his head and reassured him until he was ready to continue. "I thought I had killed him, Claire. I needed to get away, from her and from the police, and that was when I spotted the advertisement in the paper for crew on the brand-new ship, Titanic. I thought it was my chance to get away, to start a new life somewhere else, but…"

"The ship sank," Claire finished for him. "Oh, Max. I'm so sorry for what you've been through. I can see that it seemed like the final straw when Jack's grandfather didn't spot you in the water and left you to drown. But he wouldn't have seen you or heard you, you know that, don't you?" she said.

"I don't know what I think anymore," he cried, shaking his head in his hands.

"You needed someone to blame, and the obvious person was George Cresswell. But the people you should have been angry with were the ones who really betrayed you, Pauline and Joe."

"Yeah, I suppose."

Max and Claire remained seated together, Claire holding Max's hand as the past caught up with him. At one point Claire glanced up at Jemma to let her know that she hadn't forgotten her, but all Jemma could do was wait. Max and Claire talked some more, he cried some more and she comforted him. Jemma felt genuine compassion for Max now. Hearing his story first-hand had given her an insight into his bitterness and she could sort of understand how he had turned the blame onto Tom's grandfather.

Then Claire braved the subject that Jemma had been waiting for. "Max, you know now that George Cresswell wasn't to blame for your death, don't you?"

He nodded. "I suppose so."

"So you must also know that neither Tom nor Jemma are to blame for any of this."

"Hmm," came the grudging reply.

"Please let Jemma go, Max. She hasn't done anything to you, other than look a little bit like Pauline, but that's not her fault. I'll stay here with you, I promise."

Max glanced up at Claire in surprise. "Why? Why would you want to stay with me? I'm bad, Claire."

"No, you're not. I know that because if you really had wanted to hurt Tom, you would have done so a long time ago. You're a good man who just happened to have had a run of bad luck. We both have so much bitterness to work through. Remember, I need you just as much as you need me."

"You'll really stay?"

"Of course I will, but you must let Jemma go."

Max looked up at Jemma and, for the first time, she didn't feel that familiar chill of fear run through her as his gaze settled on her. Then, just as suddenly as it had appeared, the force field vanished and Jemma was free to move again.

"Go to the bench and wait for me there," instructed Claire.

Jemma didn't hesitate. She closed her eyes and transported herself back to the forest, thankful to get away from the intense atmosphere.

As she waited she paced around the bench, reflecting on both Max's and Claire's stories. Claire had been murdered by her cheating husband and Max had been betrayed by his cheating girlfriend and best friend. *Shit.* No wonder they had forged a friendship. They were two lost souls who understood each other's traumatic past.

She thought of Susie. What was she doing now? She hoped she was happy and would make the most of her life. But most of all she thought about Tom, her gorgeous lover who was now a free spirit, able to go anywhere in the universe — except to her. She sighed and wiped away a tear that had snuck out and rolled down her cheek. *I'm ready. I'm ready to go back.*

After what felt like an eternity, Claire turned up, looking exhausted.

"Are you all right?" asked Jemma as Claire sat down next to her.

"Yes, dear, I think so. I've been trying to get Max to talk about his past for a while now, but I must admit I never realized how sad his story would be."

"Are you really going to stay with him?"

"Yes, of course. Until we can both sort out our grief and bitterness we're stuck here, so we might as well help each other. Anyway, I suppose I quite like the man. I imagine we'll both be content to stay for the foreseeable future and keep each other company."

Jemma reached out and took Claire's hand. "You're an amazing woman, Claire. I always knew there was more to you than met the eye. Thank you for everything."

"Thank *you*. It's thanks to you that I met Max and I suppose I've found my soulmate." The two women sat together for a while longer, each of them wishing the other well. "Now, dear, it's time for you to go back. Are you ready?"

Jemma smiled. "Yes, I think I am."

"Good, then here's what you'll need to do. Look into the distance and fix your gaze beyond the farthest view. Keep staring at that one point."

Jemma faced away from the bench and did as Claire had said. When her eyes became bleary she nodded to Claire.

"Good, do you see those tiny strands of light flickering in front of you?" Jemma nodded again, fascinated. She had never noticed them before, they were so tiny, but they were definitely there. It was as though they popped in and out of existence. One second they were there, the next they had burst like a bubble.

"Okay, you can relax. Every now and then one of those strands tears at the fabric of space-time and forms a tiny wormhole. You need to search for the ones that become brighter instead of vanishing. That's a usable wormhole. Now, remember that you're not solid matter. You'll need to adjust your energy so that you flow into one of those tiny wormholes. You must then use all your power of thought to direct the wormhole to the right place and time. Don't forget, once you're through, you'll only have a fraction of a second to knock that drink over."

They looked at each other, both with tears in their eyes. "I'm going to miss you so much," whispered Jemma.

"No, you're not. You won't remember me, but I'll remember you, and I'll definitely miss you. I even think Max might miss you a little bit," she said, smiling.

"Oh yeah, right. Goodbye, Claire."

"Goodbye, my dear, and good luck."

They embraced, hugging each other until Jemma pulled away and turned her gaze out over the horizon in search for the strands of light she had seen a moment ago. There they were. Her gaze was drawn to one specific strand, dancing in front of her as its light became brighter. She knew that was the one. She focused her mind like Claire and Tom had both taught her to do and gradually her body become lighter, until she began to flow into the tiny strand. She couldn't deny the knot of fear in her stomach, though. After all, so much could go wrong. But she wouldn't dwell on that now.

Like liquid, she poured into the tiny particle until she couldn't see it anymore. She was inside. There was no time to waste. It was a matter of seconds before the wormhole would disintegrate and she needed to use every ounce of willpower and concentration if she was to succeed. With sheer determination, she directed her mind back to the day of her accident then, more specifically, back to the moment just before she had stood to follow those girls out for a cigarette. Then, a split second later, she was there. But in the confusion of traveling through time, she forgot what it was she had to do. Shit, the wormhole was beginning to collapse. She had to be quick. On impulse, she reached out her hand to grab hold of something from the physical world and sent a glass of Coke flying at the same moment as the wormhole collapsed.

Chapter Twenty-Four

"Oh shit, I'm so sorry," cried Jemma as the glass went flying. "I can't believe I just did that." She stared in dismay as its contents poured onto the table. She grabbed a couple of serviettes and tried to mop up some of the spilled drink while Kirsten went to get a cloth. By the time she had helped to clear up the mess, it was time to head back to class. *Oh well, I obviously wasn't meant to have that cigarette.* She grabbed her bag and followed the others, carefully dodging one of the staff who was clearing up some spilled coffee from the floor.

The rest of the afternoon passed in pretty much the same way as the morning had. At three o'clock, while Jemma was packing up her new books, her phone bleeped, telling her she had a text.

Hi hun, Fancy a takeaway and bottle of wine tonight? Can't wait to hear how you got on. C U later A xx

Jemma smiled as she replied —

Sounds gr8. Today OK. How was Jack? J x

A moment later her phone bleeped again.

Gorgeous but I'm still single

As she made her way home, Jemma tried not to think about the disappointment that was niggling away deep inside her. She couldn't put her finger on it, but she didn't feel quite as positive about college as she had that morning. It wasn't that the work was too hard. In fact, it was the opposite. She had been bored to tears when the tutor had gone over and over the same simple equation because some of the other students couldn't grasp it. She frowned. If they were struggling already, they didn't stand a chance as the course progressed. It was becoming clear that the pace would be much slower than she had thought. Still, it was only the first day and she didn't want to spoil Alice's good mood, so she put on a big smile as she opened the front door and popped the two bottles of Pinot Grigio she had bought on her way back into the fridge.

Alice was busy rummaging through the kitchen drawer for the takeaway menu. "Hi. How was it?"

"Yeah, it was great," replied Jemma. She disappeared into the bathroom for a quick shower.

Forty minutes later they were tucking into their favorite Chinese takeaway of crispy duck pancakes while enjoying one of the bottles of cold, crisp wine. "Here's to us," said Alice, clinking her glass with Jemma's.

"So what did you do at Jack's, then?" asked Jemma, taking a sip of wine. "Apart from fluttering your eyelashes at him, of course."

"Well, it was quite uneventful really. We sat in a big circle and he talked us through a meditation. I didn't think I'd be interested in that meditation stuff, but it did make me feel good. I can imagine that it would be easier to feel psychic energy when you're in such a relaxed state, so I suppose I can see the point. Oh, and that house is definitely haunted. I felt a really strong presence in one of the corners of the living room."

"Oh, hun, I keep telling you, there's no such thing as ghosts. Anyway, are you going again?" asked Jemma, stuffing her mouth full of pancake, which was delicious.

"Oh yes. I've already said I'll come to the next meeting in two weeks' time. I must remember to book a hair appointment for the day before."

"So, do you think he fancies you?"

"Oh, I just don't know. He's so lovely and he makes me feel that I'm really special when he talks to me, but then I think he does that with everyone. I'll just have to keep fluttering my eyelashes and hope he notices," she said with a dreamy expression on her face.

"Or buy longer ones. You know, like the ones Lady Gaga wears. Extra-long with silver on the ends. If subtle doesn't work, go for in your face, *fuck me now* ones."

"Sadly, I think it'll take more than a pair of fake eyelashes to make him notice me." Alice sighed. "Anyway, enough about that, I want to hear all about your first day at college."

Jemma shrugged. "There's nothing much to tell. The people were nice, but it was a bit boring. It was all really easy. I didn't learn anything new."

"Oh, that'll be to let you settle in. You'll probably find it all kicks off tomorrow."

"Yeah, that's what I thought. Oh, and you'll never guess what I did."

"What?"

Jemma grimaced as she told Alice all about the glass of Coke she had knocked over. "Oh, Alice, it was such a mess, it went everywhere. God knows what they must think of me."

"At least you made an impression," said Alice, giggling.

"Hmm. Anyway, it was okay. So, what are you up to for the rest of the week?"

"I need to find a job," said Alice as she munched on a prawn cracker. "I'm broke."

"Me too. What did you have in mind?"

"Well, I used to do some waitressing in New York, so I suppose that's my best shot. I'm going to start looking online for job ads. What about you?"

Jemma shrugged. She didn't know what she would do, but she knew that she needed to do something. "I suppose I might try some bar work or something. Anyway, hun, cheers. Here's to us."

They finished off the food and opened the second bottle of wine before settling down in front of the telly. "Have you got any homework?" asked Alice.

"Nah." Jemma still couldn't shake off the sense of anticlimax that had hung over her earlier. She'd been so excited this morning about starting college, but now she just wasn't so sure about it anymore. "I suppose in a couple of days I'll be moaning about the amount of essays I've got to do, so I shouldn't complain."

"Yes, of course."

They dumped the leftovers in the kitchen and curled up on the sofa to watch television, like they had done so many times over the last year or so. When they both drifted off to sleep, Alice had a contented smile on her face as she snored on Jemma's shoulder, but Jemma was troubled as she dozed. Even in her sleep she couldn't shake that horrible feeling of discontent.

* * * *

Two months later

"How do I look?" asked Alice. They were in the living room and Jemma was lying on the sofa, cradling her head in her hands as she watched Alice do a little twirl in front of her.

Jemma studied her and laughed. "Fine, if you're going to a woodland soiree with the local Elf Society."

"Huh?" Alice frowned and studied herself in the mirror, clearly missing Jemma's point.

"Alice, you can't go to an interview wearing that. You look like an anemic elf."

"Thanks," grumbled Alice.

"Come on," said Jemma, getting up from the sofa. "I'll help you find something a bit more suitable. Seriously, Alice, you can't wear that." They made their way into Alice's room. Jemma strode over to the wardrobe and started flicking through the hangers. Alice's room was as tidy as Jemma's was messy and for once Jemma was glad about that. She found a stylish red blouse and held it up to Alice, swinging the hanger in front of her.

"Here. This is perfect."

"Really?"

"Yep. Here, try it on." Alice took the green top off and handed it to Jemma, who dropped it into the bin when Alice wasn't looking. Alice then put the red blouse on and they both surveyed the result in the mirror on Alice's wardrobe.

"You're right. It's much better," said Alice, peering over her shoulder to check how her outfit looked from behind.

"Alice, please promise me you will never, *ever* buy anything green, *ever* again."

Alice picked up the bangle Jemma had given her once and slid it onto her wrist. "For good luck."

Jemma laughed. "What time's your interview?"

"Ten o'clock. I think I'll walk, it's only in Camden."

"So what's this place called then?" asked Jemma, following Alice into the kitchen.

Alice filled the kettle and switched it on. "It's called Glitz. It sounds great. Oh, Jem, I really want this job."

"I hope you get it, hun. Good luck." She meant it. It had been two months since Jemma had started college and Alice had been searching for a job since then. She hadn't had any luck until she had come across an ad in the window of a bistro in Camden. This job sounded perfect — good shifts, decent money and the food was supposed to be nice. Things were looking up for Alice. She and Jack were going out now and she was madly in love. In fact, Jemma had never seen Alice so happy, so getting this job would be the icing on the cake for her.

Things weren't quite so rosy for her, though. The college course had been a big disappointment. The work was too easy and she still, after two months, didn't feel that she had learned anything new. She had tried to talk to her tutor about it, but he had just said that she should stick with it because once she had the right qualifications she could access the university courses that would better suit her. He was right, of course, but Jemma was bored and had lost interest. She had started skipping a few classes and was behind with the work. On top of that, she hadn't managed to find a job and was now broke. Just to rub salt in the already painful wound, her love life was still nonexistent. She couldn't help feeling as if she was slipping back to her old life when she was at school — bunking off, smoking in secret and drinking more than she should.

After a cup of tea, Alice left for her interview and Jemma was alone, with nothing to do and nowhere to go as, yet again, she couldn't be bothered going into college. On impulse she reached for her phone, scrolled down to her Aunt Tess' number and pressed 'call'.

"Hello?" Aunt Tess' soft voice was welcoming and familiar.

"Hi, Aunt Tess, it's me."

"Hello, love. I haven't heard from you for a while, how are you?"

"Yeah, great. Well, actually I'm not sure. Are you free today?"

"Yes, I'm here all day."

"Can I come and see you?" Tears stung Jemma's eyes. She could really do with being with the closest person she had to a mother.

"Of course you can, you're always welcome here. Are you going to catch the train?"

"Yes. Shall I call you as the train approaches Tunbridge Wells?"

"Yes, love, you do that and I'll come and pick you up. We can stop off in town for a bite of lunch. See you later."

Jemma scribbled a quick note to let Alice know where she was and instructed her to let her know how the interview had gone. When she got to Charing Cross she had just enough money to buy a return ticket to Tunbridge Wells and, with ten minutes to spare before the train was due to depart, she nipped outside for a quick ciggie.

Aunt Tess was waiting for her at Tunbridge Wells station and gave Jemma a warm hug when she saw her. They decided to walk down to the Pantiles and eat lunch at their favorite café. They found a table in the corner, away from the cold draft seeping through the door, and picked up the menu, which was pointless, as they always had the same thing. After they had ordered their food, they chatted about the weather before Aunt Tess gave Jemma a serious look. "So, how are you, *really*?"

"Oh, you know. Okay."

"And college? How's that going?"

"Great."

"Then what's wrong?"

Jemma took a deep breath and started pouring it all out, everything from her disillusionment with college, her futile attempts at getting a job, her loneliness now that Alice was spending more time with Jack, and she told her aunt how much she still missed her mum. "I don't feel as if I have any purpose anymore," she finished.

"Would it help if we go and see your mother?" asked Aunt Tess.

"Yes, please," she whispered, her throat contracting as she attempted to stop her tears.

"Then that's what we'll do. Finish your lunch then we'll go and visit her."

Jemma hadn't even noticed that the waitress had brought their food, but she wasn't hungry and pushed the food around on her plate until it looked like she had eaten some of it. As Aunt Tess called the waitress over to ask for the bill, Jemma's phone bleeped. It was Alice.

I got the job! YAY! c u later. A xx

Jemma was thrilled for her friend and sent a text back congratulating her. Maybe they should go out tonight and celebrate, although it would have to be cheap. But Alice texted back saying—

I'm really sorry Jack's cooking dinner tonight. How about tomorrow? A x

Jemma sighed. Another night in on her own, which was just as well, as she had no money anyway.

"Is everything okay?" asked Aunt Tess, who had now paid the bill and was putting her coat on.

"Alice went for an interview this morning and she just texted me to let me know that she got the job," said Jemma, helping her aunt with her coat.

"Well, that is good news. It'll be you next, just you see."

Jemma wasn't so sure. She couldn't even get a cleaning job right now, so she wasn't holding her breath. She had applied for more jobs than she cared to admit, but none of them had come to anything. It didn't do much to help Jemma's confidence, especially when she had missed out on the cleaning job she had applied for last week. Every time she rang up about a new position, it was gone before she even had a chance to go for an interview.

They walked back to the car, stopping off at a florist on the way, before Aunt Tess drove them to the graveyard in Stenhurst. When they pulled up outside the church, Aunt Tess switched off the engine and turned to Jemma.

"You go by yourself, love. I'm sure you want to be on your own while you talk to your mother."

Taking the flowers with her, she smiled her thanks to her aunt and made her way through the graveyard.

As she approached the black marble headstone with her mum's name on it, a sob escaped from deep inside her. How often could a heart break before it shattered forever? Why did she feel worse with every passing day? It was as if she was missing a piece of her life, but she didn't know what.

She put the flowers, a beautiful bouquet of yellow and white roses, down onto the grave. They were her mum's favorite. "Hi, Mum," she said.

She sat next to the grave, ignoring the damp, cold ground, and closed her eyes. She told her mum about how low she was feeling. Tears poured down her face and Jemma didn't try to stop them. She was glad of the chance to let her emotions out without anyone asking her what was wrong.

Then something made her snap her eyes open and she found herself staring at the ground next to her in astonishment. Lying next to her was a large sprig of honeysuckle. *How did it get here?* She was sure it hadn't been there a moment ago.

She picked the sprig up and sniffed it, closing her eyes as she inhaled the sweet scent. When she opened them again something made her turn to her left. She could have sworn she saw the outline of a man, but there was nobody around. *How strange.* She held the sprig close to her, not sure why she was so attached to it, as a strange ache gnawed away at her heart. She shook her head. *Get a grip, Jemma.*

When it was time to leave she found that she couldn't leave the honeysuckle behind so she brought it with her as she made her way back to Aunt Tess, who was reading a newspaper in the car. "What's that, love?" her aunt asked, eying the twig.

"It's honeysuckle, but I've no idea where it came from. It just sort of appeared out of nowhere. Was Mum particularly partial to honeysuckle?"

"No, not really."

"Hmm." Jemma didn't know why, but she just couldn't throw it away so she kept a tight hold on it as Aunt Tess drove her back to the station at Tunbridge Wells.

"Will you be okay, love?" asked her aunt, looking worried, as they pulled up by the taxi ramp.

Jemma leaned over and kissed her on the cheek. "Yes, I'll be fine. Thank you for today."

"Here, take this," she said, giving Jemma a couple of twenty-pound notes. "You know where I am, just call me any time you need anything. And chin up, you'll be back on your feet in no time."

Jemma only had to wait about eight minutes for the fast train to London, and she was back in Charing Cross in less than an hour. Still clutching the honeysuckle, she jumped onto a number thirteen bus, which would take her all the way to Swiss Cottage. As the bus queued at the traffic lights by Oxford Circus, she gazed out of the window at the hordes of people rushing to get on with their lives. Tourists strolled along Oxford Street while frustrated Londoners, rushing home from work, tried to dodge past them.

When she got off at Swiss Cottage, she was tempted to walk home. It was quite a long walk to Chalk Farm, but it would give her some thinking time, like what she was going to do with her life.

Swiss Cottage was buzzing as usual, with people, traffic and bikes all rushing to get to their destinations. Jemma decided to pop into a little deli on the way home and buy something nice for her dinner with the money Aunt Tess had given her. She stepped onto the road to cross and —

Chapter Twenty-Five

Jemma blinked as tiny particles swirled around her like a swarm of bees. Muffled echoes teased her ears — voices, the screech of brakes, a scream. None of it felt real. *This must be a dream.* It had to be, because she was hovering in mid-air. A strange sense of déjà vu washed over her as her eyes focused on the body lying below in the road. The driver of the bus that had hit the girl was leaning over her, checking for a pulse. A woman nearby was calling an ambulance. *Why does this seem so familiar?*

As her eyes adjusted to the bright light shining at her from all directions, she recognized the girl. An anguished cry ripped from her throat as she stared in horror at her lifeless body still clutching the sprig of honeysuckle. No, it couldn't be. There had to be some mistake.

"It's okay," she stuttered to the shocked, gathering crowd. "I'm fine…" *Wait, I've said those words before.*

Then the light started to dim and an intense darkness closed in on her, drawing her down and forcing her back into her body. Pain. There was so much pain. It was consuming her, draining her energy.

"We're losing her," cried a voice as a siren sounded far away.

The light had now become a pinprick in the distance, getting smaller and smaller the way the entrance to a black tunnel might look from the back of a train. The voices were fading now. Then welcome tranquility enveloped her as everything became silent. A thick mist drifted in out of nowhere and wrapped its icy tendrils around her, squeezing the last rasp of air out of her lungs. There was no more pain.

No more fear. Just an ethereal sense of peace that lifted her soul out of her body, atom by atom, until she floated in the air like sparkling dust caught in a beam of sunlight. Then she sank back down like a falling feather until she landed on her feet and came face-to-face with the most beautiful boy she had ever seen. An effervescent glimmer radiated from his eyes and his skin was so pale and flawless that it was almost translucent. She stared at him, transfixed and unable to move.

"Hello, Jemma." His voice was soft like velvet and his smile reached out and warmed the chill in her blood. It was as if there was a strange kind of affinity between them, which was odd considering she had never seen him before.

"Who are you?" she whispered. She wasn't afraid. In fact, she had never felt so serene.

"I am your guardian angel. I am sorry I let you down. You should never have died last time and if Alice had not been able to convince you to return, you would have been trapped in the eleventh dimension forever. Now *is* your time, however. You have reached your destiny and my job is done. Goodbye, Jemma."

Before Jemma could say anything, the boy started to fade until he disappeared into the haze that still surrounded her. She tried to reach out to him before he vanished, desperate to hold on to his magical presence, but it was too late. He was gone. *What had he meant? Have I died before?*

Then the fog began to lift and Jemma was able to look around her. That was when she saw the man smiling at her. His body was glowing and when he beckoned her to come to him her world suddenly became complete. *Tom!* It was Tom. Suddenly the angel's words made sense as everything came back to her. Joy bubbled up and burst through her heart as she ran toward him and threw herself into his arms.

"Tom. Is it really you?" she cried, tears pouring down her face.

"Yes, Jemma. I'm here."

"Oh my God, Tom." She clung to him, not quite able to

believe what was happening. She'd thought she would never see him again yet here he was, as real as she was, holding her tightly as she cried on his shoulder. "I remember everything now. How can this be?" A sob escaped from her as elation fizzed through her veins, which felt like they still pumped blood around her body.

Without letting go of her, Tom pulled back a little so he could see her face. Then he reached up and wiped her tears away. "I'll explain everything when we get home," he whispered, his eyes glassy with emotion.

"Home?" This was all so much to take in. The angel had implied that she had died again, but there were no similarities in her experience so far. Although she had felt cushioned from the world just after she had died the first time, she knew now that that had just been because she had been in shock. This was different. Her body felt lighter and everything around her seemed intangible whereas before, the living world and the eleventh dimension had been pretty much indistinguishable.

"We'll go to Jack's house for now, but home can be anywhere you like." Tom pulled her close again and hugged her. She clung to him and buried her face in his chest. The way his arms tightened around her sent shivers tingling through her body and she took a deep breath as she basked in his embrace. She frowned as she realized that she had just felt air being drawn into her lungs.

"I'm still breathing." She gasped, looking up into Tom's face to check that he was still there. *Please don't let this be a dream.*

Tom smiled, his eyes crinkling at the corners in the way she loved so much. "No, it just feels like it. You can also feel your heart beating, but it's just your soul remembering your body's physical state while it was alive. It's quite comforting, actually."

Jemma nodded. "Yes, it is. So how come I can feel you? I haven't erected a protective barrier around myself yet."

"We don't need that anymore," said Tom as he took

her hand. "We're free entities now. We don't need to use excessive energy to move around or communicate. Your consciousness controls reality. *Your* reality. Nobody can see inside you here and no one can harm you. Ever."

You have reached your destiny, the angel had said. "Is this heaven?" she asked, still not sure if she believed in all that stuff.

Tom grinned. "I've no idea, but it certainly feels like it. Come on."

Even before Tom had finished his sentence Jemma found herself in Jack's kitchen. "How did you do that?" she cried, stunned. "What about the Star Trek thing?"

"Good, eh? We don't have to make an effort to transport ourselves anymore. We just sort of go wherever we want."

Jemma stared at Tom as he spoke. A lump burned her throat as the euphoria of seeing him again struck home and she couldn't stop another tear from rolling down her cheek as she tried to make sense of it all.

"Are you okay?" he asked with a shadow of concern furrowing his brow.

She smiled and nodded. "Yeah. I'm just a bit overwhelmed, that's all. I'm so happy to see you."

Tom sat down on a chair then pulled Jemma onto his lap. "I've missed you more than you could ever imagine," he said, his voice heavy with emotion. "Seeing you every day and not being able to talk to you or give you a hug... It was agony."

"I'd like to say that I missed you too, but I didn't remember anything. I felt really empty, though. It was as if something important was missing from my life, but I didn't know what."

"I never left your side."

"I know that now. Thanks for the honeysuckle, by the way. I couldn't understand why I was so strangely drawn to it. I thought I was going mad." Jemma chuckled as she recalled how puzzled she had been by the sudden appearance of the sprig.

"You were so sad I just wanted to do something to let you know I was there, even though I knew you wouldn't understand."

"Did you know I was going to die again?" she asked.

"Yes. Your angel came to me just before the accident," Tom replied as he brushed a strand of her hair away from her eyes.

"I saw him just after I died. He was beautiful."

"Yes, he was. If it wasn't for him you would have been trapped in the eleventh dimension forever. We couldn't have been together and you would never have been free." He ran his hand up her back, leaving a burning trail through her T-shirt. It was amazing how his touch felt even more real and intense than it had in the other dimension.

"So, are we really free now?" she asked, still not convinced this wasn't just some glorious illusion.

"Yes, we can go anywhere we like. We'll never get sick and we'll exist forever as part of the fabric of the universe."

"Can we…er…still make love?" she asked. She tried to stop the flush she knew was creeping up her neck, but the heat scorching her cheeks told her that the effort was in vain. Damn, even this death hadn't seemed to cure her habit of blushing.

Tom laughed and kissed the tip of her nose. "Of course, only now we don't have to mess around with barriers. If you want to feel me touching you, you will. If you want me to explore every part of your body, inside and out, I can. But only if that's what you want. Nobody can touch you or see inside you without your consent."

"It almost sounds too good to be true."

"It isn't. You'll love this amazing place, Jemma. It's got so many secrets that mortals have no idea about."

"I already love it because you're here," she whispered.

Tom cupped her face in the palms of his hands then kissed her on the lips. "Tonight we're going to our beach so I can remind you of just how much I love you," he said with a teasing smile. "But first, let's visit a few old friends."

"Ooh, yes please." Jemma slid off his lap, grabbing his hand as she did so. As soon as he led her through the wall into the living room she spotted Max and Claire sitting on the sofa. Max had his arm around Claire and they were both smiling. Jemma barely recognized Max, who had lost the mean scowl that had always marred his pinched face.

"Can they see us?" she asked as she crossed to the room toward them.

"No. They have no idea we're here."

"They look happy," said Jemma. She was thrilled that Claire had found someone to share her existence with. Maybe together they could heal each other and even be ready one day to make the journey that she and Tom had so they could be reunited as free spirits. Whatever she had thought of Max at the time, she couldn't deny the sparkle he had put into Claire's eyes and she was thankful to him for that.

"Would you like to see how Susie is getting on?" asked Tom after they had spent a few more minutes watching Claire and Max.

"I'd love to," said Jemma. Before she could even begin to imagine what the child would look like as an adult they were standing in front of a well-dressed lady and a handsome man sitting on a bench in a park playground. The woman was laughing at something the man was saying and Jemma recognized the infectious sound straight away.

"That's her husband, Greg," explained Tom as Jemma stared at the couple.

She was still the same Susie she remembered, only older and more refined. Gone was the cheeky child with freckles and goofy teeth. She had grown up to be a beautiful, elegant lady.

"Mummy, look at me," cried a young girl on a climbing frame. "I made it to the top."

Susie waved to the girl. "Well done, Chloe. Be careful up there."

"That's their daughter," said Tom as they watched the

young girl clamber down from the frame. He nodded toward the swings where a girl a couple of years older than Chloe was pushing a boy in a toddler seat. "That's Jodie, their oldest daughter, and that's their son, Max."

"Max?" exclaimed Jemma, laughing. "That's so funny."

Tom chuckled. "Yeah. Susie is a teacher in a primary school. She's done well."

"I'm so proud of her," said Jemma, tears welling as she watched the happy family.

"Me too. We can come and visit her any time you like." Tom put his arm around Jemma and gave her a squeeze. "It's good to see her so happy, isn't it?"

"Yes, it is. Can we stay and watch them for a while?"

"Of course," replied Tom, grinning. "We've got all the time in the world."

They sat down on a nearby bench and watched the children as they played. "Have you seen your father?" asked Jemma as Susie called out to Chloe not to go too fast on the roundabout.

Tom took Jemma's hand and entwined his fingers through hers. "Yes. I've told him all about you."

"I can't wait to meet him."

"You will, very soon."

"And how's your mother?"

"She's great. You wouldn't recognize her as the same lady you met before. She has remarried and is very happy."

"I'm so glad," said Jemma. It was incredible how dramatically people's lives had been affected just because she and Tom had escaped from the eleventh dimension. It was good to know that they were responsible for so much happiness.

Tom turned to her, his face growing serious. "There's someone here who wants to see you," he said softly. "Are you ready?"

Was she ready? She had been waiting for this moment since she was fifteen years old. She nodded and before she could blink she found herself face-to-face with her beloved mother. A deep sob escaped from her as the image of her mum blurred through brimming tears.

"Mum!" she cried as she ran into her mother's arms. "Oh, Mum, I've missed you so much."

"I know, sweetheart," whispered her mum, Caroline. "I've missed you too. It was so hard watching you suffer after I'd died."

"I never got to say goodbye to you. It all happened so suddenly," cried Jemma as she clung to her mother. Waves of joy washed away the years of pain and anguish. Her mum was here and that was all that mattered.

When they had cried, hugged and cried some more, Jemma let go of Caroline once she was sure this wasn't some cruel trick.

"Have you met Tom?" she asked, pulling Tom forward.

"Of course, we've both been stalking you. I've been telling Tom all about your escapades when you were little," said Caroline with a mischievous glint in her eyes.

"Oh, Mum, you haven't!"

Tom laughed. "No, of course she hasn't. Despite my many attempts to bribe her."

Jemma rolled her eyes and grinned. *I'm going to have to watch those two.* "Where is this, anyway?" she asked, glancing around her. They were in some sort of castle with stunning antique furniture and very large oil paintings hanging on oak-paneled walls.

Caroline blushed, something she'd never done when she'd been alive. "Well, I'm living with a count who died over three hundred years ago. His name is George and this was his castle. It's owned by the National Trust now so it's overrun by tourists during the holiday season. They can't see us, so we don't take any notice of them."

Jemma stared at her mum in disbelief. "You've shacked up with a three-hundred-year-old count? Good on you. When can I meet him?"

"Soon. You'll love him," said Caroline, her eyes glowing with happiness. "He's eccentric, charming and has a wicked sense of humor."

"It seems I'm not the only ghost to fall in love," said Jemma, looking across at Tom. As their eyes met, Jemma's stomach flipped. It was incredible how she could still feel physical sensations even though her body was now devoid of life. She couldn't tell the difference between being alive or dead. Her heart seemed to beat faster whenever she got close to Tom, fooling her into thinking it was still keeping her alive.

"You two should go now," said Caroline as she pulled Jemma back into her arms and hugged her. "You've got a lot of catching up to do and we've got all the time in the world now. Come back tomorrow and I'll introduce you to George, then you and I can spend some time together on our own."

"I'd love that," said Jemma, breathing in her mother's sweet scent.

"And then I can tell you off for all that drinking and smoking," scolded Caroline, with a chuckle.

"Sorry about that," replied Jemma, giggling. "Nothing would make me happier than to hear you threaten to send me to bed without dinner."

"Don't worry," added Tom. He gave Caroline a wink. "I'll make sure she's suitably chastised."

"Ohh," cried Jemma, laughing as Tom playfully swatted her bottom.

"Shall we head back to Jack and Alice?" asked Tom when Jemma had finished saying goodbye to her mother. "It probably won't be long before they get the phone call informing them of your death."

"Poor Alice," sighed Jemma as they materialized back in Jack's kitchen. "She's got to go through all that again."

"Everything that happened before technically never happened. And she's got Jack and her new job to pull her through. She'll be fine," reassured Tom.

"Yeah, I know. Do you think she'll be able to communicate with me this time?"

"Yes, I don't see why not. Once she's over the worst, she should feel your presence. It'll be a lot easier for you to connect with her now."

"I'll be there for her," vowed Jemma. "I'll make sure she's okay, but I don't think I want to be here when she gets the news. I couldn't bear to see her so upset."

Tom nodded his understanding. "Okay. We'll go to the beach now, shall we? You can always check on her later."

As soon as they were back at their favorite beach in Norfolk, the enormity of what had happened hit Jemma just like the wind that nearly knocked her sideways. "I can feel the wind," she cried, then burst into tears.

"You can feel everything you want to now, remember?" soothed Tom, pulling her into his arms and holding her. "You okay?"

"Yes, really I am. It's just that so much has happened since we were last here. Saying goodbye to you was the hardest and most painful thing I've ever had to endure," she said, leaning into his tall frame. "I'm terrified that I'm going to wake up and I'll still be trapped here without you."

"I promise that won't happen," said Tom as he led her across to their sand dune. He sat down and pulled Jemma down next to him.

"Sorry for crying," she said, as he put his arm around her. "The crazy thing is, I've never been so happy and yet I can't seem to stop bawling my eyes out. I'm back with you, I've been reunited with my mum, and Susie and Claire are happy. Even Alice has found love. I know she's about to get the shock of her life, but I know she'll be fine. I'll make sure she is."

"It's time to stop thinking about other people," murmured Tom as he nibbled her earlobe. "For the rest of tonight, you will only think about us and what I'm about to do to you."

"Ooh." She giggled as Tom pushed her down into the sand. "I think I can manage that."

"I'm going to show you just how much pleasure a ghost can feel then, if you fancy it, we can go for a stroll on the moon. The universe is ours, Jemma, and we have all of eternity to explore it together."

"I love you, Tom," whispered Jemma just before his lips crushed her own. His kiss awoke every nerve ending in her body, igniting them with sparks of pleasure that surpassed anything she had ever experienced. She knew then that the angel was right. She had found her destiny. She was home and there was nowhere she would rather be.

More books from Totally Bound Publishing

Book one in the Vamp Hunters series

Her life on hold for a decade, Meghan's ready to take it back and move forward. Valor is ready too. The Vampire Master won't let her disappear, not ever again.

Book three in the Blood Secrets series

As the endgame looms, choices must be made, changes must occur and skills must be refined, but as they take one last throw of the dice, everything hangs in the balance.

Book thirteen in the Sisterhood of Jade series

"When a Siren sings, best listen" — Stephano

Book four in the Magic Matched series

*In witching society, magic and politics are the only things
that matter, and marriages are arranged for advantage
rather than love.*

About the Author

Anette Darbyshire

Anette was born in Copenhagen, Denmark and now lives in Kent, UK with her husband and three children.

She wrote her first book after asking herself a simple question. She pondered on it for a few days then just had to write it down and, without even realising it, the beginnings of a book had formed. The question was, 'How would someone react if they died and woke up to find they were a ghost?' The end result was a book titled Love in the Wrong Dimension, a love story told from the perspective of a ghost.

Anette self-published the book in 2011 before writing her second book, Gowns of the Haunted. Then, in 2016, she decided to rewrite Love in the Wrong Dimension and this time she submitted it to a publisher. She is delighted that they accepted it and will be released later this year by Totally Bound Publishing. It's still the same story, but it has been polished up and has a new title, Love in Another Dimension.

Anette has always been fascinated by ghosts and has had several paranormal experiences in the past. She combines this interest with her fondness for a good love story, which is where she gets the inspiration for her romantic ghost stories. At present she is busy planning her next book, which will be set in a haunted hotel.

She loves the 4 C's: cats, chocolate, champagne and coffee. When she's not writing she spends her time as a glorified taxi driver for her children and even finds time now and then to indulge in her interests, which include Tai Chi, dance, music, aviation and reading.

Anette Darbyshire loves to hear from readers. You can find contact information, website details and an author profile page at https://www.totallybound.com/

Home of Erotic Romance

www.ingramcontent.com/pod-product-compliance
Lightning Source LLC
Chambersburg PA
CBHW020559260626
47157CB00003B/772